ELVIS ON THE EDGE OF REALITY

Giovanni Caccamo

CONTENTS

ABOUT THE AUTHOR

Giovanni Caccamo aims to become a full-time writer. His debut book, 'Martex Renver in Search of a Better Life,' was published by Austin Macauley Publishing in London on January 31, 2020.

After four decades of mastering the art of hairdressing, he has always maintained a vivid imagination and is now eager to showcase it to the world.

Giovanni and Assunta have been happily married for 30 years and are proud parents of three boys: Joseph, Pasquale, and Steven John. They live in Sydney, Australia.

He has been a devoted admirer of Elvis since 1977. When Elvis passed away, he was 9 years old, and he pondered how he would have changed Elvis's career if he had the chance to travel back in time. His new book guides you through that journey.

Chapter One

REWRITING THE PAST

A journey of redemption. The aging rock legend pondered the pivotal moments that had shaped his life. Guilt lingered from his choices, yet his insatiable desire masked the pain like a numbing drug. In 1953, he had altered his destiny, and now, in the depths of introspection, he sought a chance to redeem himself and ease the burdens that had weighed him down for so long.

Thursday, November 19, 2020, marked the day before he would forever change the life of the greatest entertainer. Positioned by the bay window in the opulent Graceland mansion in Memphis, Tennessee, he fixed his gaze on the outside world, eagerly awaiting his 19-year-old grandson, Josh Cadman. Young Josh, set to become his chauffeur for the day, would accompany him on a journey to visit the living Elvis Aaron Presley, the original king of rock and roll, who, according to this reality, had been born on January 8, 1935, but had tragically passed away on August 16, 1977, at the tender age of 42.

Confusing. The confusion may have dissipated as time passed, revealing the truth. This Elvis Presley still boasted his trademark jet-black hair and was clad in a sleek black suit adorned with 24-carat gold buttons. At least his appearance maintained the illusion. A smile crossed his face as his grandson finally arrived at the illustrious gates of Graceland. The gates swung open, and a pink Cadillac Fleetwood Series 60, one of Elvis's beloved cars, pulled up to the mansion. He had gifted this car to his grandson on his 18th birthday and witnessing him roll up to the grand entrance filled him with joy.

The doorbell chimed, signaling Josh Cadman. The family patriarch opened the door, welcoming his grandson inside. Josh sported blue jeans, a white concert t-shirt from the 2003 Elvis performance, and vibrant red sneakers. "Grandpa," he exclaimed as they embraced. "Josh, my boy, you're right on time," Grandpa Elvis replied with delight, clear in his voice. Josh inquired about his grandmother's presence, asking, "Is Grandma joining us too?" Grandpa Elvis shook his head and revealed, "No, she's out shopping with your father for my retirement celebration tomorrow."

A realization dawned upon Josh, and he said, "Yeah, Dad mentioned it. So, why did you need me as your driver today, Grandpa?" Grandpa Elvis placed a hand on his grandson's shoulder and exclaimed, "Yes, my boy, because tomorrow marks the 67th anniversary of the start of my career. You know what..." Josh playfully rolled his eyes, cutting him off, "I know, Grandpa. You were only 19, the same as me when it all began." Grandpa Elvis couldn't help but chuckle as he realized how often he must have repeated this information to his grandson. Just like any modern teenager, young Josh reacted nonchalantly. "All right, Grandson, I'm prepared for our journey."

"Yeah, Grandpa, so remind me again because you mentioned over the phone yesterday that we're going to visit Elvis Aaron Presley, who lives in Little Rock, Arkansas."

"That's correct, Josh."

"But Grandpa, isn't he the father of the late governor of Texas, Jesse Garron Presley?" Grandpa Elvis wasn't ready to discuss the purpose of their visit just yet. Not until he spoke to the real Elvis first. He realized that his curious grandson had researched the internet about the faithful Elvis and deserved some information. "Yes, he is," Grandpa Elvis replied.

Josh inquired, "Why are we visiting this dude? I checked him out on Facebook, and he used to impersonate you. But here's the weird part. He closely resembles you and is also 85 years old, just like you."

His grandfather knew the answers to all his questions, but couldn't reveal the truth. Not until he met Elvis Aaron Presley. He shrugged. "Just a coincidence, Josh," Grandpa said, "Because you know my real name is John Cadman, not Elvis Presley. That's my stage name. At birth, his parents named this dude Elvis Presley."

"So, why are we seeing him, then?"

"Listen, let's get going. If it gets too late, we'll have to stay at one of those upmarket hotels on the way back. So, have you packed your bag as I instructed?"

"Yes, Grandpa, it's in the trunk."

Grandpa Elvis picked up his overnight bag and handed it to Josh. They walked outside, and Grandpa carefully opened the passenger door of the pink Cadillac, taking a seat inside. Josh placed his grandfather's bag in the trunk, circled the car, and closed the passenger door for his grandfather before settling into the driver's seat. The car roared to life, Grandpa reveling in the engine's sound. Both men exchanged delighted glances as they set off down the driveway. The iconic gates swung open, marking the beginning of their journey to make amends for the past.

"Grandpa, we'll take Highway 55 toward St Louis."

"Sounds good, Grandson."

He knew the route like the back of his hand, having studied it countless times. He focused on the scenery where vast cotton fields once stretched for miles over the years. All that remained were rows of kale, beetroot, and cabbage. The crop for this time was significant; however, Grandpa Elvis's recollection of cotton fields and melodic tribute to them remained vivid.

In his side mirror, he glanced and discerned a black van and black SUV tailing them. Their proximity showed an undeniable pursuit. "Josh let's speed up moderately," Grandpa Elvis suggested. "Let's test the endurance of this classic beauty." Josh nonchalantly shrugged his shoulders, insinuating that his grandfather influenced his cautious driving. He firmly pressed the gas pedal, compelling the engine to emit a forceful roar as it shifted gears. Gradually, the Cadillac distanced itself from the sinister black vehicles. However, the pursuers swiftly matched their pace, confirming Grandpa's suspicion that somebody had followed them.

"Josh, you may decelerate now," he said. "I know those two black cars behind us are trailing us." Josh peered into the rear-view mirror, contemplating their next move. "Grandpa, perhaps we should return home and notify your security personnel."

"No, we shall veer sharply at just the right moment when approaching the 55 on-ramp," Grandpa advised.

Josh's eyes gleamed with excitement. "Excellent idea," he affirmed. "I will successfully elude them. Please, remain calm."

When they reached the vicinity of the on-ramp entry, he abruptly swerved, swiftly maneuvering onto the ramp. The two black vehicles missed the turnoff, suddenly braking in response, but the pink Cadillac had vanished.

"Well done, Josh," Grandpa commended.

"Thank you," he replied. "It was exhilarating, and as you can see, they are no longer tailing us. Who do you suppose they were?"

Both experienced a profound sense of relief, having evaded a potential threat. Then Elvis senior recalled that his wife Louise had insisted on arranging security because of some zealous fans. However, her husband had dismissed the idea, believing himself too old to be troubled as he was in his youth. "I'm uncertain, but your grandmother mentioned the possibility of hiring security. I hope Louise didn't engage them and we evaded their surveillance."

"Well, in that case, they should have visited our residence before our departure," Josh reasoned.

Grandpa Elvis nodded in agreement. "I suppose. I'll inquire once we arrive home," he mused, "and then we shall know."

Grandpa Elvis fell silent, sinking back into his seat, contemplating what he would relay to his idol—a secret he carried solely within himself. He pondered the chronological sequence of events, wondering if it held any relevance or if he should delve straight into the turning point that occurred 67 years ago.

Before pondering further, he fell into a deep sleep, dreaming of a significant day that had transformed his life. It happened on August 19th, 2006, when the life of a young boy named Peter Walker took a dramatic turn. Tragedy struck when his loving parents died in a car accident near their home in Nashville, Tennessee. Peter would have been an orphan if it hadn't been for his maternal grandmother, Christine Smart.

Christine stood at the burial site of her dear daughter Maxine, aged 42, and son-in-law Brian Walker, aged 44. Holding the hand of a very young Peter, they stood solemnly as the preacher concluded the funeral service. With care, both coffins lowered into the ground, and they encouraged Peter to drop a rose onto each of his parents' ultimate resting places. Other visitors offered their condolences to Christine and Peter, some shaking the young boy's hand while others hugged and kissed him. Christine Smart was Peter's sole living relative at the time; she was 75 years old, and Peter's future would take yet another turn.

By 2009, Christine had done an excellent job of single-handedly raising Peter. As Peter approached his 8th birthday, Grandma Chris (as he called her) had arranged a birthday celebration at their residence in Brinkley, Arkansas. All his classmates joined him, and a joyous atmosphere filled the house. After cutting the cake, everyone joined in singing Happy Birthday. Grandma Chris then presented Peter with a beautifully wrapped gift that would affect his future.

Standing beside his best friend, David Clements, Peter carefully untied the wrapping on a flat-looking present. As he unfolded the last side, he was surprised by what he discovered. It was his grandmother's most treasured possession—a framed Polaroid photograph of herself and Elvis Aaron Presley, dating back to 1962. Christine had met Elvis backstage at one of his concerts, and the legendary king of rock and roll had signed the photo. Rumors had circulated that Christine had a brief affair with Elvis Aaron Presley, but she remained tight-lipped about it.

"Grandpa, Grandpa." The dream abruptly ended as Grandpa Elvis heard his grandson calling out to him. He yawned and stretched his arms before responding, "Josh, my boy, was I asleep for long?" Josh chuckled and replied, "No, not for long at all. I just wanted to let you know that we're about to embark on Highway 40 and have at least 2 hours before switching to Highway 30. We should take a break and refuel because we'll be close to Little Rock afterward."

"That sounds like a good plan, but I may doze off now and then," Grandpa replied.

"That's no problem, Grandpa. I'm about to play some amazing music—one of my all-time favorite songs," Josh pressed a button on his car stereo. His grandfather's 1972 hit, 'Burning Love,' instantly filled the airwaves. As Grandpa heard the music kick in, he looked at his grandson, and they sang together.

They shared laughter and continued singing more hits from his legendary albums. After a while, Elvis Senior grew weary and slipped into another slumber where he dreamed about events from 2011. It was a time when Peter had finished band rehearsal at Partee Elementary School. Peter's love for singing Elvis songs with his grandmother led him to join the school choir. That day, Peter heard a commotion down the hallway as he walked from the music room. A group of boys was causing trouble for his best and only friend, David Clements.

Peter rushed to David's aid and intervened, pushing the boys to the side. The surprise of Peter's unexpected actions sparked a response from the ringleader, Damien Frost, who felt compelled to save face. "Here comes the singing queen of the school. Hey, this fruit belongs to the school choir," Damien taunted.

The three-boy bully gang, comprising Damien and his two sidekicks, Jack Gallon and Lance Denney, gained notoriety. They targeted anyone who didn't engage in athletic activities like football or soccer. Peter was a school choir member, while David was a tech enthusiast and was passionate about all things related to space and historical events.

"Listen, Frost," Peter said, "there's no need for this. Just walk away and leave us alone." Damien and his friends burst into laughter. Then

Damien swung his fist towards Peter's face, but Peter swiftly ducked, causing Damien to miss. Seizing the opportunity, Peter retaliated with a powerful right hook that sent Damien crashing to the floor. In shock, Damien moved his jaw from side to side while his friends helped him. The three boys formed a circle around Peter, preparing for an attack.

Suddenly, Principal Lever's voice echoed from a distance, commanding, "Stop right there!" Having witnessed the altercation, Principal Lever swiftly intervened to prevent the bullies from targeting a lone individual. "Now, the five of you march straight to my office," Principal Lever ordered. "I will deal with this accordingly."

In a crowded office, after an hour had passed, four sets of parents and Grandma Chris gathered to resolve the situation. Principal Lever started the meeting by stating, "Foremost, I witnessed the entire incident, and regardless of what your son may tell you later, I am fully aware of what transpired."

The parents were unaware of the specifics, but Steven, Natalie Clements, and Christine Smart were confident that David and Peter would not voluntarily engage in such a severe incident. Principal Lever cleared his throat and continued, "I was a short distance away in the hallway between the music and technology classes. Damien and his two companions were antagonizing David solely because he was different. At that very moment, Peter, who had just exited the music room ahead of me, swiftly came to David's aid."

Interrupting, Mr. Frost interjected, "Coming to his aid? Principal Lever, from my understanding, Damien had done nothing at that point, correct?" Principal Lever calmly stared at Mr. Frost and replied, "Oh, allow me to explain, Mr. Frost. Your son Damien deliberately targeted Peter for an unprovoked attack. Your son threw the initial coward's punch. So please, don't tell me your son has done nothing."

Curious, Mr. Frost inquired, "What exactly is a coward's punch?" Principal Lever rummaged through a drawer in his desk, retrieving four pens—three red and one blue. He arranged them on his desk, forming a triangle with the red pens and placing the blue one in the center. "A coward's punch," he exclaimed, "is when someone strikes a person, just like the blue pen, catching them off guard while trying to monitor their surroundings."

Principal Lever forcefully slammed his right fist onto the desk, causing the pens to scatter onto the floor. Grandma Chris moved to pick them up, but Principal Lever interjected, "Leave them, Ms. Smart. I'll retrieve them later." He then continued, "You see, Mr. Frost, Peter was the intended target in this case. Fortunately for him, he evaded Damien's punch."

Principal Lever intended to emphasize the gravity of bullying to everyone present in his office that day. Just a few years ago, he had been the principal of a local high school, where his and the teachers' inaction resulted in the tragic suicide of sixteen-year-old Amy Sharp. Witnessing the persistence of bullying and hoping it would eventually resolve itself. However, because of Amy's untimely death, he made a personal vow to combat bullying at an earlier stage. This commitment led him to leave the high school environment and take on the role of an elementary school principal, hoping to prevent bullying.

Now, Damien's father fell silent, directing a gaze of anger and disappointment toward his son before shifting his attention to Principal Lever, urging him to continue. "As one would expect, Peter delivered a blow to Damien's chin, causing him to collapse onto the floor. Jack and Lance promptly assisted him, at which point I intervened."

"Surely you could have intervened sooner to prevent this altercation," Mr. Frost interjected.

"Mr. Frost," responded Principal Lever, "I indeed could have intervened, but if I had broken up the fight before the first punch, it would have shifted the conflict to another area and time within the school. Once somebody used fists, we've found ourselves gathered here now. Our school strictly adheres to an anti-bullying policy. I could suspend all the boys involved, including Peter and David, who were innocent parties. However, Peter struck Damien despite being provoked. We can't condone kids retaliating with physical violence, can we?" Peter nodded in agreement as Principal Lever addressed him.

"So, what sort of punishment do you propose?" Christine Smart inquired. Principal Lever had not yet decided on a specific punishment, but an idea suddenly materialized in his mind. "All right, since you three boys targeted Peter for his participation in the school choir, I have an idea. Henceforth, all five of you will be required to join the choir. Peter is already a member, but the other four boys will join, as Mrs. Abbott has expressed a need for more male voices. Therefore, you will become a choir member whether you desire it. Failure to comply will cause a two-week suspension," he declared.

"Oh, don't worry, Principal Lever," Mr. Frost reassured. "Damien will sing his heart out in the school choir."

"Jack will, too."

"And Lance," Jack and Lance's fathers said in unison.

"Indeed, David will do the same," concurred Natalie and Steven Clements.

From that day onward, the parents agreed that bullying within the school had no place. In the subsequent years, Peter Walker and David Clements developed a close bond akin to that of brothers. Grandma Chris wholeheartedly embraced this friendship, knowing that, upon her eventual passing, Peter would find himself orphaned.

CHAPTER TWO

LEFT ALONE

"Grandpa, Grandpa?" Josh Cadman called out. Elvis Senior, awakened by a gentle poke from his grandson, slowly regained consciousness. "Josh, my dear boy," he said, "I was reminiscing about those youthful days. What can I do for you?"

"I apologize, Grandpa. I wanted to make sure you were..." Grandpa chuckled and interrupted, "To make sure I hadn't kicked the bucket, perhaps?"

"No, Grandpa, well maybe, because I didn't hear snoring." Grandpa Elvis glanced at his grandson. "I snore? How could I drown out this delightful music that is still playing?" One of Elvis's chart-topping songs, 'Suspicious Minds,' had just started playing, and the duo resumed singing. Josh, however, stopped singing when he noticed through the rearview mirror that the two identical black vehicles were tailing them not far behind. Grandpa also caught sight of them through his side mirror. "Now listen, Josh, it's possible that your Grandma Louise hired them, and maybe they're just doing their job. Having them close is fine if they don't get too close."

"Should I step on it, Grandpa? I could lose them again." Grandpa Elvis shook his head. "No, as long as they don't approach too closely, we should be fine," he replied. "Your grandma would have my head if she indeed hired them."

"All right, Grandpa, we're approximately 45 minutes from our exit onto Highway 30, where we can take a break."

"Still a splendid plan," Elvis senior mumbled as he reclined in his seat, closed his eyes, and slipped into another slumber. Josh chuckled when he heard his grandfather snoring this time, but he didn't dare interrupt him until they reached the refueling station.

Elvis Senior was now in a deep sleep, embarking on a dream that transported him back to when he found himself an orphan. It was May 7, 2015, and a young Peter woke up in bed, realizing he was late for school as the clock showed 8:48 a.m. He should have been at school. In a rush to find out why his grandmother hadn't awakened him on time, he couldn't find her anywhere. He wondered if perhaps Grandma Chris had forgotten it was a school day. A brief chuckle escaped him as he approached his grandmother's bedroom.

As he opened the door, his laughter immediately turned into sorrow, for he could see that his grandmother had peacefully passed away in her sleep overnight. Though doubtful at first, he cautiously approached her lifeless form. She appeared as though she were merely asleep, but reality dawned on Peter as he touched her arm, feeling the chilling sensation. At that very moment, he realized he was all alone. "Grandma Chris, wake up!" he pleaded. "Please, Grandma, wake up! Grandma Chris!" He did his utmost to rouse her, but unfortunately, it was too late. Christine Smart peacefully passed away in her sleep at 84.

Falling to his knees, Peter cried in agony, resting his head on her icy arm. Losing his beloved grandmother affected him even more profoundly than the tragic demise of his parents. Back then, he was merely a 5-year-old who couldn't comprehend the concept of death.

His grandmother had taken him in, his sole caregiver, and life had continued until this moment of desolation when he realized no one else would be there to look after him.

After a futile attempt to wake his grandmother, he picked up her cell phone and dialed 911. In minutes, the police and an ambulance arrived at the residence. Seated in the main living room, Peter found solace in the presence of two female police officers. His attention abruptly shifted as two paramedics carried his grandmother's covered body out, preparing to take her away. He wept uncontrollably, and the two officers spared no effort to console him until Tina Olsen from child services appeared to bring Peter into custody.

"Hello Peter, I'm Tina Olsen from child services," she introduced herself, expressing her condolences. Peter stared at the floor in disbelief as his entire world crumbled instantly. "Peter, I want to assure you we will place you in a temporary foster home," she reassured. "Maida Dall is a remarkable woman who will take care of you. She is an emergency foster caregiver. Would you mind telling me your age?"

Although Tina was talking, Peter's mind was elsewhere, consumed by the reality of his loneliness. "Peter, Peter," Tina called out, struggling to regain his attention. "Please listen to me, because I need your age to access your file back at the office."

"I'm almost 14 years old, and now I have nobody," Peter sadly replied. Tina placed her hand on his shoulder, offering support, and uttered, "Yes, Peter, I understand. However, once I gather the relevant information from our office computer, I can double-check to see if you have any relatives that your grandmother never mentioned." Peter looked up at Tina, who leaned in closer and embraced him, providing much-needed comfort. "My date of birth is September 27th, 2001," he revealed.

"Peter, that's what I needed," Tina exclaimed, gently caressing his head. Suddenly, his emotions overflowed once again. "Don't hold it in; it's OK," she assured him. "It's a normal reaction. You know, Peter, you're too young to live alone."

"So, where will I go?" Peter inquired, pulling away from Tina's embrace. Tina rummaged through her handbag, retrieved a tissue, and wiped away his tears. "You'll be staying at Maida Dall's house," she replied. Peter shook his head and said, "But you said she's only a temporary foster parent." Tina chuckled. "So, you were listening to me. Hopefully, in time, we'll find a loving family for you to live with. But for now, I need you to go to your bedroom and pack your clothes and any small belongings. We'll gather the larger items later. Come on, Peter, I'll assist you."

After some time, Tina and Peter packed some of his possessions and departed Grandma Chris's house for the last time. Upon arriving at Maida Dall's house, Maida, who was waiting on her front porch, greeted them. Maida, a fitness enthusiast with short brown hair in her sixties, was dressed in a yellow t-shirt and black gym tights. Peter remained quiet until Maida encouraged him to speak.

"Hello, Peter. I'm Maida Dall, and you'll be staying with me for now. I'll ensure you go to school every day, although it won't be your current school because of the distance. But soon enough, you'll make new friends."

"I don't want to go to a different school, and I already have friends," Peter protested.

"Listen, Peter, come inside, and I'll show you your room," Maida persuaded him. At that moment, Peter felt lost and had to accept the path before him. "Thank you, Maida," he whispered, clutching onto the guitar his grandmother had given him on his last birthday.

Although he never received formal music lessons, he taught himself to play by watching YouTube videos.

A week later, Grandma Chris was laid to rest next to her daughter, Maxine, and son-in-law, Brian Walker. Peter attended the funeral accompanied by Maida Dall and Tina Olsen. His classmates, particularly his best friend David Clements, and his parents, also paid their respects. The sun shone brightly as they lowered Grandma Chris's coffin into the burial plot. Suddenly, an Elvis Presley recording played Christine's favorite song. As 'An American Trilogy' filled the air, everyone joined in singing.

One month later, while playing an Elvis song on his guitar in his room, Peter was interrupted by a knock on the door. "Peter, you have a visitor," Maida informed him before opening the door. As Peter shifted his attention from his guitar, he was pleasantly surprised to see his closest friend, David, entering the room. "David, my man, I've missed you so much," Peter exclaimed, promptly rising from his bed to greet him with an embrace. "I feel the same way, Peter, but you can let go now," David said as he wriggled out of Peter's tightly held grip. Finally releasing his friend, Peter remarked, "What an unexpected visit!"

David shrugged nonchalantly and explained, "Well, Peter, you live quite far from me. I need you to come downstairs because my parents are waiting to ask you something." Peter's excitement grew, suggesting, "Well, couldn't they leave you here for a little while and come back later to pick you up? We could do some stuff together! There's this fantastic park nearby with one of those exhilarating zip lines."

"Peter, just come downstairs and talk to them," David urged. Reluctantly, Peter replied, "Well, all right, let's go. But David, ask them if you can stay longer because I've missed you, man."

They descended the stairs to find Steven and Natalie Clements waiting with warm smiles. Peter had yet to learn why they were there or what they wanted to discuss with him. All he wanted was for David to stay for a few hours so they could hang out. "Hello, Peter," Natalie greeted. "How are you doing?"

"Doing well, thank you, Mrs. Clements," Peter replied. "Could David stay a little longer so we can spend time together?" Natalie opened her arms invitingly and said, "Come here, Peter." Peter approached her, and they embraced, reminiscent of a mother and son. David joined his father, who placed an arm around him. "Peter, David has something to ask you," Steven announced.

Turning towards them, Peter wondered why David suddenly had a question for him, considering they had just been upstairs together. "Well, what is it, David?" Peter inquired. With a smile, David stepped closer to Peter and revealed, "How would you like to become a foster brother?" Peter heard the words, but it took a moment for their meaning to sink in. "What? But aren't we already like brothers?" Peter questioned.

As he got even closer, David beamed and exclaimed, "No, Peter, I mean, how would you like to become my foster brother officially?"

Deep down, Peter had longed for the day when a young couple would decide to take him in and offer him a proper home. Having witnessed his grandmother's passing and being aware that Maida Dall was only a temporary caregiver, he could hardly believe what his best friend had just proposed. "I would love to!" Peter enthusiastically proclaimed, prompting them to share a heartfelt hug in front of Maida Dall. Fortunately for Peter, David's parents had already applied to become foster parents.

The Public Trustee finally settled the estate of Grandma Chris, and her house was sold approximately six months after her funeral.

A trust fund was set up for Peter, containing over $600,000, which would remain untouched until he turned 18. This money would play a crucial role in Peter's future endeavors, as it would fund a year of preparation for his desired pursuit.

Josh Cadman skillfully parked the Cadillac in reverse before Sally's Diner. His grandfather was still in deep slumber, but he needed to awaken him. "Grandpa, Grandpa," he gently called out, "it's time to wake up." Elvis senior stirred, half-snoring, and fully embraced reality as his grandson prodded him. "Oh, what is it, Josh?" Grasping the situation, he quickly surveyed the surroundings and noticed the absence of the two black vehicles. "No, Grandpa, they continued driving when we entered this gas station and diner."

"Perhaps they were headed in the same direction coincidentally," reasoned Grandpa Elvis. "Regardless, where exactly are we, Josh?" Young Josh smiled and gestured towards Sally's Diner behind them. "We've arrived at Sally's Diner, close to Little Rock," he responded. "I've already fueled the car, and now we're about to dine." Still partially asleep, Grandpa comprehended their plan and questioned, "So I missed the last turnoff completely?"

"Yes, you must have been dreaming about Grandma because you kept referring to her as Grandma Chris. Who is Grandma Chris?" inquired Josh. His grandfather recollected the dream involving his grandmother, and his grandson's mention of her name stirred up some raw emotions. "Ah yes, that's right. I must have been confused in my dream," he replied. "You know, dreams, they make no sense. Anyway, let's grab some lunch inside because I'm starving." Skillfully, he diverted his grandson's question, avoiding the need to tell him about his grandmother, Christine Smart. However, he knew he would share the truth with him soon.

Suddenly, a swarm of Elvis fans materialized as they realized the legendary king of rock and roll. They eagerly requested a photograph with the king, and he graciously obliged. After a few minutes, they entered the diner for lunch. "Gee Grandpa, you still accommodated all the fans," remarked Josh.

"Naturally, I always make myself available to the fans," Grandpa replied. "You know what? One day, this may apply to you as well. Initially, we all crave fame and fortune, but sometimes, when these so-called celebrities attain such a status in their careers, they forget about those who supported them and the person they once were."

Josh directed an unfamiliar expression toward his grandfather as he struggled to comprehend the words being uttered. "Who did they leave behind?" he inquired.

His grandfather let out a disproving sound. "They left behind their authentic selves," he explained. "I'm referring to the person you truly were before stardom overshadowed everything. Nowadays, my boy, some of these so-called stars are nothing more than self-centered individuals."

"I understand now, Grandpa," Josh acknowledged. "Even though you are renowned as the king of rock, known as Elvis Presley, you are still John Cadman, the individual who walked into Sun Records in 1953 and rose to fame. But deep down, John Cadman has never truly left your mind." A smile formed on Grandpa's face as he placed a reassuring hand on his grandson's shoulder. "Finally, Josh, you comprehend," he replied, his voice trailing slightly because he knew that John Cadman himself was also a façade and Peter Walker was the actual person within him.

The two men found themselves seated in a cozy booth inside the diner, and soon after, a pleasant young waitress approached to take their order. "Hello, my name is Stacey, and I will be your server—uh, sorry, I'm nervous. Are you both ready to place your order now?"

"We are, indeed, Stacey," replied Grandpa Elvis. "Oh, and one more thing, after you've taken our order, please inform the kitchen staff I would be delighted to offer them a photo and autograph. I have some concerns about how those individuals prepare our burgers."

"Mr. Presley," Stacey asked. "Could you please sign my order pad? My parents will flip when they hear about it." Josh chuckled as he observed the youthful enthusiasm and star-struck admiration for his grandfather exhibited by Stacey, who appeared to be around his age. This was the first time in his young life that he had ventured out in public with his famous grandfather, and he quickly realized that this man was still a legendary rock icon to the outside world. "It would be my pleasure, Stacey," Grandpa smiled.

Soon enough, everyone in the diner had a selfie and autograph from the king of rock, and they both savored their burgers in tranquility, apart from one customer who audibly exclaimed when she realized the famous man. "Grandpa, I know you supposedly invented the selfie pose many years ago, but I'm curious about how you came up with the idea. Cameras were rare back then, unlike today when everyone has a camera on their cell phone," Josh inquired, his curiosity again piqued.

His grandfather pondered how he could explain that he hailed from the future and had brought forth the concept of posing for photographs years ahead of its time, all because of his knowledge from the past. "I will tell you just how I came up with the idea," Grandpa said, "only after we meet up with Elvis Aaron Presley." Josh couldn't understand why his grandfather had to wait until he met this dude with the same name but had to accept it until then. "OK, Grandpa."

Chapter Three

ELVIS, MEET ELVIS

Approaching the off-ramp on Highway 30, then continuing towards Roosevelt Road, Grandpa Elvis remained silent in the Cadillac. A sign showing their proximity to Little Rock had made him anxious as he was about to meet his ultimate idol. Just yesterday, he had spoken to Elvis Aaron Presley over the phone to discuss their upcoming meeting. The guilt he had carried for 67 years had weighed heavily on his soul, which motivated him to visit the real Elvis and propose an alternative reality once again.

"Grandpa, we're only minutes away from this dude's house," Josh said. "If you're feeling stressed, we still have time to turn back." Grandpa Elvis chuckled and replied, "Once you meet this guy, you'll understand who he is, and you won't refer to him as 'this dude' anymore."

Josh shook his head and scoffed, "I've already researched him through Facebook and Instagram, and I'm not getting too excited about meeting him." His interest had only been piqued because his grandfather had built up this meeting to where he believed they must have shared history. He glanced at his grandfather, who returned his gaze.

"The story I'm going to tell is unavailable on Facebook or Instagram," Grandpa assured him. "Eventually, you'll realize I'm not who I claim to be." Suddenly, the car swerved off the road, aggressively braked, and skidded on the gravel before coming to a halt. Young Josh needed an explanation from his grandfather. "Grandpa, you're scaring me," he said, concerned. "I've never seen you like this." Grandpa chuckled, "Scare you? If you keep driving like this, you'll kill both of us. Now I'm the scared one."

"Grandpa, I, I…" At that very moment, they both laughed at Grandpa's remark about Josh's reckless driving. "I'll have to hear your story before I judge," Josh said, "Grandpa, after the next left turn, we'll arrive on his street." His grandfather nodded, granting his grandson permission to proceed. Josh shifted gears into drive and slowly merged onto the road, "We're almost there; this is Webster Road," Josh confirmed. "And there it is, number 39. This is the house, and it looks like a beautiful mansion. I think he's wealthy, Grandpa, so at least he won't ask for a loan."

The pink Cadillac stopped on the opposite side of the road, next to the house at number 39 Webster Road, Little Rock. Grandpa Elvis surveyed the house and confirmed his grandson's observation—Elvis Aaron Presley had undoubtedly prospered financially, judging by the house's appearance. "Shall we go inside?" Josh inquired, "We can't remain here indefinitely."

"I apologize, my boy. I am simply gathering my composure as meeting the real Elvis today holds immense significance for me."

"The real Elvis?" Josh exclaimed. "Are you serious, Grandpa?" Grandpa nodded and replied, "Once we enter, I shall disclose everything to both of you. Amongst the family, apart from Grandma Louise, you shall be the sole recipient of the truth about me. Elvis Aaron Presley will be the other individual to learn of my past actions."

"I suppose it's time to enter," Josh stated, "since I am certain that the drapes covering the bay window have moved several times. This Elvis Dude must already know our presence, and judging by the cars in the driveway, he may have informed a few individuals as well." Elvis Senior did indeed notice a BMW and a Mercedes parked in the driveway. "Well, I told him I wished to avoid any media attention or the company of friends. Perhaps those cars belong to his family," he remarked. "I must meet all of them, as he mentioned over the phone, that he had five children and eighteen grandchildren."

Josh recognized the similarity and responded, "Hold on, you have the same number, too; yes, you do. 1. Aunty Lisa Marie, 2. Uncle Peter, 3. My dad, John, 4. Uncle David, and 5. Aunty Christine. You have eighteen of me."

"A coincidence," Grandpa asserted.

"Well then, let's go, Grandpa," Josh suggested. He then alighted from the car, circled, and assisted his grandfather out of the Cadillac. Slowly, they made their way across the road, and the grand estate reminded Grandpa of Graceland, owing to its size. However, it was a single-story house. The mansion boasted tan limestone cladding, with gray shutters and drapes visible through all the windows. A well-maintained hedge stood in front of an expansive veranda that seemed to encircle the house, accompanied by an impressive set of stairs leading to the front entrance. The driveway, which formed a horseshoe shape, featured an elegant fountain as its centerpiece, surrounded by lush lawns.

Ultimately, Elvis Aaron Presley lived in a colossal mansion; the distinction, however, was the absence of double gates with the iconic silhouette of the king of rock and roll. No, this Elvis lived a life of freedom, unlike the original, who had dwelled behind high fences and gate security. Understanding that the real Elvis had achieved financial success, Grandpa Elvis observed the imported cars they passed, showing that his children had been well cared for. Before they even rang the doorbell, the door swung open, and standing before them was Elvis Aaron Presley himself.

Contrary to the overweight Elvis, who had initially passed away in 1977, this version of Elvis was tall and slender. He still sported the same hairstyle, but the hair was silver and gray, and his eyes were as blue as the sky, but his face had aged over the years, as he was now 85 years old. Elvis Aaron Presley felt nervous as his namesake, the king of rock and roll, now stood before him at his front door. Both men admired each other, although only Elvis, the imposter, knew the truth.

Exchanging no words, the two older men gazed at each other intently. When Josh realized that the two aging men were afraid of each other, he chuckled nervously. Meeting each other was already quite significant for Elvis, the imposter, but his shock grew when Priscilla Presley approached from behind her husband to see why they were standing outside. Josh was about to speak when his grandfather interrupted, saying, "Priscilla Beaulieu."

"Now I see that you've done some research, Elvis, because I haven't been called that name in years," she said, "thanks to Facebook, of course." She leaned in to embrace Grandpa Elvis and kissed him on the cheek, doing the same to his grandson. "Nice to meet both of you; I'm Priscilla Presley," she said, "well, Elvis, meet Elvis."

Suddenly. Both Grandpa Elvis and Elvis Aaron Presley extended their right hands for a shake. Realizing that he had extended his idol's life, Grandpa Elvis was emotionally overcome and embraced the real Elvis. Stepping back to get another glimpse, he noticed the icon was dressed in blue denim jeans, a black short-sleeve shirt, and white Nike sneakers. Quite distinct from the images he remembered from the 1970s jumpsuit era.

"Hmm, hmm," murmured Josh as silence befell the two elderly men again. "Apologies, I forgot my manners," Grandpa Elvis said, "this is my grandson, Josh Cadman." Priscilla realized that a humorous situation had just unfolded. "Elvis, meet Elvis," she said. Laughter filled the air, breaking the tension as Elvis Aaron Presley welcomed them into his home. Some family members of the real Elvis approached Grandpa Elvis.

"Elvis," real Elvis said, "this is my eldest daughter Gladys and her husband Tom Granger." Grandpa Elvis fixated on Gladys, as she bore an uncanny resemblance to Lisa Marie Presley, the sole daughter of Elvis Aaron Presley in the past; indeed, she was the very person he contemplated silently. She had the same biological parents, albeit with a different name honoring her grandmother, Gladys Presley.

"Elvis, this is my eldest son, Vernon, and his wife Anita," real Elvis introduced, "and here is my daughter Lisa and her husband Greg Mathews."

"Dad, can you fathom your idol is in our house?" exclaimed Lisa Mathews.

"No, Lisa, I can hardly believe it, but here he stands," real Elvis replied.

"Hey, Dad," she added, "did you inform Mr. Presley that you used to be an Elvis impersonator back in the day?" Her father felt embarrassed, as he didn't wish his idol to perceive him as a mere imitating fan. "Ah, Lisa," he responded, "surely Elvis wouldn't want to hear about that." Grandpa Elvis was already aware of this. It was ironic how things unfolded, and it never ceased to amaze him that the real

Elvis had impersonated himself. "No, Lisa," Grandpa Elvis chuckled, "I guarantee he was exceptional at it."

"Yes, he was," Lisa affirmed. "Hey, we still have videos of your performances, don't we?" Real Elvis placed his hands on Lisa's shoulders. "Now, enough of this, Lisa," he said, "our guest might feel uneasy, assuming I'm some sort of obsessed follower." Grandpa Elvis chuckled, knowing that he was the one and only stalker. "No, it's all right, Elvis," he assured, "I'd be interested in seeing your videos someday." Real Elvis shook his head, "Yeah, perhaps," he remarked, "or maybe never."

"So, you're the grandson." Lisa observed intently, "So, you're the chauffeur, and your name is Josh?"

"Well, today I am the chauffeur," he replied. "My father, John, usually has the honor of driving my grandpa around." Lisa's matchmaking instincts went into overdrive. "Oh, I see the resemblance," she commented, "and quite handsome. How old are you, Josh?"

"I'm 19," Josh responded.

"I have a niece around that age," she stated. "Is Emily already here?" Real Elvis intervened. "No, Lisa, she is not," he clarified. "I apologize if my daughter had made you uncomfortable, Josh. She always acts as a matchmaker. I believe you and Emily, my granddaughter, who is Jesse Garron's daughter, share many commonalities."

"Starting with having a grandfather named Elvis, although yours is a superstar," Priscilla added, "anyway, she is undeniably beautiful."

"Soon we are expecting Karen, the wife of our son, Jesse Garron, and the rest of the family," real Elvis stated, "as per your request, Elvis, there will be no media present, only our family." Grandpa Elvis greeted everyone and upon hearing real Elvis mention Jesse Garron's widow, Karen, he felt compelled to express his condolences. "Elvis, I am deeply sorry for your loss. Your son was the most outstanding governor of

Texas during our time, unlike the corrupt individual who took his place. My apologies: I must be cautious with words."

Real Elvis likely expected discussions regarding his famous son, the late governor. However, hearing his idol speak such warm words touched him deeply. "No need to worry, Elvis," he responded. "Because I feel the same way. My son Jesse Garron did not deserve to die____."

Grandpa Elvis revealed that Jesse Garron was named after Elvis's deceased twin brother. Real Elvis was taken aback by this disclosure, wondering how the king of rock and roll could know such a private detail. "That's correct," real Elvis confirmed, "but how did you know that?" Everyone eagerly awaited an explanation, but he could not speak until he shared his story first. "I need to speak with you and my grandson to reveal the truth of my past."

Real Elvis agreed, saying, "All right, we can do that. However, we have prepared a barbecue for you and your grandson. It will take place outside under the gazebo." Grandpa Elvis felt honored by the gesture, but did not intend this to be part of his plan. "I apologize, but we did not come here for a barbecue," he explained. "I need to have a private conversation with you and my grandson. Perhaps later, if it is not too late, we would be honored to be your guests."

Elvis glanced at his wife and suggested, "Cilla, why don't you take everyone outside? The three of us can have our discussion in the front lounge." Priscilla followed his suggestion and left the three men alone. "You have a wonderful family, Elvis," Grandpa Elvis commended.

"Thank you, Elvis," Real Elvis replied. "They truly are." The three men proceeded to the front lounge, resembling more of a cinema with three red recliner lounge chairs against one wall and a massive flat-screen television on the other. However, what caught Grandpa Elvis's attention were the family photos adorning the wall between the lounge and the TV, opposite the bay windows, the same bay windows where the drapes, colored in cerulean blue, had shifted as both grandfather and grandson anxiously awaited in the car.

"Oh wow," exclaimed Grandpa, while looking at the real Elvis. "You and Red West?" Real Elvis was curious to know what was happening. "Yes, that's correct," he replied. "But how would you know that? Have you ever met him before?" Grandpa Elvis chuckled softly. "No, I haven't, but once I reveal what I have to say, you'll understand how I know so much about you and your friends." Real Elvis scoffed, "What do you know about me, Elvis? With the internet, you can dig up anyone's business. Ah, poor Red, he passed away only three years ago. We remained friends throughout our lives, and I still miss him. We still catch up with Pat, his wife, from time to time."

"Elvis, the two of you were always close. He even worked as your bodyguard once," stated Grandpa Elvis. Real Elvis shook his head disapprovingly. "What? No, he never fulfilled that role for me," he exclaimed. "He was never a bodyguard, and certainly not mine." Grandpa Elvis realized he was getting ahead of himself and held off on explaining further. "Elvis, it will all make sense once I share my story with you," assured Grandpa Elvis. However, Josh did not know what his grandfather was referring to. "Grandpa, what are you saying? Nothing you're saying makes sense."

"Josh, my boy, once I divulge the story of my past, you will understand I have been living a falsehood for far too long. Tomorrow will be the day I can finally make amends for my mistakes," Grandpa Elvis confessed. Real Elvis felt a sense of unease, even within the comfort of his own home. "Wow, Elvis, please," he pleaded. "Both of you, sit down. This talk about tomorrow is making my head spin." Josh questioned if his grandfather was losing his sanity. "Grandpa, are you all right?"

"Yes, grandson, I am perfectly fine," assured Grandpa Elvis. They settled into comfortable lounges, finally allowing Grandpa Elvis to unravel the events of the past. Priscilla entered the room, carrying a tray filled with beverages and snacks. "I hope I'm not interrupting," she apologized. "But I couldn't envision leaving our most esteemed guest without refreshments." Real Elvis beamed at his thoughtful wife. "That's my beautiful wife," he expressed. "Always thinking of everything."

"Elvis, what would you like to drink?" she inquired. His gaze fixated on a particular bottle that caught his eye. "Is that bourbon?" he questioned.

"The finest bourbon from Kentucky," she confirmed. Grandpa Elvis determined that a shot of liquor would help steady his nerves. "Yeah, I'll have a shot of that, please," he requested.

"And what about you, young Josh?" Priscilla directed her attention towards the underage grandson, uncertain of his preference. Josh, being under twenty-one, was unsure of what to say. "It's all right, Josh," reassured Grandpa, "have a drink; it will calm your nerves when you hear what I have to tell you."

"Well, Elvis," Priscilla said, "What will you be having, EP?"

"Yes, Priscilla, pour me one as well," he replied. "I could use some calming as well." Priscilla poured him a shot of bourbon and handed it over. "All right, I'll step outside," she announced. "Oh, Josh, why don't you join me? We're expecting some of our grandchildren around your age."

"No, thank you, Mrs. Presley; my grandfather wants me to hear his story."

"Very well, then I'll head outside. Just call out if you need anything," Priscilla said as she left the room.

"So, you and Priscilla must have crossed paths in Germany," Grandpa Elvis began, "during your army service."

"Yes, Elvis, but how did you come to know about our time there?" Real Elvis inquired. Grandpa Elvis crossed his legs, settling comfortably while assuring them he knew much more than expected. "In due time, Elvis," he responded, "you will come to understand. However, seeing you and Priscilla together brings me great joy." Real Elvis was still oblivious to the forthcoming story. "Elvis, I'm just an average guy," he stated, "with a famous name. Yet, you are a superstar sitting here, drinking with me in my house. All right, Elvis, what's weighing your mind?"

CHAPTER FOUR

WHO ON EARTH IS PETER WALKER

Grandpa Elvis sank into contemplation. He had rehearsed countless times over the years how he would recount the story to the real Elvis, how he had journeyed back in time and stolen his career, leaving the other Elvis unaware of his destined fame. Finally, he found himself in this moment, where he had always envisioned himself, considering what he would say next. This man, claiming to be Elvis Presley, had suddenly lost the one talent that had propelled him to a worldwide renown—his voice.

"Grandpa, Grandpa?"

"Yes, I apologize, guys," he replied. "I always had a plan until now. I need both of you to approach what I will share with an open mind."

Real Elvis leaned forward in his seat. "It's all right," he said, "just tell us what's on your mind." Josh also urged his grandfather, "Yeah, Grandpa," he said, "We're ready to hear what you have to say."

"All right then," Grandpa Expressed, "I shall begin from the start. The name I was given upon birth is Peter Walker, and my birth date is September 27th, 2001." Josh found this amusing, but his grandfather looked sternly at him. "What are you saying?" Josh interjected, "That would show that you are the same age as me, 19 years old. Are you well?" Grandpa detected his grandson's cautious approach. "Allow me to explain," he responded, "and afterward, you may inquire about anything you wish."

"Explain yourself, Grandpa, as your words seem nonsensical to me. You are 85 years old, and your birth name is John Cadman, born on February 18th, 1935. Peter Walker, who on earth is he?"

"Now, Josh," Grandpa interjected, "I did not bring you here to intervene every time I utter something that appears absurd. I implore you to let me conclude and reassure you I have not yet lost my sanity. With time, both of you will believe me, since what I am about to disclose here today is the veritable truth." Josh noticed the anger in his loving grandfather's eyes and realized that he had offended him. "I apologize, Grandpa; I did not intend it that way." Young Josh and real Elvis exchanged glances, wondering what the matter could be. Had he gone mad? Or was he unwell?

"Very well, that is who I am, Peter Walker, and I was born in the original reality of 2001. My parents' true names were Brian and Maxine Walker. Brian, my father, worked as a carpenter, primarily in Nashville. Maxine, my mother, pursued a career as a hairdresser but became a homemaker after my birth. She encountered health complications during her pregnancy with me, thus rendering her unable to bear any more children."

"I lived a normal and content life, albeit only occasionally seeing my Grandma Christine Smart. However, tragedy befell me in 2006; my parents met their demise in a car accident just ten miles outside of Nashville." Grandpa Elvis paused, overwhelmed by the emotions brought on by the tragic loss of his parents all those years ago. The two other men recognized he struggled to push forward with this extraordinary yet peculiar account, and he snapped out of his trance.

"At the tender age of five, I was not supposed to experience the untimely loss of my parents," he expressed. "On that fateful day, they were on their way to enrol me in elementary school, but as luck would have it, I fell ill. They entrusted me to my Grandma Chris in Brinkley. It was my illness that led to their demise. They would not have been on that road if I had been well. It is my fault that they perished."

Elvis Aaron Presley and Josh Cadman exchanged glances, bewildered by the overwhelming nature of these words. This 85-year-old man is burdening himself with the guilt of his parent's death over eight decades ago. Grandpa continued his narrative. "Following their passing, I lived with my maternal grandmother, my only relative. Her name was Christine Smart, a woman of 75 years. Now, Elvis, this is where your involvement in my life's reality begins. You were born to Vernon and Gladys Presley on January 8, 1935, in Tupelo, Mississippi. Unfortunately, your twin brother, Jesse Garron, passed away at birth."

Real Elvis interjected, "Elvis, can't we find all this information online?" Grandpa Elvis nodded, "Indeed, you probably can," he replied, "but what you won't find is the fact that you departed this world on August 16th, 1977, at 42."

Perplexed, Josh exclaimed, "Grandpa, this is unbelievable! Are you suggesting that this Elvis here actually died in 1977? But, if that's the case, he doesn't resemble the Elvis we know." Grandpa fixed him with a stern gaze. "Listen, it will all make sense once I conclude this account and unravel the truth behind this historical puzzle. I will explain how it came to be. So, Elvis, in the summer of 1953, you visited the Memphis Recording Services, famously known as Sun Record's Studio."

"Wait right there, Elvis," the real Elvis interjected, "that was your initial record label, and naturally, you were privy to that knowledge. Perhaps you recall our encounter at the Sun Records' Studio." Grandpa's eyes sparkled as the real Elvis mentioned their meeting. "Certainly, Elvis, I remember that moment well," he replied. "We crossed paths because I already knew of your presence there. I arrived before you since it was where Sam Phillips presented you with your record contract, signaling the start of your career."

"What career?" the real Elvis questioned. "He never offered me a recording contract. He merely mentioned that they had already signed another Elvis Presley, and initially, he thought I was joking when I revealed my name. However, he believed me once I showed him my driver's license."

"Yes, Elvis, I was present that day," Grandpa Elvis affirmed. "Allow me to explain; over time, it will become clear that I entered that studio and secured the recording contract before you. That was when I assumed your identity." The real Elvis scoffed, "I understand it was a long time ago, but according to my recollection, he only called me pretty good and said he would call me if things didn't work out with you. Elvis, we both know he never contacted me, and you became the superstar you still are today."

"Well, there's something about that," Grandpa Elvis continued. "OK, let's revert to my original childhood. My grandmother, Christine Smart, took me under her wings, and life was normal at that age. She loved you so much, Elvis, that I, too, became an avid fan despite your supposed demise in 1977. Your music remained popular even in 2006___." Interrupting, the real Elvis interjected, "Elvis, I still don't grasp what you're trying to convey. Despite our brief encounter in 1953, I, I___."

"Grandpa," Josh interjected, "you established you met Elvis briefly, but this all feels like something out of 'Back to the Future,' akin to the movie."

In grand excitement, Grandpa Elvis exclaimed, "Indeed! Like the movie, I relived my past exactly 67 years ago, and that date is approaching November 20, 2020. Allow me to elaborate before you become utterly bewildered, my dear grandson." Josh and the real Elvis chuckled, "Of course, Grandpa."

"When I was five years old in 2006," Grandpa recounted, "I went to live with my Grandma Chris. That was the year I started school and met my dearest friend, David Clements. David made it possible for me to travel back in time in 1953. However, I journeyed from the year 2020. Elvis, you were always a part of my childhood, as I would sing your greatest hits with Grandma Chris almost every night. Now, let's fast forward because sadly, on May 7th, 2015, Grandma Chris peacefully passed away at 84. This profoundly affected me, as I was now an orphan."

"From that moment onward, I felt forsaken and alone, and the future appeared bleak. I had no one left and experienced a pain I never wished to endure again. Fortunately, I was taken in by a temporary foster carer named Maida Dall, a woman with a heart of gold. I can't recall where she lived, but it was not Brinkley. She was incredibly nurturing and provided me with a sense of security. That's what I needed then—to feel safe but still lonely. About a month after Grandma Chris's funeral, I was in my room at Maida Dall's house when my best friend, David Clements, visited me with his parents."

"Steven and Natalie Clements applied to become my foster parents, and for the first time in my life, I finally felt like I belonged to a family.

They wanted to adopt me, but it wasn't necessary since I was already 14 years old. From then on, David was not only my best friend but also my brother. Life felt good, and I lacked nothing because the Clements ensured I was treated like their son. Their love for me was genuine. Over the following years, after 2015, I underwent various changes that led to an obsession with you, Elvis Aaron Presley."

"I believe you may also still have an obsession with Elvis," cheekily remarked Josh Cadman. Chuckling, Grandpa Elvis replied, "Oh, my mischievous grandson, tell me, who is your favorite singer nowadays?" Young Josh promptly pointed at his grandfather and said, "You, Grandpa."

Both elderly Elvis's burst into laughter. "No, not me," Grandpa said. "Surely there must be someone else." After careful thought, Josh finally said, "Ed Sheeran."

"All right let's pretend you were seated in Ed Sheeran's living room," Grandpa suggested.

"Well, that would be pretty amazing," responded Josh. Grandpa Elvis displayed a content smile. "Now you comprehend," he conveyed, "that's exactly how I feel sitting here in Elvis Aaron Presley's house." Real Elvis also grasped the sentiment but remained doubtful about traveling back in time. "Elvis, I appreciate the sentiment," he uttered, "but it's hard to believe going back in time only you know about."

"Elvis, I must elaborate further," Grandpa continued. "The changes I experienced in 2015 were immense. I began dressing as you did in the 1950s. In 2015, I stood out like a sore thumb; people labeled me as a weirdo. Like you, I even went to the barber to style my hair. Your signature looks throughout your career. Over the next four years, I slowly transformed into a replica of you, Elvis, the original king of rock and roll. I missed my Grandma Chris terribly, and you were my only connection with her during that time."

"Elvis, I must reiterate, it's an honor," real Elvis responded, "but time travel?"

"Well, the idea of time travel first crossed my mind when David stumbled upon some fascinating facts that occurred only every 150 years. It was during the summer of 2019, probably in June or July. I distinctly remember not having turned 18, so it must have been before September 27th. It was scorching hot that year. Anyway, David discovered that every 150 years, there is an anomaly—an anomaly as a tear in the Earth's atmosphere. A vortex allowing travel through time, but only to the past, not the future."

Real Elvis inquired, "So, you're saying it's a tear like a rip?"

"That's right, Elvis. Initially, I, too, doubted it, but David was convinced. He uncovered instances of this abnormality spanning 1000 years. Although there were documented occurrences, they didn't describe them the same way as David did—going back in time. Something undoubtedly occurred each time. Some historical events hinted at the same narrative as David, but the most recent recorded incident dates to 1870. Perhaps our advanced technology could have shed more light on these events, but it didn't exist back then."

"David referred to these tears as doorways that only opened with significant energy. According to him, when these doorways appeared in the past, they led to a different dimension in time. Let me tell you, Elvis, David's obsession with this abnormality far outweighed my obsession with you. He immersed himself in any scientific literature he could find on the subject. He even contemplated involving the government, but I spared him from potential humiliation. During that time, I pitied David because he lost sight of leading a normal life, whereas my infatuation with you, Elvis, had long been established."

"At least I went on dates with girls. It's not that he wasn't interested in girls; it's just that his project consumed him. His goal was to ensure that the right individual or government could alter the past. From that point forward, David changed, and I suppose I changed too because I missed my rock—Grandma Chris. Back then, I genuinely believed you, Elvis, and Grandma Chris were together in heaven, perhaps watching over me."

As Grandpa Elvis recounted his story, his grandson absentmindedly scrolled through his cell phone. "Grandpa," he exclaimed, "I just searched for this tear, rip, or anomaly, and to my surprise, a renowned astrophysicist named Louie Vanda Berger mentioned it in 1993. He stated that such an event was highly improbable, but he suggested that theoretically, a chance for a back in time existed."

"Well, despite the absence of Google," stated Grandpa, "these anomalies exist, as I encountered one myself."

Josh, at last, realized that his grandfather's story was not a fabrication, and never did he suspect any form of mental instability from him. It was indeed reminiscent of the concept of time travel; who knows? If his grandfather had created this tale, he would have executed it with remarkable proficiency as Elvis Aaron Presley reclined in his armchair, recounting his life. On that day in 1953, he visited Sun Records, not only to record a vinyl for his mother but also to hear his vocal abilities, driven by his ambition to become a singer. However, he never received the opportunity, for the man beside him had stolen his journey to stardom instead.

Grandpa persisted, "Months went by, and eventually, David determined when the next anomaly would occur. It was November 20, 2020, precisely at noon. Tomorrow's date, but this occurred 67 years ago. Although I remained skeptical when he initially informed me about this future date, he successfully configured a computer algorithm to calibrate a timeline for backward time travel, allowing him to select which year to visit. Through his calculations, he discovered that by channeling a specific amount of energy into an area, a portal could be opened, positioned in the same spot, but only leading to the past. David's explanation gradually made more sense, even more so than my current narrative. Hopefully, once I disclose the rest of this tale, both of you will believe me."

"Elvis," interrupted the real Elvis, "Before you proceed, I believe it's necessary to replenish our bourbons to process your back-in-time theory. Why don't you both hand me those glasses, as I suspect you too might require a refill."

Real Elvis took their glasses and poured them an ample serving of bourbon. He never expected such an exchange from his idol. And now, his aspirations of a singing career, the destiny he intended to fulfill, became validated by his genuine sentiments, ultimately erasing any lingering doubts he had harbored regarding his adequacy as a singer during his era.

Grandpa resumed, "On a particular day, upon leaving my guitar lesson, I encountered a group of individuals awaiting me outside the Brinkley music studio. Once they laid eyes on me, they started a confrontation, ridiculing me solely based on my appearance, which at the time resembled how Elvis originally appeared, with black hair and extravagant attire. They followed me everywhere I went, incessantly tormenting me. It felt like I had returned to school, reliving the same hardships. My ability to savor life significantly diminished."

Real Elvis expressed, "Contrary to popular belief, my hair was never black. It leaned towards the blonde spectrum rather than a dark hue."

Grandpa Elvis said, "Indeed, Elvis, I discovered through online research that your hair was described as blonde in your profile. However, you consciously dyed it black upon ascending to rock and roll superstardom. Thankfully, because of my Italian heritage from my father's side of the family, I was naturally blessed with black hair, thus eliminating the need for such alteration. My appearance during the year 2019, I suppose, seemed rather unconventional for that era."

"Fast forward to mid-September 2019, just before my 18th birthday. I was consistently overwhelmed by a sense of alienation wherever I went. Perhaps the inspiration to transform into the legendary Elvis from the past provoked thoughts of my late Grandma Chris. However, I had not yet contemplated the possibility of time travel, as it seemed utterly unattainable at that point."

"Eventually, David devised a method of traversing through this portal to the past, using a high-voltage metallic ring. His theory comprised drawing the tear or gateway towards us by providing an energy boost with an upright metallic ring that contained the entrance within it. It is essential to note that this journey was strictly one-way."

"Following my 18th birthday on September 27, 2019, just three days later, specifically on Monday, September 30, I received a summons to the law office of Grandma Chris's attorney in Brinkley, Arkansas. The purpose of this meeting was to facilitate receiving the inheritance given to me by my beloved grandmother. Over the years, the initial sum had matured substantially, approaching $780,000, thanks to the accrued interest. This generous amount was provided to me as a bank cheque."

"Initially, I was at a loss for how to handle this newfound wealth. However, David persistently emphasized the existence of this temporal anomaly. At that moment, burdened by the daily torment of bullying and feeling disconnected from the world around me, I began pondering the prospect of journeying back to when your illustrious career as Elvis began in 1953."

"Elvis, initially, my intention was merely to embark on a time-travel adventure to attend one of your early concerts. However, after witnessing your outstanding performance, I grappled with what I would do next. In the realm of possibilities, I contemplated becoming your confidant who could offer guidance based on knowledge of your future missteps. Yet, I also considered that our paths might never cross, and I would find myself adrift with no obvious purpose. After all, your life came to a premature end in 1977 at the tender age of 42. Despite this, an innate desire to assist you arose within me. Perhaps, in those days, I could have engaged in a conversation about your future, Elvis. However, the likelihood of a stranger heeding my fitness advice seemed improbable. You would have likely rejected my input, perhaps even delivering a knockout punch."

The three men erupted into laughter. "Perhaps I would have, Elvis," the real Elvis said, still chuckling. "So, how did I pass away in 1977 at 42? You already know that I am 85 years old, just like you, and boy, I feel it every day, but here I am, still standing."

Grandpa Elvis's laughter ceased, his expression turning serious. "Elvis, you succumbed to a heart attack on August 16th, 1977," he stated. "That was the official report then, but you depended heavily on prescription medication—uppers, downers. You had gained a substantial amount of weight by the time of your passing. You were quite a hefty man. If you had cared for yourself better, you might still be with us today."

"Well, I still am," the real Elvis replied. "Now, I don't know about your tale, Elvis, but would you have traveled back in time if I had taken better care of myself?" Grandpa Elvis was taken aback and had never pondered that scenario before. "That's a valid question," he remarked. "I can't say for certain, but I suppose you would be me, and hopefully, I would be you?" The real Elvis chuckled, "And married to Priscilla as well?" The three men burst into laughter once more.

Elvis Aaron Presley now comprehended some things his idol, who sat in his living room, had told him. However, he remained unconvinced of the truth behind the story. Grandpa Elvis sensed this and introduced his trump card. He retrieved some photographs from the inner pocket of his jacket and handed the first one to the real Elvis. As soon as he glanced at the photo, a change came over his face.

"Hey, man," he exclaimed, "this looks like me, but who is the woman here? Yeah, this seems to be my handwriting and signature. It must have been photoshopped, man. These kids can use phone apps to place people anywhere in a photo. One of my grandchildren took a picture of me, making me look younger."

Grandpa Elvis introduced Elvis to his grandmother, Christine Smart, who influenced Grandpa's knowledge about Elvis. Grandma Chris had the Polaroid picture with Elvis's signature, proving its authenticity as Polaroid photos can't be Photoshopped like digital ones. Real Elvis turned the image over and noticed the date stamp on the back: July 22, 1962. Astonished, he exclaimed, "I have no recollection of this photo, and look at me; I was dressed just like you!"

Grandpa Elvis explained, "Of course, you don't remember this photo. It was taken in my original reality, not the one we live in." Young Josh examined the image, and Grandpa Elvis handed the real Elvis another photo, a newspaper clipping from 1959 showing Elvis performing on stage. The real Elvis and Josh now had irrefutable evidence that the story being told to them was true.

Grandpa then presented another newspaper clipping to Elvis, hesitating because he knew it would be difficult to see. This clipping, dated 1976, showed the real Elvis wearing his famous unbuttoned rhinestone jumpsuit that exposed his hairy chest after a concert. The most shocking aspect of the photo was how overweight Elvis had become. Real Elvis, feeling disbelief and becoming physically ill, shook his head and said, "This is shocking! I can't believe I ended up this way. Look at my bloated face."

Concerned, Grandpa Elvis asked, "Elvis, are you OK? I apologize for showing you this photo, but that was how you turned out in my original reality." Real Elvis smiled at Grandpa and replied, "Yeah, man, I should thank you for preventing my premature death. I feel... strange, Elvis strange."

Young Josh regretted, saying, "I'm sorry for ever doubting you. Scientists worldwide are unaware of what we know here and now." The three men laughed and settled back into their armchairs. The real Elvis turned to Grandpa and said, "This is mind-blowing, Elvis. Tell us more."

Chapter Five

ELVISGATE

Grandpa Elvis, in continuation, divulged, "All right, so I came into possession of $780,000 from Grandma Chris's inheritance. I kept this money in my bank account for quite some time, as I was unsure what course to take. However, an idea struck me that would forever alter the lives of everyone involved: you, Elvis, my beloved grandson, as well as all the individuals currently outside, and even our family back home. During this period, I had too much-unwanted advice from acquaintances because of my growing fascination with emulating your image, Elvis, and my lack of living relatives who would miss my presence if I were to disappear."

"David and his parents made up my only familial connections; hence, my plan would also affect them. However, comprehending this reality was no easy feat when I conceived of transforming myself into Elvis. To gain attention, I made a purchase that would undoubtedly draw the gaze of onlookers. I ventured to David's university, patiently awaiting his emergence. Once he arrived, he sensed I harbored some plan. David frowned as he approached me, desperate for confirmation regarding the authenticity of my intentions. Seeking to execute a surprise, I positioned myself within the identical pink Cadillac Fleetwood

Series 60 that Elvis purchased for his mother, Gladys, and now it belonged to me."

"He inquired about the cost of this extravagant vehicle, to which I replied nonchalantly, Only $120,000. The seller was remarkably persistent in their pricing, leaving me no choice but to succumb to its allure. David stood in disbelief, alleging that I had lost all touch with reality. I did not expect such a reaction from David, perhaps his parents, but not David himself. And so, I addressed him, saying: David, I have devised a plan to aid you in your back to the future theory. Seeing a growing crowd caused David to grow unnerved, compelling him to join me in the passenger's seat swiftly. Perceiving the same, I started the car's ignition and hastily departed. David was correct in his assessment that the gathering crowd was too extensive, to which I should have exercised caution. Yet, my buoyant spirits overruled my better judgment."

"He inquired about my intentions before I spent all my savings. I queried when his back-to-the-future anomaly was due to occur. He explained that once a portal to the past materialized, it would only permit one to travel in that direction. Returning would require living through those years and finding a way back to the present year one initially left behind."

"After conversing, my inquiry arose: What if I could travel back to 1953? David responded with laughter, assuming I would choose a prominent era as my target. However, I challenged his assumption and questioned the significance of the year 1953. Why does it hold such importance? He inquired. Unable to reveal my motives, I informed him we were embarking on a different path. Puzzled, he asked why this was so. I disclosed that our presence on Elm Street in Brinkley was because I parked the pink Cadillac in front of an apartment building. Seeking answers, David sought clarity on our purpose there, to which

I directed his attention to the colossal green power transformer positioned just behind the ground-level unit block."

"For 18 months, I had secured the lease of the basement apartment on the bottom floor. David, gazing at the green transformer, was perplexed by the situation. Citing that our parents' house was rent-free and my decision to spend money seemed irrational, he insinuated I must have gone mad. However, his initial assumption was proven partially correct when I revealed my intention to construct a Stargate metallic ring within the confines of the apartment. Showing the power transformer next to the apartment wall, I explained we could connect a conduit to it, harnessing enough power by November 20th, the following year."

"Inquisitive about my sudden interest in creating a time travel device, David commended the plan but sought an explanation. I disclosed my desire to return in March 1953 and visit Sun Recording Studio in Memphis. I intended to record a couple of songs for a mere $4, replicating Elvis' actions that summer for his mother. He tried to unravel how I had gained such specific knowledge, and I informed him that Google had served as my source. His amusement at the revelation prompted contagious laughter, and we shared a moment of joy, wiping away tears and mucus. He resumed questioning the soundness of my judgment."

"David argued that, although I might slightly resemble a young Elvis because of my already black hair, I lacked the talent of a singer or entertainer. Then, I divulged my plans to enrol in singing lessons in the morning, acting lessons in the afternoon, and guitar lessons in the evening, five days a week, starting the upcoming Monday. Once again, David's laughter filled the air as he asserted that even if I were to gain singing skills and become a B-grade actor like the king, what would happen when the real Elvis Aaron Presley walked into Sun

Records and Sam Phillips, the owner, noticed our shared name, style, and appearance?"

"In my explanation, I conveyed that if I had arrived before the real Elvis, Sam Phillips would have already offered me a recording contract as Elvis Presley, as he couldn't possibly have two individuals by the name of Elvis. The genuine Elvis would have stepped aside to lead a regular life, while I would have become the most renowned singer of all time in his stead. Once again, David chuckled and astutely remarked that my infatuation had clouded my judgment. How could I possibly have gained legitimacy in 1953 in America? After all, my identity was Peter Walker, who was not even born until 2001. Was I going to stroll into Sun Records, sing a few songs before the actual Elvis, and somehow convince Sam Phillips to offer me a contract instead of the real Elvis that summer?"

"At that very moment, I had not fully planned, but I would eventually figure it out. Therefore, I once more beseeched David to enter the apartment so that he could better comprehend our construction of the Stargate. We made our way down a flight of stairs leading us to a door I opened, and we both entered. Inquiring about his thoughts, he approvingly observed that everything was perfect, as the green transformer was strategically behind the wall. We could erect an upright metallic ring by removing a few bricks and connecting an industrial power cable to it, taking advantage of the spacious ceiling."

"At that point, David became visibly emotional, inquiring about my ability to abandon him and his parents. Holding back tears, I explained that my unwavering devotion to Elvis was ingrained in me by my grandmother. I loved David as if he were my brother, and the same sentiment extended to his parents. I was undeniably grateful for the love I had received, but I felt compelled to pursue this endeavor. If I were to gain the contract as Elvis Presley and use the knowledge of the future that I possessed, I would conscientiously navigate the path that the real Elvis had stumbled upon."

"In this undertaking, I would never indulge in drugs, whether stimulants, depressants, cocaine, or any form of potent substances. Of course, it occurred to me that the drug known as ice may not have even existed in that era, and Elvis never succumbed to such detrimental vices. Above all, the utmost priority would be to maintain my physical well-being. I would exercise regularly and resist consuming those deep-fried peanut butter and jelly sandwiches, or banana fried sandwiches that Elvis was notorious for enjoying."

"From that moment, David fell silent and surveyed the apartment, his gaze landing on two rooms beyond the kitchen. He directed his attention to the old television cabinet in front of the wall housing the power transformer. Although he wanted to witness the outcome of his experiment, he wouldn't risk losing his closest friend and brother. I informed him that those two rooms served as bedrooms, one for myself and the other for him. We planned to move out of our parent's house and settle here to construct the Elvisgate. The name resonated with him, and I could discern his growing enthusiasm. However, I asked him again if he could accurately configure the computer to determine the correct timeline for March 1953."

"He assured me that, given enough time, he would decipher it. We had many tasks to tackle before making any computer adjustments. This was fantastic news, as he had finally agreed to lend a hand with my endeavor. Subsequently, I explained to him why our apartment was ideal for 1953—no structures were present on the same plot of land during that period. When I arrive in 1953, I will stand on empty land."

"Over the following weeks, we moved from our parents' home. Initially, they exhibited some resistance, but eventually relented, allowing us to settle into the Elvisgate apartment complex on Elm Street. My singing, acting, and guitar lessons progressed satisfactorily, and during the hour-long journey between Brinkley and Nashville, I frequently serenaded myself with Elvis' CDs. By doing so, I refined my singing skills and gradually sounded more like the authentic Elvis."

"David was deeply involved in the project as well. He extensively studied his previous findings regarding this anomaly and felt certain that the targeted date of November 20, 2020, at noon, was accurate. Subsequently, we scoured every nook and cranny for a round, metallic ring suitable for our Elvisgate. Unfortunately, nothing we discovered proved suitable. We lacked the welding skills. After weeks of futile searching, I searched eBay for any Stargate props available for sale. Miraculously, it was a life-size replica of Stargate, used in the Stargate television series during the 1990s. Its suitability was undeniable, as it was constructed from steel. However, the greatest feat was the price, a mere $4oo. But the total cost amounted to $15,000, given that the two-ton Stargate had to be delivered in sections and assembled using hydraulic lift jacks."

"After diligently following the instructions for a month and enlisting the help of fellow Stargate enthusiasts to hoist the sections into place, our lounge room was finally graced with the completed structure. Concealing our true intentions from our friends was crucial, as divulging them would have led to chaotic situations. However, we staged a celebratory gathering upon its completion. The Elvisgate was nearing its finalization, with the only remaining task being the connection of the power, a task we consciously delayed until the morning of the event."

"By December 2019, we were making significant progress on the project. However, their concerns flared when David's parents visited us and saw the Stargate. They feared that my indulgence in purchasing a pink Cadillac, and the Stargate investment were depleting my inheritance, yielding nothing tangible."

"To some extent, their concerns were valid, considering that the time travel had substantial financial implications. We deduced that the American currency had evolved since the 1950s and getting money from 2020 and using it in 1953 would cause my arrest for counterfeiting. Hence, a plan was hatched to gain banknotes from the 1950s instead. These notes were bought from collectors, and I even artificially inflated their value during some transactions because of my aggressive purchasing tactics. Ultimately, this endeavor proved to be costlier than initially expected. At least I possessed the funds to sustain myself until I secured the coveted Elvis gig. Some notes were encased in frames, causing some improvisation on my part to make them appear used."

"In February 2020, I made significant progress in my singing and acting lessons by attending additional classes. Although things were going smoothly, I had yet to devise a plan to become a legal American citizen in 1953. Initially, our idea involved seeking someone from that year who could create fake documents or birth certificates since computer systems hadn't been developed yet. However, upon researching the possibility of locating individuals with such skills from the past. David was concerned about the potential risks and legal consequences involved. Determined to find a solution, I continued searching the internet for information on obtaining American citizenship. It wasn't until May 2020 that a revelation struck me, prompting me to print out the information and hand it over to David."

"To my surprise, David praised me as a genius upon reading the materials I provided. The documents comprised a newspaper article and a birth certificate belonging to John Cadman, who had disappeared on March 15, 1953, in Nashville, Tennessee. According to the records, John was an eighteen-year-old Caucasian male, born on February 18, 1935, measuring six feet one inch in height. To my delight, his physical features resembled mine, with black hair and blue eyes. The story even mentioned that he had no living relatives and had been reported missing by his landlord."

"With this new information, my path to legitimacy seemed clear. All I had to do was visit the local DMV in Brinkley, present the birth certificate, and explain that I had been a mugging victim, resulting in my driver's license and social security card theft. Following that, they would issue me a new set of identification documents under the name of John Cadman. From that point forward, David referred to me as John to help me adjust. He was almost finished with the preparations and had set the date for March 15, 1953, three months before Elvis visited Sun Records Studio in Memphis."

CHAPTER SIX

THE ELVIS MANUAL

During his storytelling, Grandpa Elvis was interrupted by Kylie Anne, 17, and Cindy, 19, who were the real Elvis's granddaughters. They entered through the side gate and made their way through the back door to meet Elvis the Star, and a glimpse of young Josh. Priscilla followed them and gestured for them to join the rest of the family outside, leaving the three men alone to continue. It never occurred to Josh Cadman that he would find a girlfriend that day, but he found himself drawn to the two sisters as they walked away.

As the two sisters chatted and giggled, they both agreed on the undeniable good looks of Elvis Presley's grandson. Aware of their conversation, Josh wondered about Emily whom Lisa had mentioned. Being the grandson of a global superstar meant his freedom was limited—he couldn't simply go out to a movie or nightclub without being recognized. The nightclub scene was still two years away, considering he was only 19. Real Elvis refilled their glasses with bourbon, and Grandpa Elvis resumed his story.

"All right, it was September 27th, 2020. It marked my 19th birthday and my last celebration as Peter Walker. David's parents hosted my party, and some people there were confused when David referred to me as John. I explained it was an inside joke between us—David being a fan of 'The Beatles' and me, a devoted follower of Elvis. David would jokingly call me John, as in John Lennon, to tease me. Thankfully, they found it amusing."

"Although it happened over 67 years ago, this birthday remains remarkably significant in my memory. By October 2020, I had completed my singing and acting classes and was ready to embrace my role as Elvis. During this period, I extensively researched every aspect of your life, Elvis, relying on Google for information. I knew I needed something to remind me of the dates and timings of key events for the next 67 years—when Sam Phillips discovered the real Elvis, when each song was presented to him, and even when I had to prepare for every movie."

"Elvis, you starred in 33 movies, the same 33 that I also took part in. However, my most significant one was 'A Star Is Born'. It granted me the acting credentials you, Elvis, never truly gained. Please don't misunderstand me, as the beach and youthful-girl-chasing movies we both engaged in. You were never truly satisfied with your film career. You were offered the movie 'A Star Is Born' alongside Barbra Streisand, but I will discuss that later."

"David was unworried about the Elvis-related aspects of the manual, as he believed that even if someone were to get that information, it would simply be seen as pure fiction. However, his primary concern was including other significant events and tragedies in the 75 years before 2020. If someone comes across this manual, they can alter the future permanently. Although I considered making some alterations,

David insisted it was best not to, and I will explain later why he was correct."

"Now the date is November 19, 2020, coinciding with today's date, but 67 years ago, just a day before I embarked on my journey to become Elvis. We had decided that on our last night together, we would spend time at his parent's house, and oh, I almost forgot to mention Tracey Mathews."

"There was a woman who was just as old as me. We had some casual flings, but I couldn't commit to her because I wanted to become Elvis. She confessed her love for me multiple times, and I almost gave in and ended it just weeks before I stopped being Peter Walker in that reality. Even though I had feelings for her since she was perfect, it was purely coincidental that she showed up at the Clements' door that night, which was our last dinner."

"As dinner was about to be served, she entered the dining room and asked me to step outside for a private conversation. David became too invested to back out after initially refusing my plan to go back in time. However, I assured him I would talk to her privately while still going ahead with the plan. Little did I know what was about to unfold..."

Grandpa Elvis paused, choking back his emotions, and shook his head with bitterness. "Are you all right?" his grandson asked. Still lost in his thoughts, he realized he had to continue his story. "Yes, grandson, I haven't even shared this tale about Tracey Mathews with your grandmother. When I went outside with her, she dropped the bombshell that she was six weeks pregnant and wanted to know what to do."

"Man," the real Elvis interjected, "that threw a wrench into the works."

"Yes, Elvis, it certainly did," Grandpa Elvis replied. "I informed Tracey about my departure and left the decision about the baby up to her, but David would still be there for her financially if she kept the baby and sought his help."

"On the eve of the fateful day before the experiment, I told David why Tracey had come to his parents' house. I told him she was six weeks pregnant and how incredible she was. I deeply loved her, even though I could never confess it. David then wanted to abandon the experiment and begged me to stay, highlighting the promising future I could have with Tracey without worrying about my Elvis ambitions."

"I was completely disoriented, as my mind was uncertain about what course to take. I disclosed to David that I had tragically lost my entire family; hence, I had to embark on a new life as originally planned. Subsequently, I handed David a letter initially intended to be given to him just before my departure the next day. However, considering I was now responsible for a child who would not have its paternal figure present, I opted to present it to him instead."

"As David unfolded the letter, a bundle of keys inadvertently tumbled onto the floor. As he picked them up, it became apparent that they belonged to the pink Cadillac, complete with registration documents bearing his name. The vehicle had already been registered in his name at my purchase."

"Nested within the registration papers were the property deeds for the apartment on Elm Street, which I had originally purchased under his name as well. Contrary to what I had previously conveyed, no lease agreement had ever been drafted. Both David and I became emotional as tears welled up in our eyes. He called me cunning, yet we embraced one another. While his accusation held some truth, as I had meticulously planned this from the very beginning, the recent news from Tracey Mathews compelled me to make certain modifications. Thus, I presented David with a bank account statement in his name, showing that $200,000 had been reserved for his benefit. However, I now propose that he allocate half of this sum to Tracey Mathews, as she would be the mother of my child."

"As I had suspected, David had secretly harbored feelings for Tracey. He sought my consent to assume the role of a father figure to my child and become her life partner, eventually offering her the full amount, under the condition of my blessings. How could I possibly decline such a proposition? After all, David was my brother, who had solemnly reassured me he would step up as a father to my child during those moments when my self-centered ambitions had clouded my judgment. The realization that David had devised this thoughtful plan filled me with contentment. However, I also acknowledged that I would never be privy to the outcome of his plan, as I was embarking on an irreversible journey."

"Whatever became of David and Tracey Mathews would remain concealed within my original reality. Presumably, they eventually married, but who can say for certain? Perhaps David disclosed the truth about my fateful voyage to 1953 to Tracey. I left behind a part of my being, namely the potential child that, in the best-case scenario, Tracey would bear."

Chapter Seven

BACK TO 1953

"On the following day, November 20th, 2020. The basement apartment experienced the first ray of sunlight. The glimmer of sunlight reflecting from a small window reached my bedroom, where I had spent a restless night. However, my roommate David had no trouble sleeping, his snoring causing vibrations that threatened to dislodge the Elvisgate from its position. Deciding to act, I rose from my bed and resolved to remove the remaining bricks from the apartment wall just behind the Elvisgate. The goal was to create a pathway for the connected industrial power cord."

"Striking the brick repeatedly, I witnessed the sunlight grow stronger as it broke through. Strangely enough, I had no aversion to its brightness, as I knew this would be the last time I would experience this sunshine in my current reality. My persistence paid off as the stubborn brick finally gave way. The noise I made with the hammer and crowbar had roused David from his slumber, prompting him to join me in the living room. Greeting me with a yawn, he wordlessly sat down next to me. It seemed as if he had momentarily forgotten the purpose of our actions, but realization soon set in when he embraced me."

"Good job, he remarked. I chuckled, wondering if he had intentionally left the task to me, as if to imply, Let's reconsider, Peter. Who knows? However, it was too late for second thoughts. Determined to proceed, I discarded the pace of our efforts, for the electrical cable was now poised to pass through the freshly created hole in the wall. With eight o'clock in the morning fast approaching, only four hours remained until the moment of irreversible change. The morning swiftly passed, yet its memory remained vivid in my mind, even after all these years."

"David inquired about my recent printing activities last night after hearing the noise. Concerned that I had printed additional history pages, he expressed his belief that I was making a grave mistake. Assuring him that there was no cause for worry, I explained my intentions were solely focused on saving lives. My major goal was to prevent the tragic 9/11 terrorist attacks from happening; thus, I planned to inform the FBI, hoping to avert this catastrophe. However, I intended to conduct a few smaller practice actions beforehand to gauge their effectiveness."

"As David suspected, the printer had indeed been working the previous night as I surreptitiously printed out a year's worth of horse racing results. Inspired by the film 'Back to the Future' wherein Biff gains riches by utilizing a stolen almanac containing past sporting outcomes, I memorized some results as a backup plan to ensure success, even without physical documentation. Knowing David's disproval, I executed this scheme covertly."

"Time flew by that morning, and I found myself adorned in my elegant Elvis attire, prepared to witness the culmination of my endeavors. Despite the realization that David now had a chance with Tracey Mathews, as I would soon disappear, the uncertainty of each other's journeys created a difficult situation for both of us. At exactly 11:30

a.m., we positioned ourselves outside, and David, sporting heavy-duty gloves that appeared rather absurd, reassured me they would protect him from potential electrical shocks. Passing him the cable connected to the device, I jokingly remarked that, in the event his anomaly proved incorrect, at least I would still have Tracey Mathews. However, to my utter surprise, he revealed he had messaged her the previous night and arranged a date for the next day. This quick turnaround prevented any brotherly conflict, as evidenced by my ability to share this story with you."

"David unscrewed the panel on the side of the electrical transformer while I handed him the cable, retreating a safe distance in case he encountered any hazards. It is astounding to think that our meticulous planning could have been in vain if we had suffered an electrical mishap. David firmly gripped the cable with both hands in his oversized gloves, carefully wedging one end into the high-voltage element. Although not a technically advanced installation, the sight of sparks emitted from the transformer and the glowing lights within the wall where the bricks were missing proved its effectiveness. With a sense of relief, we embraced each other, fearing the worst for David. Since the lights inside had become incredibly bright, we ventured inside to switch them off to avoid drawing attention from passersby or residents in the apartment above."

"Upon entering the basement apartment, we were astonished to discover that the intense brightness did not emanate from the lights but from the Elvisgate. The entire ring glowed intensely, surrounded by electrical sparks that pulsed inward and emitted zapping sounds upon contact. Uncertain of what to expect, as this had never been attempted before, we marveled at the vibrant energy filling the room that day, realizing that it would ultimately reach its climax in the next fifteen minutes before noon."

"At that moment, memories of the television show 'Stargate' flooded my mind, recalling how individuals would disintegrate when close to the Stargate as water gushed out. Uncertain if water would burst forth, we cautiously took a step back, ensuring our safety. As the clock ticked towards 11:55, a mere five minutes remained until something significant was to occur. The Elvisgate had emitted an abundance of heat by this point, raising concerns about being caught. I unzipped my vintage leather backpack, as it blended in more appropriately with the aesthetic of 1953 compared to today's modern sports-style bags, which would have appeared out of place. Inside the backpack, I verified the fifteen thousand dollars in cash and ensured that the Elvis manual was securely stored within."

"After that, I passed my cell phone to David, since it would be useless for the next 50 years. Having futuristic technology was risky, but nobody would have believed it, anyway. My mind was now focused on the 'Terminator' movies, where Arnold Schwarzenegger would travel back in time naked. David chuckled and advised me to cover up. Luckily, I had memorized some horse racing results just in case any of this happened."

"Only 30 seconds were remaining, and we exchanged glances, knowing that this was it. As the countdown reached the final 10 seconds, we expected something extraordinary; however, nothing, I repeat, nothing occurred. Anxiety grew as the 30-second mark passed, but then, on the 40ˉsecond, it happened. Sparks finally burst forth, thankfully sparing us as we stood in the kitchen, as they traveled inches away. The interior of the ring emitted a steady white light, illuminating its metallic surface."

"David fetched a broomstick and carefully approached the ring, poking the end of the broomstick into the electrified circle. Hastily, I circled the perimeter of the Elvisgate, and to my relief, the broomstick was nowhere in sight. But what if...? The same fate would have befallen me if the broomstick had disintegrated. All worries dissipated when David withdrew the broomstick and astonished us both. Not only was the broomstick unscathed and free from flames, but there was also an unexpected layer of snow on top."

"During March 1953, it must have snowed, which is not uncommon today. I questioned David, wondering if the coordinates were accurate or if he had accidentally opened a portal to Siberia or Alaska instead. Swiftly, I sprinted to my bedroom, retrieved a jacket, and returned to the living room. David expressed concern, believing my modern Brinkley Tigers' high school jacket would attract attention, but I disregarded his worries, since I didn't want to freeze. He reluctantly agreed, advising me to replace it as soon as possible and to head directly to the local DMV."

"In an instant, the sound of the doorbell reverberated through the room, signaling that the visitor was persistent, clear from the repeated knocking on the door. Perhaps, amidst the dazzling illumination emanating from the Elvisgate and the commotion, we had finally captured someone's attention. Curiously, David approached the window and cautiously separated the blinds, ensuring that our actions remained concealed. Meanwhile, I positioned myself near the Elvisgate, ready to intervene promptly in case it was the authorities, with the realization that time was limited."

"Meeting my gaze, David motioned for me to remain calm. Then he whispered it was merely a delivery person and advised against any apprehension. He cautiously cracked the door open, allowing only his head to peek outside. He inquired about the purpose of the visitor's presence, only to receive a curious response about the humming noise resonating from within and the unexpected brightness despite the daylight. David explained it originated from the television and requested clarification regarding the reason for the visitor's arrival. The individual relayed he had a legal document intended for a certain Peter Walker, requiring his signature."

"David offered to sign on my behalf. However, the visitor insisted that only Peter himself could provide the required signature, accompanied by identification. David directed the visitor to wait monetarily while he retrieved Peter, subsequently closing the door. At that moment, as David glanced towards the Elvisgate, where I anxiously awaited, he collapsed to his knees, overwhelmed with emotion, believing that I had already departed from that reality without bidding farewell. I retreated to my bedroom to get my driver's license to present to the delivery person. Yet, initially, I couldn't help but chuckle at David's reaction, his misguided assumption I had already left. Displaying my identification to the visitor, I received an envelope, expressed gratitude, and promptly shut the door."

"Seeking to regain some composure, David concealed his emotions and assumed an air of indifference, as though unaffected by the situation. The humming of the Elvisgate persisted, its duration uncertain; thus, time became a pressing concern. Examining the envelope's contents, we noticed the letterhead showing Abercrombie and Associates Lawyers in Brinkley. David inquired whether it pertained to Tracey Mathews, although this seemed unlikely as the law firm had represented my Grandma Chris's legal matters, particularly during the handling of my inheritance. Given the imminent time constraint, I wedged the envelope into the Elvis manual, informing David that I would investigate its contents later."

"Our faces were streaked with tears as we embraced tightly, but eventually, we let go. Taking a step towards the Elvisgate, I basked in the brilliance of static light. As I glanced back at David one last time, I waved farewell before proceeding forward. My journey to becoming

John Cadman and, ultimately, Elvis Presley had officially begun. In a flash, I found myself outside in a desolate yard blanketed by snow. Although pleased that I was alive, my joy multiplied when I realized I was still fully clothed rather than unclothed."

"Determined to confirm that everything was in order, I wiggled my shoulders and felt my backpack. To my relief, it remained intact as I removed it and unzipped it with anticipation. A delight washed over me as I beheld the sight of cash, and an Elvis manual nestled within. Could it be 1953? The thought lingered in my mind, but as my gaze shifted towards the road, the sign announcing 'Elm Street' provided affirmation. Standing at the exact location I had predicted, the scenery remained unchanged, except for the absence of the apartment block. Across the street, I noticed a building that now housed a lumber yard instead of the mechanical workshop."

"Any concerns I may have had swiftly cast aside as I observed the building's familiar high-pitch roof, albeit in a much newer condition. The once-weathered corrugated iron sheets now gleamed with a fresh sheen. Patches of snow lined the roof ridges of the future mechanical workshop. The biting cold transformed my Brinkley Tigers' jacket into a pristine white. Seeking refuge, I spotted a bus shelter from where I stood across the street, the same spot where I had previously parked the pink Cadillac. Crossing over, I nestled myself inside, seeking solace from the elements."

"After enduring approximately ten freezing minutes, a vintage, robust bus pulled up at the designated stop. Its door swung open, beckoning me to embark. The bus driver sported a brown suit, complemented by a gray shirt and black tie. His hair, meticulously styled in the old-fashioned manner with a curl gracing his forehead, further reinforced the notion of a different era. Yet, until I received undeniable confirmation, caution urged me to remain silent in my quest for answers."

"The bus driver's impatience grew, prompting him to inquire whether I wished to ride or remain at the doorway like a pelican. Being called that for the first time was amusing, so I asked if he could take me to Brinkley. He assented and requested 5 cents, astonishing me with the remarkably meager fare, a rarity in this day and age. However, the driver misinterpreted my jaw drop, presuming I was challenging the reasonableness of the price when, in fact, I was not. To rectify the situation, I retrieved a $10 bill from my pocket and handed it to him."

"In response, he insulted me, calling me a smart ass and questioning if I was wealthy. This further showed that I had somehow been transported back to 1953, where even such a modest sum as ten bucks qualified as riches. Although I could have inquired about the exact year, our conversation had not been progressing smoothly. He hurled the $10 bill back at me and instructed me to sit down, cautioning that I should bring the correct fare or be prepared to walk to Brinkley the next time. Grateful for his help, I ascended the bus as the door closed, making my way to the middle seats. Along the way, I encountered individuals dressed in an unfamiliar fashion. I settled into a seat, and as the bus departed, I experienced a sudden jolt as the driver changed gears using a large manual gearstick."

"Another clue presented itself when I glanced down and noticed a discarded newspaper on the seat next to me. It was the Brinkley Daily News, dated March 15th, 1953. My excitement overflowed, causing me to erupt in exclamations of joy. The entire bus erupted in laughter at my expense, eluding the driver, who had grown weary of my freeloading ways. David, the brilliant mind behind this mysterious computer calibration, had transported me to my desired destination. He might hold the distinction of being humanity's most significant discoverer, though his contributions would forever remain unknown. Holding onto the newspaper, I gleaned it was Sunday. Naturally, the DMV would be closed, as it never opens on Sundays, even in the present year of 2020. I could only hope to go the following day."

Chapter Eight

GINO FELLINO

G randpa Elvis had made considerable progress in narrating his story to the real Elvis and his grandson. All doubts had vanished, and their curiosity had been piqued; they craved more of this extraordinary tale that was unraveling before them. Seeking their permission, Grandpa Elvis inquired, "Shall I proceed?" They realized he had captured their attention, and he continued his account.

"So, I was on my way to the town, and the landscape during the bumpy bus journey seemed familiar. However, the absence of modern structures by 2020 was clear, as they had not yet been erected. As long as I refrained from interfering with anything, everything would remain consistent. Upon entering the town of Brinkley, the snowfall ceased, and the sun cast a bright glow on the distant buildings. The bus came to a stop just outside a movie theater. The same spot where the social services were in 2020."

"In 1953, the building that I remembered looked different. I intended to visit the Social Services Department, where I would present them with a new copy of John Cadman's driver's license, thus establishing myself as a legitimate citizen of the United States. Following that, I planned to proceed to Sun Records in Memphis. As the other passengers on the bus made their way towards the exit, I remained seated, lost in my thoughts. Retrieving some smaller notes from my backpack, I prepared to pay the bus driver. Feeling guilty, I approached the front of the bus and apologized to him before handing him a $1 bill. I insisted he keep the change, as he had done me a favor by not leaving me behind to freeze in the snow."

"Wow, 95 cents, he exclaimed. Thank you, because now my family can have steak for dinner tonight. Wishing him a delightful meal, I disembarked from the bus, watching as the door closed and the bus resumed its journey. Familiar sounds revealed to me my location: the chiming of the bell from the clock at Town Hall. Glancing at my wristwatch, I encountered a major predicament. It wasn't the time, as my Apple watch, set with characters from 'Toy Story,' showed 1 p.m., matching the time on the clock. The problem lay because I had inadvertently brought a watch from the future into the 1950s. I intended to exchange it with my old-fashioned analog watch, which I had left on my bedside table after dismantling the bricks earlier that day. Alas, it was lost to me forever."

"Regrettably, I should purchase a replacement tomorrow and dispose of this one to prevent anyone from discovering it, particularly since I lacked a charger or network to update the data. Thankfully, the timer function operated autonomously without requiring a network connection, which was non-existent in 1953. In search of a place to dine, as the bus driver had mentioned steak and aroused my appetite, I strolled further down the deserted street. Wendy's Diner seemed suitable, and I approached and peered through its open doors, thanking the heavens for its availability and vacant seating. Upon entering, a refined lady beckoned me to take a seat, and I obliged by settling into a booth."

"This establishment reminded me of the nostalgic ambiance of our local Burger King outlet, adorned with antique booths, an extended counter featuring bar stools, and a jukebox nestled in the corner. It was reminiscent of Arnold's from the 'Happy Days Show,' if you will. The lady introduced herself as Wendy. Her well-kept, red hair was styled in an elegant French roll-up, and she sported a pale green tunic with a white collar and apron. Curious about what had drawn my attention, she inquired, and I expressed my admiration for her establishment."

"She said it's a diner, and they all have a similar atmosphere, but she was proud of serving the finest cuisine in Brinkley. A polite smile graced her face as she inquired about my culinary preferences, eventually suggesting her specialty: Wendy's burger and fries combo. Convinced, I accepted her offer, prompting her to relay my order to the cook before querying my beverage selection. Opting for a Coke, I leaned back, allowing myself to relax. Glancing up at the menu prices displayed behind the counter, I discovered a hamburger was advertised for a mere 25 cents, while Wendy's combo meal was priced at only 35 cents."

"My god! I exclaimed inwardly. The 15 grand I possessed nearly made me a millionaire in 1953. Reflecting on the bargain, I marveled at the enormous size of the burger Wendy brought over—it could practically rival the dimensions of my head! Such great value, I pondered. No wonder Elvis grew so large, though that was during the 1970s. I must remain mindful of my waistline, lest I outgrow him by a couple of decades. As Wendy asked for my name, I replied, Pete, momentarily contemplating slipping up to utter Peter. John Cadman, I added, handing the meal over and watching as she removed the bottle cap from my Coke."

"I was truly impressed with my first meal from this era. Its appearance and aroma were delightful. My fingers were stretched to their limits to hold the remarkably large burger. The first bite was pure bliss, with lettuce, tomato, and mayo combined in a divine symphony. The fries had an unmistakable freshness and a unique flavor, being fried in beef tallow rather than the vegetable oils commonly used today. As for the Coke, its taste had a surprising kick to it, making each sip more desirable than the last.”

“Wendy inquired about my thoughts on the meal, and judging by my reactions, it seemed she already knew the answer. The topic then shifted to my profession. Although I could have made up a job typical of the 1950s, I deemed it appropriate to embrace my aspirations of becoming Elvis and proclaim myself a singer. Little did I know that I almost made a grave mistake by mentioning ‘Elvis’ initially as my inspiration, but I quickly corrected myself, stating that I meant to say Elvis Presley. After all, how could I speak of a person who had not yet been discovered? It was apparent that I had to exercise caution and keep my big mouth shut until I truly became Elvis.”

“Fortunately, Wendy confessed she had never heard of Elvis Presley and wished me success in my future endeavors. Eager to divert the conversation, I inquired about the eerily quiet atmosphere. Wendy explained that on Sundays, most people attended church and then enjoyed a homemade lunch with their families. Having finished my entire meal by then, I asked her for directions to the nearest hotel. She recommended the Palmerston Hotel located just down the road, advising me to be cautious because of the dubious behavior of one of the staff members and his association with some gangsters. I expressed my gratitude and was pleasantly surprised when she presented me with a bill totaling only 40 cents, including her tip. In return, I gave her a generous $1 and instructed her to keep the change. Both of us were content with the meal and the gratuity.”

"Although it may have seemed inexpensive, I reminded myself not to be overly generous, as it could attract unwanted attention. Because a meal of that magnitude would cost $25 in the future, it felt only right to reward Wendy, the lady responsible for such a reasonably priced and delicious meal. Following Wendy's directions, I ventured towards the Palmerston Hotel, its vibrant sign catching my eye. The establishment appeared modern and trendy, aligning with the budget-friendly concept of hotels in the future. Upon entering, I was greeted by a somewhat suspicious-looking man at the reception desk, who introduced himself as Tony. With his Italian appearance, it was conceivable that he might have connections to some gangsters. However, I left further speculation for later."

"I inquired about a room for a solitary night and was informed by the gentleman that it would be priced at a mere $1, astonishingly cheap, even without inspecting the room itself. I tendered a $1 bill and was requested to record my name and provide a signature. Upon inscribing John Cadman and signing, the gentleman seemed familiar with the name and asked me if I was John Cadman. Another sign, though I shall refrain from elaborating until later. As I ascended the staircase towards room 13, the man's gaze lingered upon me, which did indeed unsettle me, perhaps because of Wendy's prior cautionary warning regarding him."

"The room possessed a simple yet pleasant ambiance; its cleanliness was clear. Next to the window stood a solitary bed, though no television was present, an unsurprising fact considering it was 1953 and televisions weren't as abundant. I laid on the bed for a while, contemplating the incredible feat I had accomplished earlier that day. I pondered how matters stood back home in the life I had left behind. A sense of remorse welled up within me for forsaking my adoptive family; within my heart, I sensed that this was now my predetermined path, and there was no use dwelling on the past, even if it represented the future. It may still appear perplexing, though I am confident that you both now comprehend."

"Fatigue overcame me, causing me to doze off, only to awaken around 2:30 a.m. I had slept through dinner, though Wendy's burger had satiated any hunger that had plagued me. As further sleep eluded me, I rummaged through my cash and merged the smaller denominations within my wallet, ensuring inconspicuousness in my future expenditures. Following this, I retrieved the Elvis manual. I perused certain sections, as I had intentions to venture into Memphis the following day, contingent upon procuring the documentation from the DMV and social services."

"My plan entailed locating the whereabouts of Sun Records, for I still possessed ample time before Elvis Aaron Presley arrived there. However, it remained uncertain if the timelines recorded on Google were entirely accurate. Concerns arose from the stray sheets bearing horse racing results, prompting me to puncture holes and safeguard them within the manual, for losing them would prove hazardous in the wrong hands. At present, the only detached item remaining was the legal letter, one that had arrived just before I embarked on this Elvis escapade. It remained securely nestled between the pages, with intentions to peruse its contents momentarily, though I became sidelined by my yearning to peruse additional horse racing results."

"Having examined the listings for Monday, November 21st, I espied a peculiar name in race 8, number 6: 'The Future is yours.' How ironic, considering the circumstances I had found myself in. After losing consciousness again, I awoke to the sun streaming through the window. Glancing at my Apple watch, I noticed it was 8:05 a.m., and the battery was 20 percent. Realizing it was on the verge of dying, I decided I needed to buy a new one. Bringing my backpack with me, I made my way downstairs to inquire with Tony, much to my surprise, who was still present. However, he asked me my name again, and I replied, John Cadman. Did he forget, or was he double-checking? Curious, I also asked about the location and operating hours of the local DMV. Tony informed me it opened at 9 a.m. and was just a block away from our current position. Showing my gratitude, I thanked him and set off, but before leaving, I circled back to inquire about a jeweler where I could purchase a watch; interestingly enough, when I returned, Tony was engrossed in a deep phone conversation, so I chose not to disturb him."

"I planned to find a watch somewhere without breaking the bank, opting for something affordable and straightforward. Thanks to the warmer weather, the snow from the previous day had all but disappeared. This climate consistency was typical for Brinkley. Following Tony's instructions, I arrived at the DMV office just as a staff member opened the doors at 9 a.m. Several people had already formed a queue outside, so I joined them."

"Once inside, I positioned myself behind the person at the back of the line and retrieved John Cadman's birth certificate from my backpack, ensuring I was fully prepared. Finally, it was my turn, and as I approached the man behind the counter, I noticed a peculiar expression on his face. He inquired about what help I needed, and I shared a fabricated story about being mugged the previous day, explaining that my wallet, containing my driver's license, was stolen. I emphasized the urgency of needing a replacement issued promptly."

"To my surprise, this man seemed skeptical, asking me why I didn't appear injured or sporting a black eye. I wondered what his issue was, so I elaborated, claiming that the mugger brandished a knife, leaving me with no choice but to surrender my wallet. He continued to challenge me, remarking. Just one insignificant knife and I caved?

My goodness, I couldn't believe someone like him from the past. I couldn't fathom why he expected me to be a hero and willingly endure a knife wound. Retorting, I reminded him I was still alive. Unfortunately, under his breath, he muttered that my actions were rather cowardly. Unbelievable! This man dared to call me yellow. Did he have the desire to confront me physically? Deciding to brush off his last comment, I recognized that my opportunity to perform as Elvis was swiftly slipping away without the proper identification."

"I delivered John Cadman's birth certificate to him, addressing him as sir and politely requesting his help obtaining a new driver's license. Admittedly, my approach may have lacked assertiveness, but I was on a mission and had no other choice but to comply. He instructed me to take a seat, assuring me I would eventually be attended to. However, I couldn't help but feel baffled by the intense interrogation I encountered from this self-important bureaucrat. It occurred to me then why the real Elvis had faced such difficulties during that era. As instructed, I sat down and endured an additional 30 minutes of waiting until he finally called my name."

"Remarkably, the fee amounted to a mere 25 cents, which prompted me to offer him $1 and wait for the change. It was apparent that he hadn't earned a tip. At long last, I held my freshly issued driver's license, verifying that my legal name was indeed John Cadman. My plan was progressing smoothly as I strolled out of the DMV, scrutinizing my newfound credentials. Unexpectedly, they were snatched right out of my hands by three menacing individuals dressed in pinstriped suits, excluding a distinctly Italian vibe. I couldn't help but find their choice of attire rather cliché. Their grave expressions were matched by the corpulent figure in the center, who clutched my driver's license, while the other two swiftly seized both of my arms."

"The overweight individual smiled as he read my driver's license and said they had been searching high and low for me. Eager to maintain the charade of my John Cadman identity, I inquired about their intentions, all while concealing the fact that my ID was a counterfeit. However, the confiscation of my backpack by one of his accomplices served as a stark reminder that I was in a precarious situation. I protested, but my objections were met with laughter. 'Backpack,' scoffed the overweight individual. What on earth is a backpack, John? Before I could react, his powerful right hook struck my face, leaving me dizzy but still aware enough to recall being dragged and forcibly placed into a black Cadillac."

"During the brief period of rapid driving that followed, I remained barely conscious until we finally reached the rear of an unfamiliar shop. Another blow landed on my face, causing me to lose consciousness. I realized the gravity of the situation as I found myself tied to a chair, with my hands and legs securely bound by rope. My attempts to free myself only resulted in the ropes becoming tighter. I could not escape. Observing my surroundings, I deduced I was in an outdoor section, likely next to a deli, as I faced the shop's back area. Upon glancing behind me, I noticed a mesh-wired fence containing various canned tomatoes, olive oil, and beverages."

"On the left, there was a blazing 44-gallon drum, while on the right, seated at a table that resembled a card table, was a well-dressed gangster. It seemed fitting that gangsters would occupy their spare time in such a manner. The boss or godfather, as he appeared to be, stood up and smiled when he noticed me gazing at my blood-soaked shirt, evidence of the damage inflicted on my nose and mouth. He paused by the flaming drum to warm his hands before my attention shifted to the heavy-set fellow who had knocked me out. Positioned across from me at the table, he brandished a gun. Although this situation was dire, it paled compared to the other individual next to him, who busily counted the cash I had paid extra for back in 2020."

"John, John, John, uttered the boss figure. He then said that I should have known that they were omnipresent. They had eyes everywhere. What made me think I could simply walk away from my gambling debts? I pondered the identity of the individual who had betrayed me to this mafia leader, and I realized Tony from the Palmerston Hotel must have informed them of my whereabouts at the DMV. I witnessed him making a secretive phone call when I returned. That scoundrel had sold me out. I attempted to convince the boss that they had made a mistake. However, he dismissed my claims, citing my indebtedness to Charlie Messina, an associate of his from Nashville, where I had foolishly engaged in gambling ventures and left me burdened with debts. Now, those debts were under the ownership of Gino Fellino. Yes, Elvis, you heard that right. I found myself entangled with a figure who, in that era, was the esteemed uncle of today's gangster Governor Tino Fellino."

"I had to craft an explanation, concealing the truth that I was, in fact, Peter Walker from the future. Regrettably, of all the identities I could have assumed, I mistakenly adopted that of John Cadman, a degenerate gambler. The individual counting the money informed his boss that the total amounted to $14,900, which seemed accurate after deducting the money I had spent and the small bills in my wallet. Gino Fellino revealed that my original debt to Charlie Messina was $10,000. With the addition of daily interest and a transfer fee, my debt had escalated to $14,700, leaving me with a mere $200. He inquired whether I intended to rendezvous with him right away after visiting the DMV to settle my debt, as he required a justification for sparing my life. The hefty man referred to him as Uncle Gino and asserted that

I had insisted they had apprehended the wrong person, prompting a lesson to be taught."

"Marvelous. This corpulent mass was the boss's nephew, a fact I relayed to Gino when I informed him, that I ventured into the DMV because of a recent mugging, which caused the acquisition of a new license. I assured Gino that I would promptly deliver the money after that. Regrettably, this proved to be an ill-advised decision, as the overweight nephew hastily approached and smacked my skull with the firearm's handle, vehemently accusing me of deceit. In a fit of rage, Gino Fellino, the uncle, bellowed, imploring his nephew not to jeopardize our lucrative endeavor. Although I committed errors, I derived amusement from the ponderous fellow by jestingly highlighting the remarkable rhyming nature of their names."

"He punched me once more, nearly rendering me unconscious. Eventually, the uncle intervened, urging the nephew to rein in his emotions. Meanwhile, the fleshy mass's attention was captivated by a captivating sight—my exquisite timepiece, 'Cadman,' he remarked, audaciously confiscating my Apple watch. Eager to find out the identities of the comical animated cowboy and spaceman adorning the watch's face, he inquired about their origin and their impossible movement on a wristwatch. He swiped my Apple watch, adorned with the beloved 'Toy Story' theme, from 2020. In silence, I meditated, internally correcting his ignorance—Woody and Buzz Lightyear, for your enlightenment! Keep it, you vile gangster, for the battery's demise is imminent, and good luck charging it over the forthcoming six decades."

"If matters could have deteriorated, they promptly did when Louie, the individual tasked with counting my currency, irresponsibly divulged my entire being—my trusted compendium, the Elvis manual, a most imbecilic appellation. Flicking through a handful of pages, he puzzled over the significance of such songs as Elvis Presley's 'Jailhouse Rock,' 'Love Me Tender,' and 'Suspicious Minds'—grinning with unfamiliarity. Perplexity arose when I was confronted with film titles such as 'Flaming Star' and 'Girls, Girls, Girls.' Bewildered, I found myself at a loss for words, only for the unintelligent nephew to insinuate that the latter is a pornographic film. Almighty heavens! What a dim-witted fool! Under its title, he erroneously assumed it to be a sensual production."

"All I could mutter was that it was all a figment of imagination, for I portrayed an actor in an amateur production—a text I employed to hone my craft. Remarkably, my fabrication was met with acceptance, yet the fat nephew curiously explored the texture of the paper, stroking his fingers between the pages. Inquiring about this peculiar paper, he conveyed his unfamiliarity with such a sensation. Can you fathom? This mafia affiliate had now transformed into an expert on print materials! I had swiftly printed it on my futuristic HP inkjet printer, but I lied, stating that a newspaper acquaintance assisted in its creation."

"Upon witnessing Gino's actions by the flaming drum, my heart skipped a beat. It appeared that he was about to discard the Elvis manual into the fire, but to my immense relief, he merely waved it over the drum to reignite it. Then, Louie, the money counter, presented a plate of assorted cannoli—chocolate and vanilla—and placed them on the table. Martino, the overweight nephew, laid his gun on the table and grabbed one of each flavor in both hands. This comedic moment reminded me of a scene from 'The Godfather' movie, and I couldn't help but laugh as I remarked, how original! Leave the gun; take the cannoli."

"The others joined in the laughter, oblivious that it was a line from a movie yet to be released. With his mouth full of cannoli, Martino, no longer laughing, retorted, how about I come over there with this gun and put a bullet through your skull, just like I plan to do to Sammy Navolla tonight? Startled by Martino's unexpected confession about his impending murder, Gino, the uncle, shouted, Martino! Have you lost your mind? As the uncle posed the question, a famous quote from 'The Godfather movie crossed my mind, and I couldn't resist voicing it: Never tell anybody outside the family what you're thinking."

"Astonishingly, the uncle rushed toward his nephew and struck him in the face with the Elvis manual before smashing a cannoli on top of it. Inside, I reveled in celebration, but I knew better than to make a sound for fear of Martino seeking retribution. The uncle hurled the chocolate cannoli-covered Elvis manual onto the table, then turned to me and praised, Hey John, that's a brilliant line: Never let anybody outside the family know what you're thinking."

"Grinning to myself, I pondered how Marlon Brando had won an Academy Award for uttering those words, unbeknownst to the world until the 1970s. Despite being physically restrained by a genuine mafia gangster, Gino's compliment fostered a genuine connection, prompting me to ask if I could leave. Go? He responded, contemplating the proposition. I'll tell you what, John. I'll keep the $200 as a credit for future bets. Future bet? I questioned silently, realizing that my mission was to become Elvis, not succumb to the vices of a degenerate gambler. I inquired if I could place that bet immediately, driven by a stroke of luck."

"Can you believe it? I recalled some horse racing results from that day. So, how could I possibly fail? Everyone burst into laughter because of a degenerate gambler, bound to a chair, feeling lucky. As a reasonable man, Gino asked me which race I wanted to place my bet on. Completely clueless because of my share of concussions, I asked for the time. At that moment, the fat nephew shouted, Hey Uncle! Cadman, what happened to the funny cowboy and spaceman cartoon? Ha, the Apple watch just ran out of battery, and good luck charging it for the next 60 years, I thought."

"Boss, it's 12:55 p.m., Louie declared. Lost in my thoughts, I pondered, was it race 8, number 6, or race 6, number 8? Gino grew impatient and demanded to know why I was delaying. In response, I inquired about the upcoming race. Louie said, Race 6, Boss, in five minutes. Right, it must be race 6, number 8, I concluded. Thus, I requested to place the entire $200 on number 8. Martino, the obese cannoli muncher, laughed and mocked that 'Lucky Lucy' is a donkey. It's a 100 to 1 shot! I couldn't recall that name. What had I gotten myself into? I was about to lose all my money, and then what would I do?"

"Initially hesitant, Gino reconsidered when his nephew pointed out that if the donkey won, they would owe me $20,000. The uncle beamed with pride as he proclaimed that his nephew's logical reasoning skills resulted from his college education. That's why he's good at math. I wasn't impressed, as a ten-year-old could have done the same calculations. Growing impatient with Gino's indecisiveness, I remarked that Mr. Messina would gladly accept the bet if Gino didn't. Finally, with only a few minutes left, Gino accepted the bet, taking the bait."

"Louie produced a radio, or Gino called the wireless, and switched it on. Initially, a static sound filled the air, but as Louie found the right station on the dial, the radio announcer announced that the race was about to begin. Doubt crept into my mind as I recalled that the horse I had studied was named 'The Future is Yours'. What had I done? I had confused this horse with a donkey. The race began, and as expected, 'Lucky Lucy' lagged dead last. Gino Fellino grinned while his nephew, Martino, chuckled with delight. Then, just 100 yards from the finish line, 'Lucky Lucy' surged forward and won by a nose."

"The Rock and roll industry might have been forever changed in that very instant when I regained my money. With his mouth agape, Gino dropped his cigar, and Martino, filled with disgust, pounded a brick wall, potentially injuring his hand. Only Louie, wearing a smug grin, truly grasped the impossibility of my accomplishment. Although I wanted to cheer exuberantly, my jubilance was curtailed because I was still bound to a chair. After a brief pause, I wondered if this mafia boss would renege on our bet and simply have me killed. It was at that moment I erred on the side of caution."

"Initially, I prayed to him to release me from my restraints, and a wave of relief washed over me as he motioned for Louie to do so. I flexed my stiffened limbs to restore blood circulation while offering him an opportunity to save face. All I desired was the sum of $14,900 and, above all, the Elvis manual. I inquired if I could take the money present on the table, leaving the remaining $5,000 that he owed me as credit for future bets. Seizing the money that was rightfully mine seemed reasonable, but taking the additional 5K from his pocket could create complications. To my satisfaction, he consented but asked if I could replicate such a feat for his benefit. I swiftly reminded him that my initial success was a mere fluke, as I had always been on the losing end."

"Proceeding to the table, I snatched the cash and hastily tucked it into my backpack. Much to my surprise, Martino was perched on the table's edge, concealing the Elvis manual under his backside, only revealing a corner. The importance of this manual propelled me to act swiftly—I deftly extracted it from under his considerable frame. The evidence of a chocolate cannoli stain, which I assumed had been obliterated from his rear end, surely would have led people to believe he had soiled himself as he walked about. Gino, the boss, extended his hand, and we shook in agreement. He acknowledged my audacity and even proposed I join his ranks, but I declined respectfully."

"Louie, ever cool, simply smiled as I departed the enclosed premises of the shop and embarked down a narrow lane that led to the bustling main street I glimpsed ahead."

CHAPTER NINE

THE PINK CADILLAC

"After that encounter with a gangster, John Cadman was finally out of trouble. From then on, I steered clear of any troublesome individuals. It turned out that the obese Martino Fellino was the father of Governor Tino Fellino. It's incredible to think that if only I had known, I could have somehow dealt with Martino and prevented Tino's birth. But that's a story for another time."

"Exiting the alleyway, I found myself on the main street and glanced back at the storefront; a sign reading 'Gino's Deli' caught my eye. It was quite amusing to see a mob boss owning a deli, just like in the movies. Tired and needing to catch my breath, I settled down at a bus stop not far from the mob-run deli. I was alone and checked if my earlier assumption about the race and horse numbers was accurate."

"Being paranoid about someone abducting me again, I looked around cautiously. Retrieving my backpack, I pulled out the Elvis manual, which now had chocolate cannoli stains, and flipped to the back pages. My initial fears were confirmed as I read about race 8, set to start soon, with the winner number 6, 'The Future is all Yours.' That was the one I remembered. However, race 6 showed that number 8, named Lucky Lucy, emerged as the victor. How fortunate was I to have won back my money? But the stroke of luck did not end there, for a shining reflection across the street caught my attention."

"The dazzling reflection emanated from a vehicle sale in a car dealership across the street. Call it what you may, as this seemed too good to be true. However, it was true, for the reflection originated from a pink Cadillac positioned on a tilted ramp for display. Without hesitation, I arose from the bus shelter and traversed the road, coinciding with a bus from my previous location. As I approached, I noticed the license plate number JPS-123. Yes, Grandson, the same license plates your car possesses to this day. I could hardly believe my eyes, for this was the identical car I purchased in 2019 for $120,000 after inheriting Grandma Chris's estate. I was dumbfounded, or perhaps still feeling the effects of Martino's punches."

"The salesman approached to negotiate a deal I intended to accept regardless of the cost. I made an impulse purchase of the car on the spot. However, there were a couple of distinctions between this pink Cadillac and the one I surrendered to David Clements. First, this one was impeccably new, unlike the sixty-six-year-old vehicle in David's possession, as well as yours, Grandson. Second, the price was a mere $1,675, a true bargain, albeit not in 1953. I drove away from the dealership in my brand-new pink Cadillac, much to the delight of a salesman named Phillip Brown, who didn't even have to reduce the price because of my remarkable savings of $118,325 compared to its future value. What a steal!"

"The car handled the roads with greater ease than it did in its later years. I passed by a prestigious establishment called the Brinkley Arms, where the grand columns in the front foyer reminded me of

Graceland. I securely parked the Cadillac in the lone available spot at the Palmerston Hotel. Perhaps I had taken a risk with this vehicle, as it seemed to attract some unwanted attention. A group of young individuals approached to get a closer look, but the expression I received from Tony upon entering the Palmerston conveyed all the information I needed."

"The three gangsters who accosted me outside the DMV office were tipped off by someone aware of my identity and whereabouts. Judging by the treacherous countenance of this hotel concierge, I knew who the informant was. The astonishment on his face suggested he did not expect me to be alive. I recall seeing this traitor on the phone when I almost inquired about a jeweler's whereabouts. He was in communication with Gino Fellino, and given Tony's Italian appearance, I could make a connection. The following move I made was a risky one, as my goal was to evade trouble until I became Elvis."

"With my singing career, the possibilities would be endless. However, sometimes, in life, it becomes necessary to set things straight. Uncontrollably, this idiotic man fell to his knees and began babbling, ultimately confessing to informing the mob about me. This was the amusing part as I reached into my pocket. I intended to retrieve the room key so I could throw it at him in a manly manner, if workable. Unfortunately, this fool assumed the worst, believing I had reached into my pocket for a gun. I kept the key in my pocket, expressing my thoughts to this snitch with a choice selection of words instead."

"I demanded an explanation, questioning why I shouldn't end his life. You, you cowardly and deceitful swine. He was left speechless. His fear escalated as he urinated all over the floor. I continued, reminding him that despite his Italian name, he was far from being a tough man, a worthless nobody without a spine. If our paths ever crossed again, I threatened to retrieve the gun from my pocket and blow his head off, you insignificant coward. I derived great pleasure from the encounter as I frightened the creep to where he pleaded for a second chance. With my right hand still in my pocket, I confidently left the Palmerston Hotel and climbed into my Cadillac, making my way to the luxurious Brinkley Arms hotel."

"This was the establishment I could easily become accustomed to, complete with a parking attendant, to ensure my pink Cadillac remained hidden from prying eyes. From now on, room service will be my sole means of dining, eliminating any risk of unwanted encounters with gangsters. Upon entering my room, I couldn't help but notice the bathroom. As I gazed at myself in the mirror, I couldn't help but notice that my eyes were as black as the ace of spades. I had gained a swollen lip from the blows I had received."

"I postponed my audition for Sun Records because I didn't want to give Sam Phillips the wrong impression and consequently miss out on the opportunity to perform as Elvis. That evening, I ventured down to the hotel shop in search of attire for 1953. Fortunately, I stumbled upon a remarkable bargain—a complete suitcase filled with clothes, undergarments, and socks, all for a mere $80. I used an inexpensive wristwatch since Martino Fellino let my Apple watch perish. An exquisite Rolex for $895 caught my eye, but ultimately, I opted for an Omega that cost me a mere $12."

"The following day, I embarked on a journey to the renowned Memphis Recording Services, Sun Records. I only wanted to scope the place out for my future visit. After referring to the Elvis manual, I discovered the studio was at 706 Union Avenue in Memphis, Tennessee. I had even printed a map from Google, effortlessly using modern technology in this primitive era. After an enjoyable drive in the pink Cadillac, spanning an hour and a half, I arrived in Memphis. Initially, I noticed the local Social Services building upon entering the town, prompting me to stop there to complete my credentials. The experience was vastly superior compared to the Department of Motor Vehicles. Within 15 minutes, I got valid proof of my social security and tax number, unless the true John Cadman were to resurface."

"Now fully prepared, I searched for the Sun Records studio. To say I was anxious would be an understatement, as this was the very reason I had traveled from the future. I pursued the career of the most legendary singer of all time. As I turned onto Union Avenue and neared the storefront building on my left, my eyes were captivated by the sign for the first time. Astonishment washed over me—this was where Elvis Aaron Presley was discovered."

"On that day, driven by curiosity, I stepped out of my car and confidently walked across the road towards the studio. However, my timidity prevented me from venturing inside, so I retraced my steps and headed back towards the car. Coincidentally, a remarkably attractive young lady emerged from the recording studio and gracefully crossed the road in my direction. She was adorned in a vibrant yellow floral dress, her stunning red hair glistening in the sunlight. I couldn't help but notice her captivating, sparkling blue eyes as she patiently awaited service at the front counter of a nearby coffee shop. Completely enamored by this woman, I found it nearly impossible to divert my gaze, as she had effortlessly stolen my heart."

"In a moment akin to being struck by lightning, I felt an undeniable connection with her. She was unlike any woman I had ever encountered before. Perhaps Tracey Mathews possessed a similar allure, but there was an undeniable elegance about this woman. Admittedly, I recognized the stark contrast between our respective eras, yet she remained awe-inspiring, destined to affect the course of my life profoundly. As she returned inside the studio, I briefly contemplated following her, consumed by infatuation, yet ultimately decided it would be wiser to retreat before potentially making a fool of myself."

"Considering Graceland was just a brief 12-minute drive away, I determined it was worth exploring. Armed with the address I had carefully printed, 3734 Elvis Presley Boulevard in Memphis, I embarked on my journey. Unfortunately, I could not locate the exact address of the future iconic dwelling. Thus, I resorted to relying solely on the guidance of a Google map found within the Elvis manual. Traveling on the southbound lanes of Highway 51, I soon faced Graceland. Curiously, I parked my car across the road, for it appeared somewhat distinct from the photo I had in my possession. As there was no sign of traffic—not even a vehicle in the distance—I descended from my car, compelled to explore the premises. With the side of the house in my line of sight, I confidently crossed the road in search of a better vantage point."

"Upon reaching the front of the grand estate, the commanding columns greeted me. Despite the absence of the towering walls and the renowned musically inspired gates that would adorn the property in the future, the mansion kept its majestic aura on its sprawling 14-acre grounds. Consulting the manual, I learned Elvis had acquired the mansion for a staggering sum of $102,500 on March 19, 1957. Proclaiming to myself that I must excel in my endeavors, lest this part of my plan crumbles, forcing me to settle for an alternate option."

"It is common knowledge that I currently live in Graceland, the property I acquired. The details of how I got Graceland will be disclosed later in my narrative. Having spent half an hour exploring my future residence, I departed from Memphis. I returned home to the Brinkley Arms to prepare myself for the most significant rehearsal in my pursuit of becoming Elvis."

Grandpa Elvis was interrupted during his storytelling by the real Elvis, who had always harbored suspicions that Tino Fellino, the incumbent, orchestrated his son's death, and now he realized that his intuition was correct. He posed the question to Grandpa Elvis and was initially hesitant to respond to his narrative. He acknowledged he believed the Fellino family had some involvement.

Josh inquired of his grandfather whether the woman with the red hair who worked at Sun Records and had captured his heart was his grandmother, Louise. During his storytelling, Grandpa Elvis deliberately refrained from mentioning her name, as he wanted his grandson to learn about his journey of falling in love with Louise by chance and when it occurred. After all, they belonged to different eras. His grandson knew well that his grandparents' marriage remained strong even in the present day, but hearing about his grandfather's encounter with the love of his life and how infatuated he was at first sight further reinforced the concept of love at first sight with him as well.

The real Elvis rose from his reclining position and refilled their glasses with additional bourbon. "So, you stalked Grandma Louise?" inquired Josh. Grandpa Elvis gazed at his grandson and chuckled, saying, "You're quite cheeky. Yes. I did indeed pursue her, but it nearly jeopardized my entire journey towards becoming Elvis."

"What?" Josh questioned.

"Listen," Grandpa explained, "I disclosed the entire story to your grandmother, just as I am sharing with both of you now, but only after she accidentally stumbled upon the Elvis manual, which forced me to confess. Fortunately, the part about stalking that you mentioned brought her joy, and she realized the impact she suddenly had on me. However, I will delve further into this later."

CHAPTER TEN

SUN RECORDS

"On the following day, after having breakfast at the Brinkley Arms Hotel, I checked out of both the hotel and Brinkley itself because I intended to be in closer proximity to Sun Records and Graceland. I then checked into the Hotel Memphis Belle, where I ended up staying for an extended period. Now, I know that what I am about to disclose would likely result in legal consequences today, given that my motive for relocating was not solely to be closer to Sun Records and Graceland. I continued what you may refer to as stalking your grandmother Louise. However, my dear grandson, it was not a malicious act, although I must admit that the gorgeous lady from Sun Records remained in my thoughts. Louise embodied everything I could ever desire in a woman. For approximately a week, as my black eye transitioned from yellow to its normal state, I returned to Sun Records every day solely to glimpse Louise as she left the studio to grab lunch from the establishment across the street."

"Without fail, I would always be a step ahead of her, and on one occasion, I even stood directly behind her in line as she patiently waited to be served at that coffee shop. The scent of her perfume gracefully floated in the mild breeze, and her hair seemed as if it had just been styled for a professional photoshoot. Her voice, soft, would play in my mind as I attempted to find sleep each night. The original plan remained intact; however, instead of dedicating my time to practicing the guitar that I had purchased from a Nashville store, I would daydream about her. I have often pondered whether I missed out on becoming Elvis and if having Louise in my life would have been enough. Honestly, she would have sufficed, but as you already know, I had both."

"The day had finally arrived—Monday, March 30th, 1953. It signified the beginning of a new era for me, one that I quickly adjusted to. My plan for the day was to walk into Sun Records and lay down two songs for a mere $4, just as the legendary Elvis Presley would do in approximately three months. I hoped that by then, I would have transformed into him, and he would become a regular guy with occasional singing gigs at churches or weddings. Who could have predicted such a twist of fate? Nervousness consumed me that morning. David Clements and I had previously discussed this and deemed it a normal reaction. But why was I so anxious? Was it because I was about to alter the history of rock and roll? Or was it because of the woman who was employed at Sun Records? This encounter marked our first meeting and conversation."

"Strangely, my biggest concern was not if she would appreciate my talent but if she would like me as a person. The fear of being disliked by her weighed more heavily on my mind than the fear of receiving disapproval from her boss, Sam Phillips, regarding my singing ability. At exactly 8:55 am, I parked my vibrant pink Cadillac a few blocks from the Sun Records studio."

"Was it an attempt to prepare myself mentally for everything that was about to unfold? Or perhaps I needed to gather enough courage to approach the woman who had captured my heart? By parking the car some distance away, I ensured that Sam Phillips would not catch sight of the flashy vehicle. In doing so, I hoped to avoid him mistakenly perceiving me as self-sufficient, potentially retracting his offer for a small percentage deal that he had extended to the real Elvis. I realized now that the thought of meeting Louise for the first time plagued my thoughts. In all our planning alongside David, we had never accounted for this scenario. How could we have foreseen such an unexpected complication?"

"Exiting out of the vehicle, I clutched my guitar and ventured towards the entrance of the recording studio, fully aware that my grand ambitions took precedence over any fleeting emotions. As I neared the front door, I noticed Louise stationed just outside the recording booth, diligently carrying out her duties as a receptionist. There was a momentary hesitation, but it quickly dissipated when Louise directed her gaze toward me, radiating an inviting smile. The warmth emitted from her smile only intensified the sweltering sensations coursing through my body. Sweat enveloped me as if I were perspiring profusely at this stage."

"Amidst my approach, I nearly fumbled with the guitar because of the sheer presence of this captivating individual. Then, for the first time, Louise started a conversation with me. Hello, she warmly greeted me, and welcomed me to the Memphis Recording Studios, otherwise known as Sun Records."

"A-ah, hello, I responded with a gradual pace, my speech faltering because of the entanglement of my tongue. I was rendered foolishly inarticulate, as this enigmatic woman had rendered my ability to converse completely inept. Even the mere act of communication became an impossible feat, let alone the prospect of securing a contract that would catapult me to the summit of musical fame."

"The delightful receptionist inquired; May I be of help? Are you here to perform as a singer? In response, I could only fathom the absurdity of my actions at this precise moment. So, you are a singer? She probed. Is your purpose here to record your musical prowess? Frozen in place like a bewildered goose, my thoughts remained coherent while the words escaped me. What on earth was I doing? Sensing my anxiety, she acknowledged my state of distress. I am Louise Baker, she imparted. And you are? Summoning up the courage to seize control of the situation, I realized she had rolled her eyes, silently signaling her perception of me as a fumbling buffoon. Oh, heavens above, I finally mustered the words. The flutter of her vibrant azure eyes served as a catalyst, driving me to respond."

"I am John Cadman, and I would appreciate the opportunity to record two songs. Very well, John, Louise assured me, I am more than capable of assisting you with your recording endeavor. So, tell me, who do you aspire to sound like? Ah, nobody, I confessed. In that case, she remarked, who would you say your vocal style resembles? Ah, nobody but myself, I replied. Now, from my original reality, I recall that this line of questioning is the identical one you, Elvis, were asked back in August 1953. However, Sam Phillip's original receptionist posed the inquiry, and her name was Marion Keisker, not this lovely woman named Louise Baker. It is conceivable that the original receptionist was absent, as she worked there at a later stage. On that day, I did not want the disturbance of these emotions since I desired to secure the Elvis gig."

"Then Louise said that she was confident that Sam Phillips could assist me with everything. After I completed a form, and paid $4, which I could pay overtime since they offered a payment plan. With certainty, I withdrew a $20 bill and handed it to her. The substantial denomination impressed her, and she had to search through the entire cash drawer to retrieve the $16 in change. I sat in the lounge area to fill out the form. Shortly after, Louise approached me, handing over a receipt. Coincidentally, Sam Phillips emerged from the recording studio booth at that exact moment and introduced himself. I felt no apprehension as we shook hands. He informed me he owned the studio and was there to provide guidance. Following that, he inquired about the song I wished to perform."

"I conveyed to him I would like to sing 'My Happiness' for the A-side and 'That's When Your Heartaches Begin' for the B-side. I'm familiar with all the lyrics and want to hear how it sounds. He said no problem as he noticed that the payment had been made, so I trailed behind Sam as he opened the door to the recording studio, but before doing so, I had to pass by Louise, who was seated at her desk. She smiled and gestured with her thumbs for good luck. I reciprocated with a smile and a cool nod. Upon entering the modest studio, the acoustics proved excellent as our voices resonated clearly. The sound produced by my guitar was astonishing when I strummed a few chords for practice. Sam left my side and entered the booth, informing me that once I was ready, he would flick the switch. The recording sign would illuminate, signaling me to begin from that point onward."

"During practice, I impressed Sam with my guitar playing. It's no wonder after dedicating 14 months to intense training. Finally, the moment had arrived. Sam started counting down from five, and my readiness stemmed from visualizing this very moment countless times while lying in bed at the Elm Street Apartment. Just as I was about to sing, Louise unexpectedly entered the control booth where Sam was seated and gave me a wave. Unfortunately, my words came out differently, and I made a mess of it. This woman, Louise, had utterly ruined me with her presence, causing many mistakes. It's astonishing to think that I had intended to leave a lasting impression on Sam Phillips."

"My endless takes to complete the A-side left him feeling frustrated. By the time the B-side was finished, we were all relieved that it was finally over. Sam swiftly left for lunch, leaving me stranded in the front foyer, while Louise, with her deceptively friendly smile, sorted out the final version of my vinyl. She handed it to me, reassuring me that nerves could get the best of anyone. Perhaps that's true, but it shouldn't have applied to me, the man who traveled from the future, to become the king of rock and roll."

"Despite the indirect role in all of this, I thanked her. The true fool was me, incapable of controlling the emotions I had for Louise Baker. I returned to my hotel room with a bottle of bourbon to drown my sorrows. That night, I was convinced that I had ruined my only chance. So, I delved into the Elvis manual and read the Google printout detailing how the real Elvis had been discovered in August 1953."

"Was my approach that day completely unrealistic? As I read through the printout, I discovered that the real Elvis had recorded those two songs. However, Sam Phillips didn't offer him a recording contract until 1954. It was only in July 1954 that he teamed up with Winfield Scotty Moore and Bill Black. Mind you, Elvis had gone into Sun Records for a second recording in January 1954! Now, I realized that my nervous performance that day wasn't the sole reason for my failure. Sam wasn't even actively seeking a singer like Elvis during that time."

"The following morning, I arose with a hangover resulting from the consumption of a bottle of bourbon. I sat up in bed and made the decision that, within a week, I would embark on another recording session. However, this time, I intended to provide Sam with what Elvis had previously provided him, ultimately securing him for the gig in July 1954. The real Elvis was not scheduled for his recording until August 1953, affording me approximately 3 to 4 months to attain the gig. In the event of my failure, the real Elvis would assume the role."

"Following a week of practice and introspection, I determined that Monday, April 6th, 1953, would be the day I would venture into Sun Records for another attempt. I endeavored to compose myself and finally remove the image of Louise Baker from my thoughts. It was precisely 11:50 a.m. A mere 10 minutes before Louise's lunch break. This was part of my strategic plan to ensure her absence, as I believed it to be the optimal course of action. The street upon which Sun Records lived was teeming with a multitude of cars, causing me to park approximately half a mile away from the studio. Initially, trepidation consumed me as I wondered if all the vehicles were there for the recording studio, given that many renowned singers had already signed with the Sun Records label."

"To my relief, my concerns eased as I entered the vacant recording studio. Oh, Louise, the woman of my dreams, the one whom I thwarted attempts to forget her appearance for an entire week, was standing before me. My hands sweating, and I felt my heart racing faster than ever, threatening to burst from my chest. Louise looked up upon hearing my entrance, and upon spotting me, she gave a smile. What was I to do? I could not afford to derail another recording, as doing so would cause Sam Phillips to shun our future dealings."

"Louise greeted me and recalled my name while I unquestionably remained mindful of hers. Before I could even inquire about a recording with her boss, a clean-cut, attractive gentleman entered the room behind me. Oh, honey, she exclaimed, you're early. Meet my fiancé, Grant Oliver. Grant, this is one of our clients, John Cadman. This, undoubtedly, was the most devastating news I could have received as we exchanged handshakes. This handsome gentleman was Louise Baker's future husband-to-be. I was heartbroken. She referred to him as honey. However, what did I expect? This stunning woman named Louise Baker was not only captivating for me but also for everyone else. This gentleman, with his chiseled jawline and impressive physique, was already intertwined in Louise Baker's life as her fiancé. They were destined for marriage, leaving no genuine opportunity for someone like me."

"Grant inquired about my contractual relationship with the label, a rather audacious question considering he had already secured the girl, and I had nothing. It seemed he took great pleasure in rubbing this in my face. I responded negatively, subsequently approaching Louise to inquire about the possibility of recording with her boss once more. She informed me that Sam Phillips would not be in town until the 20th of the month, approximately two weeks away. This news left me feeling disheartened, as my aspirations of impressing my crush were fading away with Sam's absence. My determination to land the Elvis gig remained unwavering."

"I assured Louise that I would return on the 20th, only to have her inform me that Sam was already fully booked. Disappointed, I accepted the alternative arrangement she provided: an appointment on Monday, April 27th, at 11 a.m. because 9 a.m. was already booked for Scotty Moore and Bill Black. However, I secretly planned to arrive early, eager to make the most of an opportunity. Although Louise was no longer a part of my future, I found solace in the prospect of working alongside the authentic members of Elvis's band who were booked in for 9 a.m. With this newfound clarity of mind, I bid farewell to Louise and the enigmatic Mr. Chisel Chin as they headed off to lunch. Though still burdened by an aching heartache for Louise Baker, I hoped that in due time, the pain would gradually diminish."

Chapter Eleven

THAT'S ALL RIGHT

"During the following three weeks, I dedicated my time to constant practice. Some of the other residents in the building seemed to be bothered by my singing, as the police were called once. However, when they entered my room and saw that everything was normal, they asked me to lower the volume. Just like the original Elvis in 1953, I encountered failure. He made another recording in January 1954. I reviewed the guidance provided in the Elvis manual and realized that I needed to make Sam Phillips interested in me—he had to desire my talent. Otherwise, I would lose any chance of negotiating on my terms."

"Ultimately, Sam Phillips offered Elvis the contract. I questioned whether I had missed any crucial details or if I was attempting to alter history before it had even been written. Who can say? I persisted in analyzing the connection between Sam Phillips and Elvis. Further along, I learned that Elvis Presley had made a second recording in January 1954, which included the songs 'I'll Never Stand in Your Way' and 'It Wouldn't Be the Same Without You'. Yet again, nothing came of it. It was disheartening to discover that even Elvis Aaron Presley faced failure twice and struggled to secure a gig."

"Then, finally, I found the answer when I uncovered what made Sam Phillips extend the contract to Elvis. It all happened on July 5, 1954, during an evening session. In that session, Elvis, along with Scotty Moore and Bill Black, had already played everything, but nothing stood out. They were about to call it a night when Sam Phillips asked them to perform one last song. Elvis picked up his guitar and enthusiastically started playing a blues number from 1949, Arthur Crudup's 'That's All Right.' He began by acting foolish and jumping around, and Bill joined in, mimicking Elvis's playful behavior. Eventually, Scotty Moore also joined in, imitating their antics."

"In the control booth, Sam Phillips has the door open. When the original song, which he was familiar with but had never heard, played at a much faster pace, and reached his ears, he became excited and requested a recording of it to be made. Three days later, he had it played on the radio alongside Memphis DJ Dewey Phillips. Non-stop, he played 'That's All Right,' launching the career of the most renowned singer of all time from that moment on."

"It's incredible to consider that the answer had been present all along, and it was fortunate for me that Gino Fellino had not accidentally dropped that manual, which I referred to as 'my everything,' into the burning drum. I now knew what my course of action would be when I entered Sun Records on the morning of April 27th. However, I would not arrive at 11 a.m., as Louise Baker had booked for me. Instead, I would arrive at 9 a.m. hoping to audition with Scotty Moore and Bill Black. The pieces were falling into place, and for the first time, I felt content, both in my current life and the one I had left behind. During those three weeks of practice, I embarked on a few road trips.

I recognized that once things escalate, my freedom, just like the real Elvis, would be restricted because of fame."

"Louise Baker was almost removed from my thoughts, and the catalyst for this was that I discovered she was engaged to be married. I continuously reminded myself that Louise was merely an attractive woman who worked at Sun Records. I moved forward and vowed that the next time I returned, I would not succumb to the emotions of a love-struck puppy. No, not this time. It would be a strictly business endeavor, as I had now devised a plan to secure the Elvis gig."

"Well, that day arrived, and the morning of Monday, April 27th, 1953, was cold. I arrived at Sun Records at 8:30 a.m. and parked my car just a few yards from the recording studio. Because of the chilly weather, I waited inside my vehicle, eager to catch sight of Sam Phillips and Louise Baker. Oh, Louise, despite persuading myself to move on mentally, my heart still longed for her. However, I would never interfere with her future, as I was not even supposed to be there."

"At 8:43 a.m., the bus dropped Louise off, and she made her way towards the studio, clad in a lengthy pink coat that almost matched the shade of the Cadillac parked nearby. Upon entering, Sam Phillips arrived in a black convertible Chevrolet at 8:48 a.m., choosing to park just a few spots away from me. Perhaps he didn't mind the cold, as the top of his car was down, or maybe it was just a deliberate image he wanted to portray. Regardless, it was a relief to see Sam present, unlike three weeks prior. Moments later, Bill Black and Scotty Moore emerged from a taxi, venturing to the trunk where the driver retrieved a couple of instrument cases. One was undoubtedly Bill's upright bass, while the other contained a guitar for Scotty Moore. I questioned whether I was engaging in some form of stalking, though now I possessed the elements required to transform into Elvis."

"After waiting an additional five minutes, it was now 9 a.m., the appointed time I had been anxiously expecting. With determination, I snatched my guitar and made my way to Sun Records. I had attempted this venture a few times previously, yet my courage vanished each time my hand touched the doorknob of the renowned recording studio. However, today was different. I reassured myself that my nerves were under control, and even my usual perspiration seemed absent—perhaps because of the chilling temperatures preventing sweat from forming."

"Finally, I entered the studio, causing Louise Baker to wear a surprised expression upon seeing me walk through the front entrance. I casually approached her desk, exuding confidence, as if I had arrived punctually for my 9 a.m. appointment. One notable difference this time around was my lack of nervousness compared to the previous encounters. Perhaps it was because I had moved past my infatuation with this stunning woman. She greeted me with a simple hello and stated that there must have been a mistake, as my booking was for 11 a.m., not 9. This proved to be one of the few occasions in my life where I concocted a lie to deceive Louise. However, my sole purpose was to become Elvis, and at that moment, I was desperate enough to do whatever it took."

"With confidence, I dismissed her assumption and reminded her of my confirmed appointment with Sam. To my surprise, she informed me that Sam was already occupied with a band. In response, I resorted to my puppy dog expression, unbeknownst to me, that Louise harbored a secret crush on me, just as I did for her. Because of her engagement to Grant, also known as Mr. Chisel Chin, she had kept her feelings suppressed. However, her affection for me prompted her to lend a helping hand that day."

"She instructed me to take a seat in the lounge area while she conversed with Sam in the recording booth. After a moment, Louise and Sam emerged from the recording booth, with Louise settling down at her desk and offering me a smile and a small wave. Making his way over to me, Sam expressed his delight in my presence, as he required a lead singer for a band he was forming. He claimed that my timing was coincidental, although I had planned it. Sam's desire for my musical talents aligned perfectly with my aspirations. I maintained a composed demeanor, masking my eagerness."

"Nervousness overwhelmed me once again, not because of Louise, but because I was about to meet and join the original members of the Elvis band for the first time. I followed Sam into the recording studio, where Louise greeted me with a smile. I composed myself, reminding myself that she was already spoken for. Upon entering the studio, Sam introduced us, and we exchanged handshakes. Scotty Moore and Bill Black, who were not much older than me, exuded youthful energy, fostering an instant connection. They graciously offered their help if needed, happy for me to assume the lead position in our three-piece ensemble."

"Sam informed them of my potential as an up-and-coming vocalist, causing me to wonder if he genuinely liked me based on my initial attempt or if he used the same praise for all inexperienced singers. Only time would reveal the truth. Sam retreated into the control booth while the boys inquired about which songs we should work on. I challenged Sam's patience initially, ensuring that when I burst into the lively performance of 'That's All Right,' it would evoke excitement reminiscent of the original recording."

"If anyone from the future could effortlessly maneuver through mediocre songs, it was me. After two hours of grueling patience, I felt prepared. Although my bandmates were unsuspecting, the outcome awaited them. Then, my personal Achilles' heel, Louise Baker, entered the glassed control booth to convey a message to Sam, leading to a familiar occurrence. Louise gave me a smile and a wave. Initially, I was paralyzed, much like before, but this time, I had no choice but to engage in foolishness."

"So, this time around, I instructed the band members to observe me closely and attune themselves to a refreshing rhythm. I began playing the song on my guitar with a swifter tempo, as I had rehearsed, and delved into the lyrics, frolicking and leaping around the recording studio. I unintentionally toppled some chairs. To my astonishment, the two musicians remained motionless, merely spectators to my self-inflicted embarrassment. Oh dear, what have I done? This was not how I had intended it to be. They stood there, sharing laughter, as I exposed the fool within me."

"Then, finally, the turning point arrived when Sam appeared from the recording booth, radiating excitement, and exclaimed, Now, John, you've finally got it! The original version of that song was mundane, but with the sped-up tempo, it's astounding. I'm going to record this rendition. Wow, Sam was genuinely enthralled by my singing, and Louise, my enchanting Kryptonite, bestowed upon me a radiant smile and two thumbs up from behind the glass partition. We launched into 'That's All Right' and executed it flawlessly, exceeding all expectations. Then we seamlessly transitioned into 'Blue Moon of Kentucky,' also maintaining an invigorating pace. Finally, our performance concluded, and Sam complimented us, saying, Nice Job, guys. And that was it, no contract, no offer."

"Had I misinterpreted his intentions? Or was I once again attempting to manipulate the course of history before it unfolded naturally? Scotty and Bill were engaged in a separate discussion with Sam, leaving me clueless about my next move. Thus, I surrendered at that moment.

Sheepishly, I strode out of the recording studio, bidding farewell to Louise for the last time, before shutting the front door behind me and making my way towards the pink Cadillac. I entered the vehicle and was enfolded by its comforting warmth, a stark contrast to the chilly outside."

"It is with utmost conviction that I currently hold the belief that the genuine warmth I experienced emanated from the sight of Louise emerging from the recording studio. She paused momentarily, surveying her surroundings before briskly making her way towards the car. With agility, she entered through the passenger door, swiftly sealing herself inside. It had always been a dream of mine to witness Louise occupying the seat next to me in my car, creating an intimate setting for the two of us. However, this interaction did not make up a romantic rendezvous, as she merely sought refuge from the cold and had a pressing question to ask me. Louise conveyed Sam had engaged in discussions with Scotty and Bill, affirming that each of us possessed a potential that could be realized to its fullest extent. In Sam's own words, he urged her to retrieve the young man in question, for there was work to be done."

"Louise expressed astonishment at the car, never having expected that I would be a proud owner of such a flashy vehicle. As she gently caressed the dashboard with her right hand, I ought to have been overwhelmed with joy at the news relayed by Sam. However, Louise's repeated praise for the Cadillac rendered me once again entranced by her allure, as if she possessed an irresistible power over me."

"Returning to the studio, Scotty Moore and Bill Black bid us farewell, assuring me of the promising future that awaited us. Merely days later, a recording contract was signed, and Sam Phillips inquired about the name I wished to adopt. Without hesitation, I expressed my desire to go by the name Elvis Presley. Sam voiced his approval, remarking that the name flowed smoothly and carried an air of originality. Little did he know the moniker held personal significance to me alone, for it hailed from a realm far removed from where I came. Subsequently, Louise was enlisted to ensure the legal registration of my newfound identity with the help of lawyers."

"Within three days, Sam arranged for our two songs to be broadcast on WHBQ radio in Memphis, Tennessee, courtesy of DJ Dewey Phillips. Interestingly enough, the track 'That's All Right' garnered incessant airplay for many weeks, continuously looping through the station. From that moment onward, John Cadman ceased to exist, as Elvis Presley became the name on everyone's lips."

Chapter Twelve

A Love Crush

At long last, Grandpa Elvis reached the point in his narration where he transformed into Elvis. The two men beside him were completely captivated by the tale. Suddenly, the doorbell chimed, abruptly interrupting their conversation. Priscilla hurriedly dashed past them, exclaiming, "I'll get it!" Meanwhile, Elvis Aaron Presley wriggled in his recliner, admitting, "It's quite a struggle for me to rise from these chairs nowadays." As Grandpa Elvis and his grandson shared a chuckle, the real Elvis sank back into his comfortable chair, having initially struggled to stand and answer the door. Priscilla then entered the living room accompanied by a striking young lady who instantly captured the attention of young Josh Cadman.

"Grandad," the young woman uttered, planting a kiss on the real Elvis's cheek. "My love, my angel," replied the real Elvis, addressing Emily. Emily Presley, after all this time, had finally come to visit. Emily possessed an impressive stature and an immaculate pear-shaped physique. Her long, sandy blonde hair cascaded in medium ringlet curls, gracefully draping over her shoulder. Her eyes shimmered with a blend of blue and green when struck by the light.

"Elvis and Josh," Priscilla introduced, "allow me to present my granddaughter, Emily Presley." Grandpa Elvis extended his hand for a shake, followed by a kiss on the cheek. When Emily locked eyes with Josh for the first time, it felt as though a bolt of lightning had coursed through both of them. They stood silently, gazing intently at each other. After a few moments, they extended a handshake and gave each other a mutual kiss on the cheek. Lisa Mathews had previously informed Josh how well-suited he and Emily were to one another, and even though he hadn't set out that day to find love, love had serendipitously found him instead.

On that day, Aunty Lisa, who played the role of Cupid, had been in contact with Emily. Despite recently getting over a previous relationship, Emily expressed her lack of interest. However, upon meeting Josh Cadman, she felt a certain something. Could it be love at first sight? Perhaps. Priscilla inquired when they would be ready to join the rest of the family outside for a barbecue. In response, Elvis, her husband, informed her they needed more time because Elvis had yet to finish speaking with them. Priscilla wondered about this important conversation between her husband and the world's most famous person.

Both Emily and Josh experienced an awkward moment as they discreetly glanced at each other. Being fully aware that they were being observed by everyone present, they had to remain composed for the time being. Priscilla smiled and then guided her granddaughter towards the back door, giving Elvis more time to continue his tale. Josh followed Emily with his gaze as she walked away. She paused, looked back, and caught him observing her. Both grandfathers shared a laugh.

"You know what?" the real Elvis stated, "I believe your grandson has been struck by the same lightning bolt that struck you all those years ago." Grandpa Elvis chuckled and agreed. Josh was unfazed, lost in his admiration for Emily's beauty and imagining a future with her. The three men took a seat.

"All right then," Grandpa Elvis continued. "We were signed to the Sun Records label and started gaining significant interest across the nation and abroad. We performed concerts nearly every night throughout the United States. However, I deliberately refrained from showcasing the iconic Elvis hip-gyration dance style. That was all part of a bigger plan, which I executed later during my first appearance on the Ed Sullivan Show. But more on that later."

"In the famous Grand Ole Opry, we had already performed gigs by June 1953. This was quite an accomplishment considering that it was only a year later, Elvis; you made your debut there and were rejected by the traditional officials. One of them suggested you stick to truck driving at Crown Electric Company, where you were employed."

Real Elvis couldn't help but smile as he added, "Indeed, I recall working as a truck driver there. I continued in that line of work for another three years until I got my full qualifications as an electrician. In 1962, I even purchased the company and successfully managed it until my retirement."

Grandpa Elvis, having been updated on the real Elvis's progress at the time through private investigators, was already aware of Elvis's Crown Electric career. He was content knowing that Elvis had achieved financial stability, which made him feel proud that he didn't have to support him despite his initial intention to assist. Grandpa Elvis refrained from interfering because of the real Elvis's success.

"Yes, and your Crown Electric career brought me joy," stated Grandpa Elvis. "Although my career seemed to be filled with happiness and success initially, I encountered a few obstacles. However, I received a completely different review from the Grand Ole Opry officials, who even recommended that I make regular returns. Looking back, I now believe that they were unnerved by your provocative hip movements and leg gyrations. Those actions truly spooked them. I purposely held back those moves for a grander occasion in the future."

"Now, this is when my heart felt an overwhelming burst of excitement," he continued. "It was late June 1953, and I was in my dressing room at the Grand Ole Opry, preparing for another performance. Sam Phillips, my manager, walked in to have a conversation with me. At first, he mentioned things were progressing rapidly. I suppose he was correct, considering the knowledge I had from the future. He then informed me I had been booked for a two-song performance on the Ed Sullivan Show. My fame was about to go global."

"In the Elvis manual, it stated that you didn't appear on the Ed Sullivan Show until September 9th, 1956, where you performed 'Hound Dog.' However, this was three years later. The issue for me was that back in 1953 when I didn't have Colonel Tom Parker as my agent, that song wasn't offered to me. I was concerned that my career trajectory had deviated too quickly from yours. Then I realized I couldn't have the same experiences as you. I believed that my career progressed at a faster pace because I attracted not only the youth but also the conservative parents of that era, all thanks to my restraint in performing provocative hip movements."

"During his visit, Sam informed me that the purpose of his visit that day was to share some news about Louise. Initially, I feared the worst, thinking perhaps she had abruptly left Sun Records and disappeared from my life forever. However, Sam revealed Louise had taken a leave of absence because she had broken off her engagement with Grant, the guy with the chiseled chin. Initially, I was elated, but I remained composed. Then, Sam disclosed that Louise had fallen in love with someone else."

"I couldn't comprehend what was happening because Louise had broken up with Grant because she loved another person. Sam then grinned and shared that the person she loved was me. He chuckled because he was aware of my awkward behavior around Louise and knew about my feelings for her. He knew Louise would only suggest me as the lead singer for any band if she had an ulterior motive. She always vouched for me."

"Finding Louise became my priority after realizing I had a chance with her. I informed Sam of my search for her and expressed my inability to go on stage. However, he reassured me that there were still thirty minutes left before showtime and advised me not to waste time looking for Louise, as she was already waiting in the hallway. As Sam opened the door, a delightful smile greeted me from Louise. Subsequently, Sam excused himself, leaving her to enter the dressing room and shutting the door behind her. At that moment, my heart raced as I approached her, embracing her for the first time and sharing a kiss."

"Grandson, that is the story of how your grandmother, and I came together. Although I still aspired for my career, we couldn't ignore the love we felt for each other. Unlike the original plan, my path as Elvis took a different route to its rapid progression and momentum. I deeply admire Louise's integrity, even though I came from the future, which prompted me to realize that marrying her soon was essential before it became too late. Naturally, her traditional-minded parents would not have approved of us living together before marriage."

"I was determined to have her in my life and marrying her would ensure our lifelong commitment. Grandson, as you are already aware, our love for each other has endured to this day. I now firmly believe that our union was, despite the contrasting eras from which we emerged, meant to be."

Chapter Thirteen

Meeting the Real Elvis

"Louise and I were deeply immersed in love, however, like any ordinary couple. We encountered a few challenges. We had engaged in discussions about our impending nuptials with her parents, yet I, along with John Cadman, lacked any identifiable relatives. Hence, I initially assumed his identity. Louise's parents initially harbored reservations about me. They believed I ought to have at least one remaining family member. Aside from Sam Phillips, who served as my manager, and band members Scotty and Bill, I had a shortage of genuine friendships. This raised concerns."

"Curiously, though, I could have confidently confided in them that such a predicament had indeed befallen me in my real life. When I was Peter Walker in 2020, I was, in fact, an orphan. However, divulging the truth to them, including Louise, would have complicated matters excessively. Thus, I had to endure their mistrust. Still, I had ample tasks to accomplish. Therefore, I decided not to disclose the truth to Louise.

I knew she would inevitably dissuade me from pursuing a career as Elvis."

"Now, as for meeting you, Elvis, it occurred in August 1953. I cannot recall the precise date, although I vividly remember the occasion. I was at Sun Records alongside Scotty and Bill, recording 'Hound Dog.' We aimed to have it readily available on the market for sale before my appearance on the Ed Sullivan Show. By this point, Sun Records' studio had attracted several additional vocalists seeking to record their material. Sam Phillips had to bring his long-time receptionist, Marion Keisker, to assist Louise in managing the overwhelming workload resulting from the success of Elvis Presley."

"On that day, Elvis, you entered the Sun Records studio to pay for your recording session, eager to listen to your voice. It was during this moment that our paths crossed for the first time, just as you had already mentioned. Marion attended to you at her reception desk, since Louise was inside the control booth with Sam Phillips. With the recording session nearly complete, Marion acquainted Louise with the form you had completed. Upon discovering your name, Louise became excited, speculating a family connection between you and me."

"Approaching you with a warm greeting, Louise inquired about our potential relationship. Elvis, you assured her that no such relation existed as you had already consulted your parents, who confirmed this. At that instant, the door to the recording studio swung open, and Louise hurriedly approached me, informing me about a man with the same stage name as mine who had arrived. Without even asking if we were linked, Elvis, I caught sight of you seated in the lounge area, leaving me stunned. There you were, the genuine Elvis Aaron Presley, the same Elvis Aaron Presley whom I was acquainted with in the future, and the same Elvis Aaron Presley whose singing career I had traveled back in time to appropriate."

"In that surreal moment, I almost felt compelled to urge you to pursue your singing career and rectify the wrongs of your original past, as I knew it from my reality. However, I ultimately chose the other path—to claim it for myself. I overheard Louise mentioning that your name closely resembled mine, yet all I desired was to approach you, introduce myself, and shake your hand. The frenzy of the ladies screaming upon witnessing me exit the recording studio meant nothing to me."

"Elvis, you are now aware of the truth behind my actions, but my career was only just beginning, and I had yet to achieve significant success—not in terms of finances or celebrity status. No, no, I possessed a knowledge of the future, thanks to my best friend from the future, David Clements, who had warned me to be cautious about altering too many aspects of the past, fearing that something worse might replace it. Well, taking over your career, Elvis, was merely the initial step. Later, I will explain how events unfolded differently from the original timeline."

"Initially, Louise held onto the notion that some familial connection must exist between us. Her parents had been pressuring her about my identity, and they were correct in their judgment. However, I hailed from a future era, not a deceitful imposter as they had feared. Perhaps being labeled a con artist would have been easier to accept than the truth of my temporal abilities. Credit to Louise for her unwavering loyalty, standing by my side when most would have abandoned me. Unyielding to the interference of her parents or any other obstacles."

"David recognized the necessity of establishing a legal identity for me in the past, as it was crucial for my pursuit of the Elvis opportunity. However, the idea of constructing a family lineage solely to satisfy a potential spouse had never crossed our minds. Marriage had never been part of my plans, as you are already aware. Yet, I must apologize for continually reiterating the profound impact Louise had on me; meeting you, Elvis, at Sun Records that day was always part of my plan. At that stage in your life, your talent was still unrefined, but with time, you would become the greatest singer of all time. It is true when they say that sometimes, all a person needs is to be in the right place at the right moment."

"From my advanced knowledge of you, Elvis, from the future, I had an advantage. We have crossed paths both then and now, but I have always remained closely connected to your life. Over several decades, I engaged various private investigators from different agencies to unearth information about you. This was driven purely by my curiosity, as well as my desire to provide any possible financial help. However, the reports consistently affirmed that you were thriving. News reached me about your acquisition of the Crown Electric Company, where you employed a workforce of over 100 individuals. You had achieved financial success, which somewhat eased my guilt, albeit not entirely."

Real Elvis interrupted, "Elvis, you looked surprised when you saw my wife, Priscilla. Surely, your investigators would have given you this information."

"Good point, Elvis," Grandpa Elvis said. "They could have, but I specifically asked them not to divulge anything personal, like relationships. I only wanted to make sure that you would be OK financially. Elvis, I informed you about your original demise, which occurred at 42 on August 16th, 1977, because of a heart attack. And yet, here you are, 85 years old and still alive. The considerable alteration I had made in your original reality, alongside your prosperity, should have absolved me of my wrongdoing. However, guilt remains guilt, so I am here today, seeking your forgiveness. Yet even that gesture may not be sufficient."

"Now, let us return to that noteworthy day when Sam had you in the recording studio. While you were performing the two songs that I had previously sung just a few months prior, I was positioned at the front counter, signing autographs for fans. Inadvertently, I overheard Sam disclosing to you after you had completed the recording session the unusual coincidence of your name being Elvis Presley. He had already signed another Elvis Presley to the label. Sam expressed his belief that I would be the next significant sensation in the industry, but he acknowledged that your vocal sound and style resembled mine, and he commended it. Thus, he kept your name on record, and if my career trajectory faltered, he would invite you."

"When I encountered Sam's words that day, it became apparent that you were talented. As I knew from my experiences, you were the true king of rock and roll. Hence, I consider myself the impostor, while you embody the genuine Elvis. Fortunately for me and my plan, there was never a need for Sam to call you back and replace me because I reached even greater heights when I implemented modern marketing strategies. Using this knowledge, I garnered positive media attention on a near-daily basis. It was common knowledge in 1953 that I was the one who first invented the concept of selfies. Initially, this idea originated in the early 2000s when camera phones became commonplace."

"In those days, whenever someone encountered a famous person or celebrity, they would extend their arm and capture a photo of themselves together with the celebrity, much like what we do today with family and friends. In 1953, I unknowingly started this trend with a fan's camera, and soon, everyone began referring to it as a selfie photo years before it became widely recognized. By engaging in this practice, my fame skyrocketed. Even professional photographers would take selfies to include themselves in the frame."

"From that point onwards, I gained confidence in altering a part of my past that had no negative consequences. Introducing the concept of the selfie provided me with a platform in the lives of everyone, propelling me forward. I knew that Sam Phillips had praised you as being genuinely talented, which is why he promised you another opportunity if I were to fail. This promise only fueled my determination to succeed, and succeed I certainly did."

"Louise's parents, too, worried that once my rock and roll career took off, I would succumb to the temptations of other women, as many stars before me had. While that was always a concern and still is, Louise wanted me in her life, and I wanted her in mine, so we remained united. As my career progressed, encounters with groupies came and went, but I was already aware of the difficulties you faced in your marriage to Priscilla."

The Real Elvis found himself in a state of disbelief as he leaned forward on his lounge chair. "No way, not me and Cilla," he exclaimed. "We have never done that, man." Josh comprehended the message his grandfather was conveying to the authentic Elvis. "Elvis, trust me," Grandpa Elvis stated. "This occurred when your daughter, Lisa Marie, was just five years old. It may seem unimaginable, but your current wife has always kept your legacy alive. Elvis, both you and Priscilla, lived in Graceland, which is why I had to live there as well."

"That's why, upon my arrival in 1953, I made it a point to visit Graceland. After all, it was the residence of the king of rock and roll. You and Priscilla lived there, and later, after your passing, she transformed it into a museum so that fans from all over the world could see how you lived. It was truly remarkable how she kept your

Graceland mansion open to the public for paid tours, and the revenue generated benefitted your daughter."

"It's difficult to believe this, considering that you two are still married, and it's all because of my actions. However, in my original reality, you and Priscilla divorced in 1973. Elvis, I consider myself fortunate because of the love I felt for Louise. With that, along with the knowledge of the consequences of infidelity and the havoc it can wreak on a couple, I attempted to avoid getting involved in any affairs. Throughout the years, such opportunities presented themselves to me, but I always thought of Louise and the children we would have together in the future."

"In my pursuit of self-care, I dedicated myself to maintaining a healthy lifestyle through proper nourishment and physical activity, Elvis. Judging by your current state, your lifestyle in the 70s, before your demise in 77, differed significantly. You were grappling with personal challenges, seeking support for mental well-being, yet you never received the help you needed. Back then, Elvis, you indulged in self-destructive behaviors, particularly drug use. Throughout my career, I was tempted by drugs but consistently declined. If any member of my team ever offered or partook in such substances, they were promptly dismissed. As a result, some of the wisdom gained from your troubled past enabled me to become a more virtuous individual, renowned for my unwavering integrity."

"Now, even at the same age of 85, I can hold my head high despite encountering a few delicate moments throughout my life. Though I faced my challenges with drugs and weight gain, the reasons behind my struggles differed from yours, Elvis. Regrettably, I took a regrettable path, but I will elaborate on that stage of my life shortly. Ultimately, Elvis, we must acknowledge our shared humanity, understanding that

experiences alone do not possess the power to alter our present emotions."

CHAPTER FOURTEEN

THE ED SULLIVAN SHOW

"During the peak of my career, I performed at the Louisiana Hayride in late August 1953. It was around three years before Elvis originally released 'Hound Dog' with Sun Records. However, because of my upcoming appearance on The Ed Sullivan Show on September 9, 1953, I insisted on releasing the song before that date. I wanted to hold on to the song because I recalled that during your initial appearance, you sang 'Hound Dog,' but the television camera only captured you from the waist up. Despite performing your signature hip gyration, the audience at home had no way of witnessing it."

"This was my chance to showcase your infamous hip gyration and leg dance movements for the first time. If you can recall that performance, you will understand what I am referring to. You, Elvis, pioneered this style from the beginning of your career, but I saved it specifically for this occasion. Ed Sullivan, the show's host, had invited you because he recognized you as a budding superstar. However, Sullivan himself was a conservative man who refused to allow any explicit performances on his show. Therefore, he filmed you from an angle that hid your lower body because he already knew what you would try to do on live television."

"That day is still vivid in my memory when I entered the New York studio and received a warm welcome from Ed Sullivan. He embraced me, knowing that I was about to elevate his show to new heights. That day marked a turning point for American television, propelling it to unparalleled global popularity and making it the most-watched television show in history. Even by today's standards, the significance of the inaugural show on September 9, 1953, can't be overstated. I remember that you were previously restrained from showcasing this dance move because of societal objections. The constraints imposed by the moral guardians back then were formidable."

"Such evolutions would have been unfathomable to them. To maintain secrecy, I deliberately withheld my plans from Scotty and Bill. It wasn't a matter of distrust towards them, but a desire to surprise everyone, including my band members. My aim on that day encompassed the promotion of my career on a global scale. Nowadays, with technology, the internet, and social media, younger generations can effortlessly reach a wider audience. However, during the year 1953, such resources were non-existent. I exploited the Ed Sullivan Show as my means of widespread exposure, akin to the role the internet plays in contemporary times."

"Preparing for the show made up most of the day's activities. Naturally, I refrained from executing my planned gyration move during the afternoon rehearsals. Ed Sullivan, supervising my performance, added an extra layer of importance, as he held reservations towards the rock and roll genre. Supposedly, he had an unpleasant encounter with a previous rock and roll artist. His presence during my rehearsal aimed to ensure that my performance would meet his expectations. Did I deceive Ed Sullivan on that day? Perhaps. Without a doubt, I strategically incorporated a few rhythmic foot taps during rehearsal, testing whether he would notice, but he didn't."

"In due course, the opportunity presented itself for me to unveil my undisclosed dance routines to the global audience and establish my distinct style of rock and roll. On that day, the crowd attending the show was the largest it had ever been, most likely because of the anticipation of my live performance. The enthusiastic audience added to the grandeur of my act. Eventually, the moment arrived, and I made certain to don my most comfortable footwear, as I intended to go all out with my moves. Just before the commercial break, Ed Sullivan announced that Elvis Presley would grace the stage with two live song performances."

"During the break, the three of us proceeded to the stage and positioned ourselves accordingly. Scotty and Bill sensed that something was amiss when I moved one light from the designated area, creating some much-needed space for my dance routine. What followed the break took them by surprise. The producer started the countdown, and we were live on air. Ed Sullivan stood before us and uttered only two words. 'Elvis Presley.' The female audience members went into a frenzy, and the atmosphere turned electric even before we began performing 'Hound Dog.'"

"As the song began, I executed my moves with finesse. Initially, I swayed my legs back and forth while maintaining balance on the balls of my feet at the end of each leg turn. The cameras captured the entire performance. Midway through the song, I removed the microphone from its stand and approached the crowd, combining my infamous hip gyrations with my leg movements. The cameras broadcast the entire spectacle live across the world. Upon the culmination of the 'Hound Dog' rendition, some of the female audience members became overwhelmed with excitement, causing a few to faint momentarily. Concerned, I temporarily halted the performance, but they quickly regained composure and continued enjoying the show."

"My career began with the song 'That's All Right,' where I incorporated dance moves and hip gyration into my performance. The cameras focused on me throughout the entire song, and I had an incredible time dancing like you used to, Elvis. The lively music compelled me to do more than stand still, as I had done before appearing on the Ed Sullivan Show. From that moment on, I continued to showcase my moves everywhere, although there was a difference in how the American adults perceived it compared to the scrutiny you faced."

"Ed Sullivan, a hands-on professional, recognized the impact of my dance moves on his television show, which was considered the best show ever. Despite any personal reservations he may have had, Ed expressed admiration for my style. He even attempted to join me during the break in the show. The subsequent interview with Ed Sullivan lasted twice as long as usual because of the constant screams from the audience, making it difficult to engage in conversation."

"For me, the Ed Sullivan Show became an influential platform, like the internet and social media of today. I made many appearances on the show in the following years, primarily to promote my albums and movies. Despite my initial concern, they would only film me from the waist up. The producers insisted I showcase my trademark hip gyration and dance moves, fully acknowledging its sex appeal."

"Following my first television appearance. Record sales skyrocketed, resulting in continuous royalty earnings. I saved enough money to purchase Graceland, and in January 1954, I expressed my interest in buying the property. Unfortunately, it was not for sale even though I will surpass the reported $102,500 original price paid by Elvis in 1957. I remained determined to get into the house. Finally, in February 1954, three years before Elvis purchased Graceland, I bought it at a final price of $267,000, which was significantly higher than the market value at the time but still considered a great deal in my eyes."

"There is always a prospective buyer for every residence, and the reason I ended up paying the price above market value was likely because it wasn't even for sale. The presence of Elvis Presley's interest in purchasing it undoubtedly inflated the price, but it's not like the king of rock and roll would live elsewhere, right? Now, the plan I had carefully crafted for my future was progressing exceedingly well, perhaps even too well. The pace at which things were moving forward was unsustainable in the long run."

"During that time, Louise noticed how I meticulously strategized every single step of my career, although she remained unaware of my ability to foresee the future. She wasn't particularly fond of the way women reacted to my dance moves, but I assured her that such reactions were necessary to gain visibility in a wider global audience. Louise was experiencing some pressure from her parents back then, which led me to propose to her in April 1954. Thankfully, she accepted. However, my manager, Sam Phillips, expressed concern that my career might decline because of my forthcoming marriage. Regardless, I was undeterred because my love for Louise was profound, and I was ready to settle down, even though we were both just 20 years old."

"It wasn't until I drove Louise and her parents to the property that she discovered Graceland. Extensions and renovations were being carried out throughout the entire mansion, including the construction of the guitar-shaped swimming pool. I vividly remember that late April day in 1954 because Louise's parents were seated in the back of the Cadillac, perplexed about where I was taking them that morning. When we arrived at Graceland, they noticed the famous gates with musical notes and a guitar player on each side being installed. Curious, Louise inquired about the owner of the residence. I informed her it belonged to a famous person."

"By this time, her parents were also pondering the same question. As the gates opened for us to enter, the revelation became apparent when Sam Phillips emerged from the house to greet us. As we stepped out of the car, Louise asked Sam if it was his house. He chuckled, regarding me with an odd expression. Then he realized I hadn't revealed to Louise and her parents that the house belonged to me. There was no choice but to explain to Louise why we were there. Nervous and bewildered, she implored me to clarify the situation."

"Our new home awaited us, and I held Louise tightly, gazing into her eyes. Once the renovations were complete, we could marry in this magnificent mansion. As Louise and her parents stood in awe, I assured her that by living here, we would have the privacy and normal life we longed for. I revealed that there was ample space for the large family we envisioned in our future, shocking her,"

"Charles Baker, Louise's father, finally broke his silence. I could sense his initial reluctance to trust me, fearing I would abandon his daughter, but his words now conveyed approval. He acknowledged that this would be a beautiful home for us to start our married life. Meanwhile, Sam Phillips gestured for Louise's parents to explore the interior while we leaned against the pink Cadillac, admiring the Graceland mansion."

"Louise expressed her apprehension about the speed at which everything was happening, concerned that I had exhausted my finances to buy the mansion. I assured her that this house would serve as our sanctuary, ensuring our cohesion and normalcy. Gradually, a smile appeared on her face as she realized my meticulous planning for a large family, despite not yet consulting her. I unveiled the name of the house, 'Graceland,' which she instantly adored. I informed her that interior designer Cathy O'Brien awaited inside, ready to involve her in selecting colors and flooring."

"As we entered Graceland, we crossed paths with Louise's parents, who stood by the guitar-shaped pool in the backyard. I clarified that the pool's design was non-negotiable, as it mirrored the one owned by the real Elvis in my alternate reality. Perhaps Louise harbored doubts about marrying a rock star, knowing that fame would impede our chances of a normal family life. Our commitment and deep love for each other prevailed. Today, we remain steadfast in our devotion, though we've had our fair share of challenges over the years. I will delve into those hardships later, which may not align with your initial assumptions."

"The Graceland mansion's renovation works were completed by the beginning of June 1954. Throughout the years, the place underwent multiple remodels to keep up with the prevailing styles. Louise, known for organizing noteworthy events during her lifetime, kick-started her passion for making every occasion extraordinary with our wedding. That year, we had planned for our wedding to take place at Graceland on Saturday, September 25th."

Chapter Fifteen

THE COLONEL

"Arriving back at Graceland in early December 1954, after embarking on a two-month honeymoon trip encompassing various destinations worldwide, Louise and I had the privilege of exploring places the real Elvis never could witness. Despite being a renowned American singer, I knew how to interact with fans of all types once they recognized my identity. After providing the media with a photograph and a brief interview, they refrained from invading my privacy. Being aware of the intricacies of public life that awaited me in the future, I comprehended that people's treatment towards celebrities differed significantly back then."

"Witnessing the excitement that would ensue upon my appearance among the crowd, I realized from the future knowledge that aggressive behavior towards ordinary individuals and the media, under the assumption of one's special entitlement, would deteriorate public opinion towards such a celebrity. This understanding shaped my decision to allocate my time to them generously. Our travels from one place to another were prolonged, but we explored many renowned cities around the world. By the end of 1954, my Elvis career was solid, with over 30 songs released under the Sun Records label. Most of these tracks achieved the pinnacle of success, securing the number-one spot on various charts. Remarkably, within the early stages of my career, I became the most sought-after entertainer of all time."

"In March 1955, Sam Phillips, my manager, was flourishing. It occurred to me that perhaps I did not require Colonel Tom Parker to propel my success further. Sam, with my future knowledge and particularly my innovative marketing techniques, provided me with a distinct advantage over the real Elvis's career trajectory during that time. Destiny has a way of aligning events, regardless of the path one is deliberately laying out. Sam arranged a meeting between Colonel Tom Parker and me at the renowned Lombardo's restaurant in Nashville."

"That day, Sam and I went together, and he recounted to me how he had almost gone bankrupt because of a previous artist's copyright infringement before I came into the picture. Before our meeting, I had already familiarized myself with the situation through the Elvis manual, so I expected what he was about to say when he mentioned wanting me to meet someone significant and keeping an open mind. He was referring to none other than the Colonel. Throughout the drive to Nashville, Sam continuously expressed how he saw me as a son and emphasized that I could always rely on him for anything. However, I understood his underlying message was that he had already sold my contract."

"As the journey progressed, conversation dwindled, and we fell into a comfortable silence. We observed the surroundings, such as the traffic and the weather. I pondered over the reasons behind Sam Phillips selling my contract since the money he was making could have easily resolved his financial troubles. Perhaps his decision stemmed from concerns about my marketability as a married man, considering I had gotten married at a young age. In the music industry, marital status hadn't proven beneficial for many rock stars. I paid no mind to this, as my heart was content with Louise, and that was all that mattered to me."

"Upon reaching our destination, Sam parked the car just outside the restaurant's entrance. A valet took over to park the car, and we stepped out. This establishment was synonymous with luxury and fame, making it the perfect place to be spotted by the media during significant business dealings. I suspected that some representatives of the press would be present. As we entered, the photographers went into a frenzy. We were then guided to a private room towards the rear of the bustling restaurant."

"Inside, I spotted Colonel Thomas Andrew Parker seated at the table adorned in a light gray suit and matching hat. Upon our entrance, the 44-year-old manager rose from his seat, respectfully removing his hat. Sam introduced us to each other, but I already possessed the essential knowledge about this renowned manager, as I had thoroughly researched him in the Elvis manual. Ultimately, this encounter was bound to happen, as he held the key to securing my recording contract with the RCA Victor record label and the Hollywood movie contracts."

"Upon meeting the man, I couldn't help but notice the stark contrast in the size of our hands during our handshake. Seated at the table, the Colonel, with his round figure, directed his attention towards me and declared himself a devoted admirer. I was genuinely impressed by his words. He astutely observed that I strategically saved my signature hip gyration and dance moves for my first appearance on the Ed Sullivan Show. His awareness of this left me even more amazed. Though I had no response to his assumption, I conveyed my agreement with a slight nod."

"The Colonel explained how my performance on the show had captivated him, catapulting me onto the international stage. It almost seemed as if he possessed some profound insight into my future. How was this possible? He must have possessed a brilliant intellect. To divert attention, I credited my manager, Sam, acknowledging his exceptional work. The Colonel then placed a large cigar in his mouth, igniting it and engulfing our surroundings with smoke. He concurred with my praise for Sam, revealing their agreement regarding my future endeavors."

"Curiosity sparked within me as I inquired about this supposed agreement. However, I feigned ignorance, not wanting to reveal my knowledge of events yet to come. Subsequently, Sam spoke, and I already expected his words. He explained he had taken my career as far as he could, and by selling my contract to the Colonel, he secured his financial well-being while ensuring that I would achieve the utmost success under the Colonel's guidance. I was no stranger to the fact that the Colonel had initially paid Sam Phillips $35,000 for your recording contract, Elvis."

"Elvis, Sam Phillips had not been your original manager. He had signed you to his record label under a standard contract. It was only after Sam encouraged guitarist Scotty Moore to become your first manager. So that you had someone to protect you from deceitful music promotors. Following that, Bob Neal took on the role of your manager. Bob had experience managing other bands that worked alongside the esteemed country singer Hank Snow. To be exact, Hank's jamboree attractions belonged to him but were overseen by Colonel Tom Parker, a former carnival barker. In August 1955, Colonel Parker assumed the position as your manager."

"In contrast to your experience, Elvis, my management approach differed, as I persuaded Sam Phillips to take charge of my career. Initially, he hesitated because of a conflict of interest stemming from his ownership of the recording studio. However, he eventually agreed, and together we tried to avoid any involvement with the Colonel until this point. Although Sam was competent, he never possessed the same connections as the Colonel."

"I pleaded with Sam because he allowed me to kick-start my career. I had to make it appear genuine, thus preventing the Colonel from gaining an advantage in future negotiations. Sadly, Sam seemed disheartened, suggesting deep down that he knew it was an unwise decision, yet he still had to persuade me. He explained he had already sold my recording and management contract and had received appropriate compensation, which he believed would secure the survival of Sun Records."

"The revelation evoked a strong emotional response from me, and I expressed to Sam that I understood why he had taken such actions. I vowed not to forget our conversation in the car, as I always regarded him as a father figure. This was an intense and difficult situation, but it must be done. The Colonel addressed me as his son, effortlessly maintaining his deceptive façade as a cigar-smoking manipulator. He extended his right hand, and we shook hands. He then uttered, welcome to the fold. At that moment, I comprehended the necessity of the Colonel's connections and influence. However, it's crucial to remember that being from the future, although my contract had been sold to the Colonel, there was still no formal agreement between myself and his management, namely the Colonel."

"Following this encounter, we enjoyed our meals. The food was superb, and my memories of the place remain extremely precious. As we finished our meals, the contract was presented for me to sign. The Colonel displayed signs of impatience, urging me to sign on the spot and placing a folder on the table in front of me. The Colonel orchestrated the entrance of newspaper reporters and photographers into the private room. This was a planned move, as I was aware of the excessive percentage the Colonel initially took from the real Elvis's contract. Allocating 50 percent of one's earnings to a manager was an unreasonable demand, especially when I was the one doing most of the work."

"But no rational person would willingly surrender half of their earnings. However, during Elvis's era, that was the norm. The subsequent events had the potential to derail my career because, with the media present, the Colonel expected me to sign the contract without hesitation. I firmly refused to put my signature on the document until my lawyer had carefully reviewed its contents."

"The transfer of management was of utmost importance, according to the Colonel's words. It was crucial! Despite his attempts, I remained unyielding and, in a gesture of respect, refrained from reciting the section in the contract that outlined the exorbitant 50 percent management fee. The Colonel continued to persist, only to discover that I was a young man, but far from a fool. On that fateful day, he tried to coerce me into compliance, but I stood my ground. Subsequently, I granted him an opportunity to discuss the matter privately, away from the prying eyes of the media whom he invited, but he declined."

"It was truly a sight to behold as the Colonel nearly choked on his cigar upon hearing my unequivocal statement that I would never agree to the terms that demanded 50 percent of my earnings be surrendered to him. The reporters, upon hearing my words, became positively jubilant, with the cameras zooming in on the Colonel's astonished countenance. To his credit, the Colonel refrained from denying my claim about the contractual percentage that I had not even perused. I believe he was genuinely surprised by my knowledge of the contents inside the folder, which prompted him to gaze at me with a smile while simply puffing on his cigar. As previously mentioned, I allowed him to converse privately, yet unbeknownst to him, his tactical attempt to pressure me into signing dissolved before it could even take hold."

"On that day, I embarrassed the Colonel, thwarting his plan to bind me to the same contract as the real Elvis had in my previous life. I possessed knowledge of his substantial gambling losses, and for that reason, I vehemently refused to pour my blood, sweat, and tears into work that his racetrack would squander exploits. A stalemate ensued for an entire week between the Colonel, me, and Sam Phillips, who depended on this deal to come to fruition. He even comprehended my unwavering stance. Seeking legal counsel, I presented the contract to a lawyer who confirmed my suspicions that the Colonel would receive half of my earnings. Having traveled from the future where the fine print continued to harbor many betrayals, I remained steadfast in my decision."

"The Colonel and I reached a deadlock despite the absence of a contract between him and me. This was because the Colonel possessed my original agreement with Sam Phillips, granting him authority to prohibit my performances and recordings. He even had the power to prevent me from singing without charge. The notion of trade restriction was not considered, as a contract was still considered binding. Later, I discovered the Colonel had paid Sam Phillips over $100,000 for both agreements. Eventually, he would have to either return the contract to Sam or reduce his initial percentage fee."

"I was aware of a future management fee, which was approximately 10 percent, and was the highest amount I would pay. Many weeks were spent negotiating, but we eventually reached an impasse because I offered 8 percent while he insisted on 15 percent. Eventually, we settled on 12 percent; I included provisions for overseas touring with or without my manager's presence in my contract. Was this a stroke of genius? Not exactly, as I possessed crucial information about the Colonel's identity within my Elvis manual. It was revealed that Colonel Thomas Andrew Parker was originally Andreas Cornelis Kuijk, born on June 26, 1909, in Breda, North Brabant, Netherlands."

"Since the Colonel never held an American passport, he could not travel abroad. It was later mentioned that this explained why he couldn't leave America and opposed your overseas tours, as it would mean relinquishing control. I ensured I had no such restrictions, as I had aspirations of performing in major cities worldwide and exploring many unknown places during my tours."

"In retrospect, I believed the Colonel would have settled for a 10 percent fee, but the sticking point was the provision regarding overseas touring. Despite the prolonged negotiations, I viewed this as a reasonable compromise. I regarded Sam Phillips as a father figure, as aside from Steven Clements, David's dad, I had never truly had one. Although three months of stalemate may have seemed unproductive, it resulted in the conception of our first child, who was born on April 11, 1956."

"We welcomed a daughter whom I named Lisa Marie. I wanted to keep the same name as the original Elvis had given his only daughter. I also aimed to curry favor with the Colonel by incorporating his wife's name, Marie, as our daughter's middle name. From that moment onward, the Colonel and I treated each other as father and son. The man had the greatest management skills of all time, and by June 1956, I had signed a recording contract with RCA Victor Records, just like the real Elvis had that same year. Hit after hit came my way, and things were going better than expected."

Chapter Sixteen

Fun in Acapulco

"Immediately after I joined with the Colonel, Hollywood came knocking on my door. While we were at a standstill, he was fervently working to secure my future. In July 1956, I put pen to paper and signed a contract, subsequently landing a leading role in the film 'Love Me Tender.' I vividly recall watching the original movie starring Elvis from the past. While it was a big hit for you, my rendition was well-received, earning me critical acclaim. I attribute this success to the intense acting lessons I received from the future and avant-garde techniques that were yet to be invented during the 1950s. Those experiences laid the foundation for my flourishing movie career."

"This phase of my professional journey proved to be the busiest period. In 1957, two more films, 'Loving You' and 'Jailhouse Rock,' were released concurrently with the real Elvis. You were correct, Elvis, when you opined early on these movies all shared a similar trajectory. I found tremendous joy in their production, and let's be honest, who could complain about a movie salary of $1 million per film?"

"Another phenomenon that typically accompanies rising stardom is the intrusion of women into one's life. On two occasions, I experienced this firsthand. This instance transpired in 1959. Joe King, one of my tour managers, had arranged for a group of attractive ladies to be present in my caravan on the set of 'Flaming Star.' When I entered the caravan and saw what was happening, I immediately dismissed the women. I needed to take such action, as I was all too aware of the consequences of becoming entrapped in such behavior. Observing what had befallen the real Elvis throughout his career, I resolved never to entertain such distractions. I promptly ended Joe King's employment, ensuring that such situations would never arise again."

"I was honored that Louise had selected me as her life partner, and if I had performed such actions towards my heavily pregnant wife and one child, it would have completely shattered everything I believe in. However, there are individuals in the industry who cannot comprehend this concept. Despite giving the example of Joe King in 1959, another manager, Tony Lawrence, committed the same offense in 1962. It occurred on the 'Fun in Acapulco,' set where three attractive ladies awaited my arrival in the caravan. Perhaps Tony assumed I desired to have fun in Acapulco, but not in this manner, as I had always remained faithful to my wife and children."

"By 1968, four more children had come into this world. Peter, born in 1959, was always intended to be my first son's name since it symbolized my original birth name, Peter. I suppose it was a way for me to connect with my true self, something that no one else could fully comprehend but that held great personal significance. In 1960, John was born, and he is your father, bearing the identity I assumed when I traveled back in time. The Cadman surname was chosen to embrace my identity and ensure that I remembered who I truly was. Hence, my children and my wife kept the Cadman's name, as the famed Presley name did not belong to me, but to you, Elvis."

"I believed that this was a manifestation of my past guilt, both back then and presently. Hence, I was the only one who used your name, associating it with the rock and roll persona I developed starting in 1953. In 1963, David came into this world, and I named him after my best friend as a reminder of the brother I had left behind. Fortunately, Louise allowed me to name our children, and later, when she discovered the truth about me, the significance of the names became clear to her as well. Finally, in 1968, Christine was born, and now you know she was named in honor of my grandmother, Christine Smart, from my original life."

"Having achieved everything, much like the original Elvis, I found myself engrossed in a movie career and a series of concerts throughout the United States. However, as any artist would understand, the overwhelming demands of my work left me with no time or energy to schedule performances overseas. In 1969, I completed my final film endeavor 'Change of Habit,' just as the real Elvis did. I needed to alter my usual routine of starring in movies. Meanwhile, my record sales continued to thrive, resulting in many gold records that I had run out of space to display."

"Subsequently, the landscape of the music industry transformed with the emergence of chart-toppers such as the Beatles, the Rolling Stones, and the Beach Boys. Similar to the fate suffered by the original Elvis, I experienced a gradual decline in importance. With no promising movie scripts or hit songs to revive my standing, my popularity plummeted. Desperate for some respite, I yearned for a break. Unfortunately, the Colonel, my manager, had unique plans, constantly exploring alternative avenues for my career. He worried I was ready to retire prematurely; how could I possibly retire at such a young age? I was only 35 years old as February 1970 approached."

"Persistently, the Colonel presented me with more of the womanizing films that had once garnered success. Yet even the broadest audience had their fill of these productions. While the Colonel insisted, I continue working, I found solace in the comfort of my home alongside Louise and our children. We possessed all that we needed, and finances were not a concern. I had accumulated enough wealth to lead a comfortable life for the rest of our days. Royalties far exceeded what was necessary, but the Colonel's unwise investments caused him financial troubles. To appease him and rid myself of his constant badgering, I reluctantly agreed to increase his percentage from twelve to twenty-five. Similar to the real Elvis, I was his sole client. Even if he were to take a quarter of my royalties, I still possessed more than sufficient means to sustain myself without engaging in any further endeavors."

"The Colonel continuously released a series of my prior albums, but their sales remained mediocre. This lackluster response could be attributed to the influx of talented artists in the music industry during the 1970s. In this era, one could go from being at the top of the charts to disappearing completely in a matter of moments. Undoubtedly, the seventies marked a time of immense innovation within the realm of rock music. However, my predicament arose from my semi-retired status, which made it challenging for me to adapt to this period despite my advanced knowledge of what lay ahead."

"In January 1971, I recorded songs that were presented to me by various songwriters. My compliance with the Colonel's wishes was driven by a desire to maintain my extravagant lifestyle and the financial responsibilities that came with raising children. I realized the importance of continuing to generate income and making the most of the remaining talent at my disposal. Growing apathetic and in need of a new endeavor, perhaps my career had grown stale by this point, and my confidence in delivering live performances had waned; interestingly, I had included an overseas clause in my initial contract with the Colonel, yet I no longer possessed the motivation to embark on tours."

"Instead, I revisited my Elvis manual, and despite having promised Davis Clements not to interfere in any world-changing events, I had already made a few alterations that had turned out to be successful. Secretly, I had always intended to intervene in two significant tragedies that were yet to occur in the United States. The first tragedy that compelled me to take action was the catastrophic explosion of the Space Shuttle Challenger on January 28, 1986, resulting in the loss of seven astronauts, one of them being a high school teacher. However, it was the second event that held the utmost importance. September 11, 2001, known as 9/11, claimed the lives of nearly 3,000 individuals because of a terrorist attack."

"These two tragic events had constantly occupied my thoughts, and I had a fifteen-year window before the Challenger Space Shuttle disaster. To ensure success, I needed to conduct a few trials involving minor tragedies. I needed to remain inconspicuous in my actions, carefully delaying or thwarting events before they unfolded. My first target was a mere two weeks away: the 'New Orleans Mardi Gras massacre.' This dreadful incident occurred on February 2, 1971, when a man named Victor Hanson embarked on an 11-minute spree through the narrow streets of the French Quarter, armed with a 12-inch hunting knife. Tragically, his rampage resulted in the deaths of eleven individuals and left eighteen others injured."

"On that day, as the event began, Victor Hanson, a deranged individual, entered the French Quarter amidst the Mardi Gras floats. In broad daylight, he embarked on a killing spree, targeting innocent participants of the Mardi Gras. It is important to note that any attempt to find information about this incident through online searches will be futile, as I successfully prevented this tragedy from occurring."

"This marked the first instance where I could alter history with success. However, it was no simple task, as I could not simply call the police and request the arrest of a man solely on speculation about his potential actions. Despite knowing the deranged killer from the Elvis manual, it would have been ineffective. Although he had a previous criminal record, it was unrelated to any threats or assaults. He had remained under the police radar. I realized I needed external help while also ensuring that I kept myself away from any suspicion. How could I explain my knowledge of certain events, considering I was from the future?"

"Turning to the Colonel, I inquired if he knew of someone trustworthy. The Colonel introduced me to Max Tiller, a private investigator, who he considered reliable. One evening in late January, just about a week before the Mardi Gras massacre, the Colonel brought Max Tiller to Graceland. Max Tiller was a solidly built man in his mid-forties with dark eyes that bore a resemblance to a wrestler. I believed him to be the ideal person for the job, given his experience as a former police officer and the connections he maintained within the Memphis police station. Realizing the sensitivity of our conversation, I asked the Colonel if I could speak with Max in private, ensuring that the Colonel would not be implicated in any of this covert work."

"A few days later, Max returned to Graceland, bringing a folder detailing information about Victor Hanson. It revealed that Hanson had a history of drug-related offenses and had already spent time in the county jail. This information presented us with an opportunity to halt his planned actions in New Orleans on February 2nd. The only viable method was to orchestrate his arrest, taking advantage of his previous incarceration for drug possession. We devised a plan to set him up by planting approximately ten pounds of cocaine."

"Let me explain my recent actions to both of you. Effectively, I gave Max the sum of $25,000 in cash, along with sufficient funds to buy drugs. These drugs were subsequently planted inside Victor Hanson's residence in New Orleans, after which Max discreetly alerted the local authorities. On January 31st, 1971, law enforcement forcibly entered Hanson's abode, successfully locating the drugs and $25,000 in cash. Naturally, the currency was mine. As a result, Hanson was apprehended and officially charged with engaging in drug-related activities and unlawful possession. Following an extensive examination of his residence, the authorities discovered a note that explained Hanson's motivations behind his projected actions to take place in two days. A year and a half later, Hanson was convicted and subsequently sentenced to twelve years of incarceration."

"The police captain received abundant accolades for his role in subduing a deranged murderer, and I would venture to say that such commendations were rightfully deserved. However, this endeavor cost $50,000 besides Max's remuneration fee. The significance of the matter lies because of these efforts. I saved eleven lives and prevented eighteen individuals from suffering injuries. This brought me immense happiness, for I felt akin to the legendary superhero known as Superman, who valiantly safeguards the planet from imminent dangers."

"This triumphant rescue mission further solidified my decision to keep Max Tiller as an integral member of my workforce for the following fifteen years. Throughout this period, I allocated approximately $20 million towards this noble cause, thus preserving the lives of over 556 individuals from similar catastrophic events transpiring worldwide. Although Max remained oblivious to the truth behind my actions, I could not help but think that he must have sensed something peculiar. He never inquired about my intentions or the nature of my activities, a testament to my wise selection of an apt candidate for the task at hand."

Chapter Seventeen

A Star is Born

"During the years 1971 to 1975, my touring schedule was relentless. However, unlike you, Elvis, your performances were limited to America. I embarked on a global tour fueled by overwhelming demand. I devised a cunning plan to market myself that would captivate audiences across the globe, beckoning them to witness my concerts. The concept was simple yet revolutionary—I implemented a uniform price for all my shows. Thus, regardless of the seat location within the venue, a ticket to my concert would only cost a flat rate of $20. Whether attendees were seated in the prestigious A reserved area or nestled in the distant bleachers, the cost remained the same. The early bird catches the worm, as they say."

"Admittedly, this approach presented challenges. The astute colonel rightly pointed out that charging a mere $20 positioned us at a breakeven point after considering expenses. In certain venues, we even faced losses depending on the location of the concert. I felt compelled to reclaim my position at the pinnacle of the music industry, and in due course, this strategy proved immensely successful. The Colonel, pleased with my revived passion, skillfully capitalized on the opportunity, amassing millions upon millions of dollars through merchandise sales at each show. Being well-versed in economic principles, I understood that in 2020, attending a concert starring a renowned artist could set one back anywhere between $500 and $1,500, figures people will pay."

"However, even in 2020, $500 remained a considerable sum. During my younger days, I would eagerly spend my hard-earned money on concert tickets, only to leave the merchandise booth empty-handed, unable to afford a memento to commemorate the exceptional performances by the artists I revered. Therefore, when individuals attended my affordably priced $20 concerts, they freely embraced the opportunity to splurge on merchandise, resulting in substantial profits for us. The Colonel marveled at my intelligent marketing strategies and insight, basking in the success they brought, making him a content man."

"To support my heroic feats as Superman, I embarked on a tour. Simultaneously, the release of some of the real Elvis tracks provided me with renewed inspiration, putting me back on the right path. I came across an article depicting a decline in the real Elvis's health during the same period, just two years before his passing. However, I defied the odds and enjoyed improved health. As a forty-year-old man in 1975, I refrained from resorting to the prescription drugs that dragged the real Elvis down to the lowest point of his life."

"Similar to the real Elvis, my film career ended in the '60s. While perusing the Elvis manual, I hatched a plan. The manual presented conflicting accounts of an incident that occurred in 1975 when the real Elvis found himself backstage after one of his concerts. Barbra Streisand and her then-boyfriend and hairstylist, Jon Peters, met with

Elvis and proposed that he take on the leading role in the upcoming film 'A Star Is Born.' Now, this is where the stories diverge, but it is said that at that specific moment, Elvis was fervently eager to accept the role had Streisand offered it."

"This role ended up being given to Kris Kristofferson, who later won a Golden Globe for Best Actor in a Musical in 1976. Streisand herself also won a Golden Globe for Best Actress, and the song 'Evergreen' secured the Academy Award for Best Original Song. During that time, Elvis experienced great heartbreak, as this role could have potentially reignited his acting career. It was a serious and substantive acting role, distinct from the beach romp, high-speed car chases, and speedboat adventures that both of us eventually resorted to."

"Various theories circulated, yet only the real Elvis knew the truth. One theory suggested that the Colonel, Elvis's manager, desired top billing for Elvis in the movie credits. However, Streisand had already garnered an Oscar for 'Funny Girl' in 1968 and received a nomination for 'The Way We Were' in 1974. Given that it was her motion picture, she insisted on top billing, resulting in Elvis being denied. Another theory implied that Elvis woke up the following morning, realizing his lack of motivation to pursue the role, and requested the Colonel to make the opportunity vanish."

"The Colonel, wanting a $1 million upfront fee and $100,000 for expenses, made these excessive demands as a starting point. He insisted on receiving 50 percent of the profits. It's quite astonishing. The team ultimately decided against casting Elvis because the movie's total budget was only $6 million. Despite this, the film performed very well and ended up grossing $80 million worldwide. Not too shabby. However, the Colonel's demands would have incurred significant costs. What Barbra didn't know was that if Elvis had played the role instead of Kristofferson, the revenue could have been much higher."

"Opinions regarding the matter varied. Some believed the Colonel asked for the standard fee that he genuinely thought was fair for that time, while others believed he intentionally inflated the figures to discourage Streisand. As an avid reader of the Elvis manual, I was aware of this. However, I needed this film to align my acting career with my original plans from the beginning. Keep in mind that the rigorous acting lessons I had previously undergone were meant for a more serious acting career than what the real Elvis truly had or aspired to have. That's how I secured the role in the movie, and as you already know, the rest is history. Until now, nobody knew how I ultimately got the part. Like the real Elvis, I too went backstage after a concert in Vegas around January 1975, where both Barbra Streisand and Jon Peters were present."

"They approached me directly, but unlike the real Elvis, who gave Barbra unsolicited advice about her hand movements while singing, I kept my suggestions to myself because I wanted her on my side—and she was. Then she offered me the same deal that was originally proposed to you, Elvis. Naturally, I knew about the original agreement. I verbally accepted the role only after receiving a written offer from her and ensuring that everything was checked out. I was thrilled to take on the role in the movie."

"Upon arriving at Graceland three days later, the Colonel presented me with the contract, which immediately caught my attention. I noticed my name was being credited lower than Barbra Streisand's, and there seemed to be a lack of specifics regarding my payment for the role. Deep down, I believed that the sheer fame of Elvis Presley alone should have propelled this movie to even greater heights than the original. This film surpassed all expectations. It became a massive success, partially because of Barbra Streisand's insistence on having

Elvis play the role, knowing that his involvement would skyrocket the movie's popularity."

"During this time, a stark contrast became clear between the real Elvis and me. Unlike him, I was in impeccable physical shape. Perhaps Barbra had noticed Elvis's decline in the past, witnessing his slurred speech and the diminishing sex appeal that accompanied his aging appearance. Conversely, I was the complete antithesis of the original Elvis, which led me to believe that this movie had the potential to receive critical acclaim and recognition. Although I acknowledged that Barbra Streisand deserved top billing, I felt I deserved it even more and was determined to secure it, despite not having ownership over the movie."

"To gauge their response to the demands of the planet's most famous rock star, I requested the Colonel approach them and propose placing my name at the forefront of the credits. I was eager to discover the financial offer associated with the role. Approximately a week later, the Colonel returned with news that top billing was non-negotiable because of Barbra's stellar reputation as an actress. Her Academy Award guaranteed her the first position, regardless of any counteroffers. Therefore, I had no choice but to find contentment with second billing."

"The Colonel informed me they had offered the customary fee of $500,000 for the role, along with a percentage of the box office revenue. Monetary concerns were of no issue to me, as I will take on the role and fully embrace the persona of Elvis, a name recognized by every individual on this planet. However, there was no way my ego would settle for anything less than top billing; I craved the recognition and acknowledgment it entailed."

"I presented them with an offer they couldn't turn down, a proposition that would have been agreeable to anyone. My proposal con-

sisted of working on the movie for free and receiving only 5 percent of the box office gross earnings. Initially, they hesitated to grant
me top billing and declined my proposal. However, they eventually
recognized the value of my deal, and I officially signed on for the
role. Shooting the movie later that year was an incredibly enjoyable
experience for me, as it allowed me to portray my true self effortlessly,
thanks to the chemistry between Barbra and myself."

"Hence, you now understand how I secured the part and the existence of an alternate version of this movie. When the film was released
in 1976, it drew massive crowds to the theaters because of the hype
surrounding my role. Towards the end of that year, I was honored
with a Golden Globe award for Best Actor in a Musical. And as you
may already be aware, in 1977, I won the Oscar for Best Actor for my
performance in 'A Star Is Born.'"

"I would like to take this opportunity to offer my sincere apologies to Peter Finch, who originally received the award for his role in
the movie 'Network' that year. I must also extend my apologies to
Sylvester Stallone, whose 'Rocky' movie initially won the coveted best
picture award in my alternate reality. However, as you already know,
'A Star Is Born' ultimately claimed this honor. The 'Rocky' films have
enjoyed considerable success, with several installments being released
since then, reaching the impressive count of seven or eight by now.
Anyway, my apologies to you, Sylvester. Now, you are aware of the
truth behind the original events as opposed to the version you were
familiar with."

"Ultimately, this movie shattered all box office records by grossing
over 555 million dollars, a feat that remained unsurpassed for a significant period. The Colonel, once again, found himself in high spirits
as he received a substantial payday from the 27 million dollars from
my share of the box office earnings. I had accomplished my long-held

desire to be recognized as a highly accomplished actor. This success propelled my acting career, leading me to star in many other films until I retired from Hollywood in the mid-90s."

"There was one script I couldn't turn down; it was for the role in the movie 'The Godfather 3'. Being a huge fan of the 'Godfather' movies, I was ecstatic to play the character of Johnny Fontane. This opportunity arose because Al Martino, who originally portrayed the role in the two previous movies, was unavailable for the scheduled shooting date of this picture. As a result, they approached me, and I took on the part. Interestingly, my portrayal in this film differed from Al Martino's original performance. I believe the producers must have been admirers of my acting, which led to an expanded role for me in the movie. Ultimately, I earned my second Oscar in 1991 for Best Supporting Actor."

"If anyone could go back in time, they would have something to say. However, my dear grandson, I already did that. Time catches up with us all, and even though I once could turn back the clock, I no longer possess my youth. Hollywood has always been a place of wonder where dreams come true, yet one is often remembered solely for their most recent film."

"Working alongside the talented Al Pacino, Joe Mantegna, Diane Keaton, and Andy Garcia made my last movie truly delightful, as they treated me as one of their own. This pleased me greatly, as it showcased my ability to perform in a serious role. In the end, I concluded my acting career on a high note, retiring after 'The Godfather 3' because of my firm commitment to my singing career. In winning another Oscar, I had nothing more to prove."

Chapter Eighteen

A Triumph and Tragedy

"Max Tiller, a highly innovative individual, possessed the ability to swiftly adapt to technological advancements and computer skills that would prove helpful in the future. Having arrived in 2020, I comprehended the significance of technology as we ventured toward the next phase. As the early 80s rolled in, I found myself on yet another break from touring. My musical endeavors, such as the songs 'Breaking Bad' and 'Losing the Faith,' had attained some success, and I discovered myself in unexplored territory within the music industry. The 80s were a mixed bag of highs and lows. However, a radiant moment emerged on February 18th, 1985, when I, as John Cadman, celebrated my 50th birthday at Graceland. This naturally was my newly assumed birthdate. Although, in secret, I would still commemorate September 27th as it held my true birthday, but for the rest of the world, it was John Cadman's special day."

"This occasion was even broadcasted, captivating a substantial audience. Many individuals from Hollywood and the music industry attended, totaling a staggering number of 2,500 participants. The most notable aspect of my 50th birthday celebration was the noteworthy gifts I received. Among the presents, one stood out, mirroring what the real Elvis had also received in the past: a gun from Colonel Tom Parker. The gifted firearm was a 1971 Colt Lawman Mklll 357 magnum revolver. Currently in my life, emerging from a future inundated with news of gun violence, I possess no interest in firearms. However, once I visited a firing range and gained some proficiency, I became captivated."

"The real Elvis had possessed multiple guns, owing to his hobby of collecting them. There was even an infamous incident where he shot all his television sets at Graceland upon catching sight of Robert Goulet on the screen. Now, let me explain the reasoning behind sharing this story. Less than a year after commemorating my 50th birthday, I, too, replicated Elvis's actions and shot all my television screens. Louise implemented a permanent ban on guns within the confines of Graceland."

"The following narrative discusses the significance of the recounted episode involving a firearm, to show that possessing knowledge of past tragedies is not always helpful. David Clements had cautioned against altering past events, as even the most minor adjustments might lead to outcomes worse than the original. How accurate were David's words, considering my perpetual yearning to rectify the 1986 Space Shuttle Challenger disaster? Upon viewing the original footage on YouTube and subsequently getting Wikipedia information, which I added to the Elvis manual, my ambition grew stronger."

"On January 28, 1986, NASA's Space Shuttle Challenger plunged the world into despair with a devastating accident claiming the lives of seven astronauts. Among the victims were Challenger commander Dick Scobee, pilot Michael Smith, mission specialists Judy Resnik,

Ronald McNair, and Ellison Onizuka, payload specialist Gregory Jarvis, and Christa Mc Auliffe, a soon-to-be pioneer as the first teacher in space. It was for her sake alone that I desired to alter the course of events on that fateful day. The complexity of the task made it nearly impossible to convey the details to NASA."

"Planning the daring Superman rescue proved to be the most intricate challenge, for I could not involve Max Tiller in this endeavor. Figuring out how to justify my knowledge of such a momentous event without involving Max created a problem. As I delved into the report, I discovered that the Space Shuttle had disintegrated 73 seconds after liftoff. Following this, the then-American President Ronald Regan started the Roger's Commission to find out the cause of the catastrophe."

"Further examination of the report revealed that the cold weather that morning had caused the rubber O-rings connecting the fuel segments of the solid rocket booster to stiffen. The Morton Thiokol factory had constructed four hull segments using powdered aluminum fuel and ammonium, the technical terms of which escaped my memory. The report also clarified that the O-rings had never undergone testing in extreme cold weather. On the day of the launch, the temperature hovered around 30 °F."

"Goodness, what kind of text was I perusing? The content surpassed my comprehension, and even if I were to reach out to the engineers at mission control discretely, they would disregard the futile ramblings of a concerned citizen. During that time, I was in turmoil because I desperately wanted to prevent this impending disaster. Eventually, I realized that rewriting the Roger's Commission report, word for word, and secretly sending it to the engineers responsible would be my best course of action. With any luck, they would attentively assess the condition of the O-rings, resulting in a launch delay and the salvation of those seven lives."

"And that is precisely what I did, although it consumed approximately two weeks of my time to transcribe the report from the Elvis manual manually. I took utmost care, for I could not afford this information as I was prepared to divulge it to NASA to come back and incriminate me. I foresaw a future where a single hair or fingerprint on any of those pages could betray me with DNA identification. However, back in 1985, I was uncertain whether the FBI possessed such capabilities. Given their penchant for secrecy, it was impossible to know if they wielded similar tools as they do today, but I was unwilling to take any risks."

"During my planning phase, I involved Max Tiller but refrained from disclosing any specifics regarding the Space Shuttle Challenger or NASA. I requested that Max Tiller purchase an unassuming typewriter, namely the 1984 Olivetti Lettera 25. This red typewriter was basic, ensuring it wouldn't attract undue attention. As I handled each page and typed, I donned gloves and even wore a hairnet to prevent any mishaps with the envelopes. If the FBI were to investigate the typewriter model used to produce these letters, they would discover that it was widely available to the public, and they would find no trace of fingerprints or hair samples. After diligently completing five sets of the Rogers Commission findings, I was prepared to have them dispatched to the authorities."

"Max was entrusted with delivering the letters to various destinations worldwide, while I compensated him handsomely. To avoid suspicion, each letter was sent from a different location: Rome, Paris, Sydney, Beijing, and Berlin. By adopting this strategy, it would be nearly impossible to trace the origin of the information. Max took great precautions by wearing gloves and ensuring the letters were devoid of any incriminating evidence. As the days went by, the Christmas of 1985 approached, and my anticipation grew as I diligently followed the news. To my astonishment, there was no mention of the letters disclosing the imminent problem with the O-rings."

"In my TV room, affectionately referred to as the jungle room in Graceland, I had arranged multiple television sets. Six televisions were relics from a more primitive era compared to the future I hailed from. Being in tune with the evolving times, I eagerly awaited the new year in 1986. Sitting before the array of televisions tuned to different news networks, I continued my search for any shred of information. Yet, disappointingly, no news of the letters materialized. By January 26th, my desperation grew to the point where I contemplated using the telephone, as the intended impact of my five letters had not been achieved. Recognizing that tomorrow would be the 27th, I concluded there was no alternative but to contact the recipients directly."

"On the evening of January 26th, it finally occurred. Every TV station on the evening news broadcast the cancellation of the scheduled Space Shuttle Challenger launch, which was originally planned for January 28th. The launch was postponed indefinitely, with reports attributing the cancellation to the frigid weather and potential manufacturing defects in the rocket boosters. Jackpot! The mission had been called off, and the lives of the seven astronauts were saved. Naturally, I was overjoyed by the news. Although the children and Louise couldn't fully comprehend my excitement, I knew that this was where I truly saw the significance of my ability to travel back in time, beyond just assuming your gig, Elvis. By altering the course of events, I had made a difference for the greater good, and it was an incredible feeling."

"Now, let me transport you back to my 50th birthday, specifically the significance of the gun gifted to me by the Colonel. It was Monday,

April 21st, 1986, nearly three months after my intervention prevented the original Space Shuttle Challenger disaster. On that morning, I returned inside after some target practice in Graceland's backyard. As I meticulously cleaned my gun, I sat before the television. Every channel that day was broadcasting the eagerly expected Space Shuttle Challenger launch, scheduled for 11 a.m. While I carefully oiled the empty gun, I overheard some commentators discussing how they had resolved the O-ring issue that led to the initial cancellation of the launch on January 28th."

"What an incredible feeling it was to hear the news reporters announce the problem had been fixed and the seven astronauts would now embark on their space mission, with the weather being favorable. Little did they know that by this point, they would have perished tragically. The most satisfying aspect of my knowledge of the future was that I saved these seven individuals, along with the 556 lives from the past. The tally now stood at 563 lives. However, only I was aware of this, and it was worthwhile and fulfilling."

"Now, I am inclined to believe that you both have already been exposed to the final version of this Space Shuttle launch and now you understand why events unfolded in this manner. It all happened because I intervened and altered the natural course of history. Recall that I was cleaning my gun, but I paused and carefully placed it down on the coffee table as the clock neared 11 a.m. Nervous yet filled with a deep sense of delight, I watched all six televisions simultaneously broadcasting the imminent launch. After the countdown, the engines ignited, and the rest, as they say, is history..."

After concluding his story, Grandpa Elvis pondered his actions while the real Elvis comprehended the profound impact of this tragedy on his idol. Josh, his grandson, searched for information about the tragedy on his cell phone. He also experienced a profound sense of remorse for his grandfather. "That day will forever haunt me," Grandpa Elvis expressed. "I apologize because what I am sharing with both of you is not so much a significant accomplishment as it is a confession."

"Once the engines were ignited, a rupture occurred in the changed solid rocket boosters, whose O-rings had recently been replaced based on the information I provided NASA from the Rogers Commission. Unfortunately, an oversight resulted in the explosion of the rocket booster on the launch pad, as new O-rings, although stronger, failed to seal between the segments properly. With the increased heat from the engine ignition, the ill-fated Space Shuttle Challenger exploded before it even took off."

"After all, the seven astronauts I had previously saved perished. However, the tragedy did not end there. Debris from the space shuttle scattered outward at ground level, obliterating a section of the crowd that had gathered to witness the launch over three miles away from the launchpad. Although this distance was considered a safety requirement back then, it proved inadequate because_____."

"I am deeply sorry because, as a result, I caused the deaths of another 1,293 individuals and injured an additional 3,235. David was right all along. By altering the original tragedy, I inadvertently created an even more devastating outcome. This remains one of the darkest periods of my life. Yes, I confess to both of you, and now that I bear responsibility for the deaths of 1,300 people, men, women, and children."

"I have been keeping this burden inside for a long time, as the memories remain fresh in my mind. Years after the Space Shuttle Challenger tragedy, the FBI released to the media the tip-off letters they had in their possession. These were the letters I had sent to NASA, yet they never discovered the responsible party. They used the information I provided, which initially yielded positive results. However, they later realized that their efforts to address the first issue with the O-rings led to an unimaginably worse outcome. That ill-fated mission became the 25th and final launch of the Space Shuttle."

"The information in my Elvis manual revealed that the Space Shuttle program endured for another 25 years after the initial catastrophe. The 135th mission was started on July 8, 2011, marking its last endeavor. However, as both of you are aware, these missions never took place because I meddled. On that day, I also succeeded in permanently ending the space shuttle program."

"Hey Grandpa," Josh Cadman inquired, "whatever happened to the gun you mentioned concerning this tragedy?"

"Now, let us revisit the matter of the gun. I had just finished cleaning it moments before I witnessed the unfolding tragedy. Yes, I had almost forgotten about the gun. My state of mind was far from rational, and one can only fathom the emotions I experienced as I witnessed the event before my own eyes; consumed by anger and remorse for my actions that day, I swiftly loaded the gun and aimed at the six televisions. Just as you did initially, Elvis, albeit not for the same reason."

"Louise, who was in the kitchen, dashed in to witness the aftermath of my actions. Upon seeing me, gun in hand, directed at six smoky and dim television screens, she became unhinged. It nearly cost me my marriage, as I refused to divulge the reason behind my firing of the gun at the television sets. That night, she packed her bags and sought refuge in a hotel in Memphis."

"I could not disclose the truth to Louise, for I hailed from the future and had endeavored to alter history for the better. Instead, as warned by David Clements from the past, I had only worsened the course of history. Christine, our youngest, was the only one living at Graceland, and it was exceptionally challenging for an 18-year-old to witness the downfall of her father. Despite the efforts of her older siblings to assist me, I merely withdrew myself."

"In my quest to maintain a blissful union with Louise, Elvis, I attempted to steer clear of unfaithfulness. However, my secret, which I feared would overwhelm her, nearly jeopardized our relationship. Despite my attempts to avoid certain aspects of your history, I have encountered strikingly similar experiences, albeit in different manifestations. This has led me to embrace the notion that some occurrences will unfold and evade them futile. As my narrative progresses, you will come to acknowledge this truth as well."

Chapter Nineteen

DRUGS, BOOZE, AND ROCK

"Following that fateful day in 1986, the subsequent eight years marked my most somber period, despite narrowly evading the same fate as the real Elvis, thanks to my knowledge of his impending demise. I succumbed to the allure of excessive drug and alcohol consumption to numb the anguish of my actions. Before this tragedy, drug abuse and alcoholism were realms I had always avoided. However, by 1988, I spiraled into a state of freefall, unable to function without the reliance on prescribed medications and alcohol, much like the original Elvis."

"My physical appearance significantly altered over this time frame, as I could not engage in exercise or any form of physical activity. Retreating into isolation, I scarcely ventured beyond the confines of Graceland, and my once-thriving career had all but dissipated. Other performers rose to prominence, while I experienced a continuous decline with each passing day. Yet, if I exposed myself to the public eye, I would have become a subject of ridicule. Swiftly, the media began speculating about the downfall of what was formerly the world's greatest rock vocalist."

"To her credit, Louise returned to live at Graceland following a year-long separation, with the condition that the firearm had to be eliminated. I obliged, destroying it and subsequently shunning any ownership of guns. Both Louise and my adult children made valiant efforts to lift me out of this abyss. However, akin to many rock stars from that era dependent on substances and alcohol, I would exhibit signs of improvement only to regress and find myself in an even worse state."

"The nadir was reached in July 1992, when I resorted to selling some of my prized gold records to collectors solely for the sake of financing my drug habit. My family intervened, assuming control of my finances. The Colonel, despite no longer being my manager, recommended seeking professional help. Subsequently, in August 1992, I experienced a drug overdose, teetering on the brink of death. At that moment, I yearned for death, and as I candidly reveal to you, I attempted to take my life."

Josh Cadman experienced a surge of emotions upon discovering the harsh reality surrounding the demon of suicide. Two years prior, one of his classmates had tragically chosen this irreversible option, prompting Josh Cadman to exhibit maturity by advocating for the importance of mutual support and open discussions about emotions. However, news of his own grandfather's attempted suicide came as a profound shock. This grandfather, whom Josh Cadman admired for always exuding a positive demeanor, had concealed this dark chapter from both his family and the prying eyes of the media.

Curiosity piqued, and young Josh inquired, "Grandpa, my parents have never mentioned these troubled times. Would one find such information if they were to conduct an online search during that period?" In response, Grandpa Elvis warmly chuckled and said, "Indeed, my boy. During those years, I was depicted as a fallen rock star, a recluse. Although certain rumors circulated, the Colonel suppressed them."

A mixture of concern and guilt washed over the real Elvis as he confessed, "It has just dawned on me, Elvis, that I have indulged you in excessive amounts of bourbon today, and here you disclose you were once plagued by alcoholism." Grandpa Elvis, amused by this revelation, reassured him, "No need for apologies, dear Elvis. I have since recovered, and at our age, what is there to lose?"

The real Elvis breathed a sigh of relief, realizing that he no longer had to fear facing Grandpa Elvis's wife's wrath. "Ah, Elvis. No need to worry about that," Grandpa Elvis chuckled. "Back then, you would have been in quite the predicament. After my failed suicide attempt in September 1992, I voluntarily admitted myself to a top-notch rehabilitation facility in Dallas. A year later, I returned home, having successfully conquered my battles with drugs and alcohol. While I continued to enjoy moderate drinking, I never stooped as low as I did during that dark period. I have steered clear of drugs and rebuilt my life from the depths of despair. In 1994, at 59, I embarked on a remarkable comeback journey."

"The original comeback that took place in 1968 was executed by none other than you, the authentic Elvis. Commonly referred to as the '68 comeback special, this event occurred during a period in Elvis's career where he faced various challenges. After concluding his involvement in movies, the real Elvis became dissatisfied with the path his career was taking. Determined to make a resurgence, you took the stage wearing black leather pants and a jacket, captivating your devoted fans. From that point forward, you experienced a rebirth, as you had secured a contract to perform in the iconic Las Vegas casinos."

"Despite my comeback special occurring in 1994, a staggering twenty-six years later than yours, it ultimately didn't matter because my loyal fan base remained intact. Like you, I also welcomed back the Colonel as my manager. However, by 1994, the Colonel was eighty-four years old, and his vitality had significantly diminished. He struggled with various health problems, such as diabetes, which forced him to spend ample time at home. Having the Colonel back in my career was the sole aspect that made it feel authentic once again."

"The pinnacle of my comeback was in December 1994, when my highly anticipated special aired. Although live television was not as significant during that period, my comeback special garnered the largest live viewership ever recorded, a record that stands even to this day. It is worth mentioning that I felt an overwhelming nervousness when I stepped onto the stage that had been meticulously designed according to my wishes. This coincidence with the real Elvis's experience added another layer of similarity between our respective comeback specials. The only difference is that mine took place in 1994, while yours occurred in 1968. The outcome proved beneficial for both of us, as we both required this style of comeback."

"By March 1995, I, too, had secured a residency contract in Las Vegas; however, unlike your original arrangement with the International, Elvis, I inked a deal with Caesar's Palace casino. I desired to cater to a larger audience, initially considering a ticket price of $20, reminiscent of past years, to ensure accessibility for the masses. However, given the economic climate of the '90s, charging $20 no longer seemed workable, as it barely covered the expenses. Ultimately, we negotiated a flat $60 that solely aimed to cover the production costs. Las Vegas proved to be a favorable environment for both Louise and me, as she lived in the hotel and attended each of my performances."

"In our relationship, Louise and I reignited the flame, affirming our commitment to never part ways again. Despite the modest income from my performances in Vegas, I invested in prominent companies such as IBM, Microsoft, and Apple. These investments were executed with insider knowledge of the future trends, although proving such accusations would prove futile, wouldn't it? Throughout the ensuing years, this was the avenue through which I reconstructed my career, skyrocketing into the fame of rock and roll history while amassing a billionaire status."

"David Clements also expressed concern when he discovered my inclusion of historically significant stock dates until the year 2020. As I explained to him, I intended to divert funds from the fraudulent individuals inhabiting Wall Street, ensuring minimal impact on regular investors. Why not use this foresight for the greater good? Subsequently, I made substantial investments in Facebook, Instagram, Google, and Bitcoin. As you both are aware of my past, I then diligently allocated billions of dollars to many charitable organizations funded by the Elvis Presley Foundation."

"It all makes sense now," Josh remarked, "it all makes sense how you navigated the intricate world of investment so effortlessly, and now I comprehend your methods."

"Indeed, Josh," Grandpa acknowledged, "you now possess an understanding of my strategies. With my career firmly back on track through my residency at Caesars Palace in Las Vegas, the demand for my shows reached unprecedented heights, causing two performances per day, akin to the original Elvis. Because of the demanding workload and the Colonel's compromised health, our face-to-face interactions became infrequent. Knowing his proximity as a fellow Las Vegas resident instilled a sense of closeness, offering the reassurance that his advice was readily available if needed."

"In December 1996, the doctors delivered discouraging news, and during Christmas, I took time off from my show to be with him and his family. As 1997 began, the Colonel showed significant improvement, leading me to return to Caesar's and resume a demanding schedule of performances. However, his health deteriorated, and on January 20, 1997, I lost the man who had been like a second father to me. Colonel Tom Parker passed away at 87 in a Las Vegas hospital because of complications from a stroke."

"While some may assume that I had issues with the Colonel throughout our manager-artist relationship, this couldn't be further from the truth. To me, he was a father figure I had always longed for, especially after losing my biological father at the tender age of 5 in 2006. Even when the Colonel and I faced a contractual dispute early on, I harbored no ill feelings towards him. Our disagreement arose solely because of my advanced knowledge of Elvis's prior contract."

"When the Colonel moved on without me, I still thrived, thanks to Louise, my rock. Eventually, the media revealed details about the Colonel's life before he arrived in the United States. However, I had already known that information through the Elvis manual and played the part of someone surprised every time it was brought up. My previous acting lessons certainly came in handy. Despite reporters attempting to provide me with information about the Colonel over the years, I never paid much attention. I continue to miss him deeply."

"After the Colonel's passing, I realized that I no longer required a manager since I was doing well on my own. However, Sam Phillips from Sun Records became a consultant for my media and marketing team at Caesar's Palace. This team was led by John, Peter, and Lisa Marie. My eldest children joined as ambassadors for my ever-expanding charitable endeavors. David and Christine joined the team shortly before the turn of the century. As my vast fortune grew, my five children invested in its success. They became an essential part of my life, offering their support and remaining close to me."

Chapter Twenty

Uncovering the Mystery of 9/11

"Grandson, my story now is to talk about the year 2001, the monumental year of our births, despite the peculiarities of our age difference and generational gap. It is only through my ability to travel back in time that this extraordinary circumstance unfolds. While your arrival brought us immense happiness, the year itself was tainted by a series of four meticulously executed attacks on the United States by a terrorist group on Tuesday, September 11, 2001. The focal point of this horrific event was the World Trade Center in New York, where American Airlines Flight 11 and United Airlines Flight 175, both hijacked, crashed into the North and South towers, respectively, resulting in devastating consequences."

"This calamity, which I had always intended to prevent, claimed the lives of 2,996 individuals and left another 6,000 injured. I vividly recall this tragedy, as I was born merely 16 days later in the same year. The news of the 9/11 terrorist attacks on the World Trade Center dominated my upbringing. The thought of journeying back in time and averting such an immense catastrophe consumed my mind. However, this endeavor nearly cost me my life, as I will now divulge."

"However, Elvis," the real Elvis interjected, "your account aligns closely with the actual events, as the same number of casualties were reported as you have described." Josh promptly consulted his cell phone's Google search to corroborate his grandpa's narrative. "Indeed, Grandpa, my search on Google confirms your words. Wikipedia states almost verbatim what you just shared. It even provides the staggering figures of 2,996 deaths and over 6,000 injuries."

Grandpa Elvis let out a chuckle and remarked, "Once again, it's Google's fault. But my knowledge, dear Grandson, belongs to the past, and from the future, I too have searched on Google. I had embedded this very information in the Elvis manual."

"So, Grandpa, you mean you couldn't rescue all these individuals?"

"No, I didn't, Grandson. My courage wavered after the Space Shuttle Challenger disaster in 1986, causing me to cease my Superman-like rescues. That initial rescue had gone wrong, plunging me into a nightmarish struggle with drugs and alcohol. By 2001, Max Tiller had ceased to exist because he had succumbed to cancer in 1995. We saw very little of each other after the Space Shuttle tragedy. However, I knew I had to prevent the events of 9/11 from unfolding as they loomed in the future. I contemplated restarting my rescues because this was not an accident but a deliberate act of mass murder against American citizens on American soil."

"On February 18th, 2000, I marked my 65th birthday in Hawaii with a live concert. My thoughts centered on how I could alert the FBI about the imminent attacks involving two planes targeting the New York World Trade Center. A third plane, American Airlines Flight 77, crashed into the Pentagon in Arlington County, Virginia. In contrast, a fourth plane, United Airlines Flight 93, was initially headed towards Washington, D.C., but ultimately crashed in a field in Stoney Creek township near Shanksville, Pennsylvania."

"Initially, I considered employing the same tactic I had used in 1986 by mailing warning letters to the FBI. However, technology has advanced significantly, and DNA testing has become highly sophisticated. Most agencies were not yet taking such threats seriously. My only option was to contact them directly. I gained untraceable cell phones on the black market, specifically for this purpose."

"By August 2001, my plan was almost set, yet the premature celebration following my initial Space Shuttle Challenger rescue continued to haunt me. Insecurities once again dominated my thoughts, fueled by the upcoming 9/11 terrorist attacks. I recognized the risk of spiraling downwards if I failed once more. Even Louise noticed my descent back into the dark mental state of 1986, which nearly destroyed our marriage and my life."

"My sole source of solace during this period was my determination to avoid relapsing into prescription drug abuse, knowing it would devastate Louise and our family. On September 1st of that year, I observed that these terrorists were already deeply entrenched in the planning phase. What if I could somehow convince the FBI that an impending disaster was on the horizon?"

"In less than two weeks, my primary aim was to persuade the FBI to investigate the individuals accountable for the tragic events of 9/11. However, my thoughts kept drifting back to that fateful day in 1986 when I bore the weight of causing the loss of 1,293 innocent lives. As time passed, my condition worsened, reaching a point where getting a decent night's sleep seemed impossible by September 8th, 2001. I resisted the use of medication as sleeping pills had previously ensnared me, leading to an unrecoverable state."

"Louise, perceptive as ever, recognized the inner turmoil I was enduring as I fixated on an unattainable goal. I needed to persuade the FBI somehow to acknowledge the imminent attacks and prevent the looming danger of 9/11. Who knows what catastrophic schemes could unfold in the future? A football stadium with a crowd of fifty or sixty thousand people might fall victim to an airplane-turned-weapon, a concept that had not even been conceived before 9/11. Adhering to a normal existence without acting upon my knowledge of America's most significant terrorist attack on its soil was inconceivable."

"Many scenarios flooded my mind at that moment, but the opportunity to save the lives of 2,996 individuals and an additional 415 first responders could not be dismissed. Even if I were successful at thwarting this initial attack on 9/11, what about subsequent ones? Regardless, an attack could still take place because of intelligence agencies' inaction until after such a catastrophic event. One change that would follow was the implementation of heightened security measures as a direct consequence of 9/11."

"On the morning of Monday, September 10th, 2001, the day preceding the 9/11 attacks, stress consumed me, leading to an argument with Louise. She insisted I seek medical help for my unconventional behavior, even threatening to leave if I did not confide in her, reminiscent of the aftermath of the Space Shuttle Challenger disaster. How could I disclose everything? I had grown weary of the constant anxiety over potential future deaths for which I might or might not be held accountable. Ultimately, fate would determine the outcome."

"I had to contact the FBI and request their help in shutting down the airports and investigating the 19 individuals involved in the ongoing planning stage. Despite being aware of the need to explain my knowledge to the FBI, I believed that as the most famous rock star of all time, my warning would be taken seriously and result in the suspension of all flights across the United States. The goal was to prevent the unfolding tragedy by identifying and stopping the culprits involved."

"However, the events that followed only emphasized the need for more change or intervention. As I glanced at my cell phone, it showed that it was 9 a.m., less than 24 hours before the first plane was scheduled to impact at 8:46 a.m. I hesitated, aware that once I made the call to the FBI, there would be no turning back. Yet doing nothing was no longer an option. With determination, I began inputting the FBI's phone number into my cell phone. Precisely as I concluded dialing the last digit, the phone emitted its first ringtone."

"The significance of the situation weighed heavily on me, and suddenly, I suffered a heart attack. Intense pain pervaded my chest, extending down to my left arm. Collapsing onto the floor of the jungle room at Graceland, I grappled with the enormity of the situation. Fortuitously, my call established contact with the FBI. The voice of a lady on the other end of the phone echoed in my right hand, which clutched the device tightly. The FBI receptionist, noticing an obscured noise during my unsuccessful attempts to communicate, traced the call."

"Meanwhile, police cars and ambulances hastily made their way to Graceland, coinciding with Louise's return from her shopping trip. As she approached the renowned gates, flashing lights surrounded her. They discovered me lying unconscious on the floor, but still alive. The paramedics swiftly revived me, and while I remained horizontal, I realized I could not warn the FBI about the looming attacks. Once again, I was consumed by a sense of failure, unable to utter a single word as I hovered near the edge of death. I could faintly hear Louise inquiring about my intentions, but I could not provide an answer."

"After an interval, my condition stabilized, and I was transported to Memphis Regional Hospital. En route to the hospital in the ambulance, I experienced another episode, causing Louise and the children to follow, fearing the worst, hurriedly. I became more distressed when I tried to alert the ambulance personnel about the events of 9/11 tomorrow, and for them to notify the police. In my mind, I was vividly conveying what would occur the following day, but my words became jumbled, and my message was lost in translation, resulting in nothing more than murmurs."

"Subsequently, I was admitted to a hospital bed where I lay in a stable condition. Louise and my children ventured out into the hallway to receive an update from the chief physician. Although I couldn't hear the exact details of what the doctor conveyed, Louise informed me later that the surgeon had inquired whether I had been under significant stress during that time. In response, Louise retorted to the surgeon that he is a renowned rock star who has undergone similar challenges in the past. The surgeon explained that the heart attack was likely stress-induced, as the scans showed the healthiness of my heart and arteries. Stress appeared to be the only plausible explanation."

"Upon recovery from this episode, they advised I seek mental evaluation at a clinic to determine the cause of my stress. However, there was a predicament: Would anyone believe me if I were to disclose the burden of knowing what lay ahead in the future? The stress of it all had led to this point, illustrating how my attempt to save those lives had failed. Yet, the situation wasn't over, because a nurse approached Louise and made inquiries about me. Despite being acquainted with me as the famous rock star Elvis Presley, she required my social security number, driver's license, and proper identification under my real name, John Cadman. Louise assured the nurse that she would bring the identification the following morning, which was September 11, 2001."

"On the evening preceding the assaults in New York, as the last child departed Graceland and Louise found herself in solitude, she recollected retrieving my identification for the following day. This was imperative so that the nurse could input my information into the hospital's computer system. Holding onto a glass of red wine that she had nearly consumed after an eventful day, she entered our shared bedroom. With determination, she accessed the entrance to our walk-in secure chamber, the designated location for safeguarding our valuable possessions. Taking deliberate steps within the confines of the safe, she directed herself towards the shelves that proudly presented my cherished gold records and the two Oscars that only lay for our visual delight."

"Subsequently, a series of events unfolded, ultimately exposing my well-kept secret. Fortunately, fate played its part in this manner, for which I am immensely grateful. Louise, standing on her tiptoes, reached upwards towards the uppermost shelf, vigorously attempting to access a flexible file that contained our imperative documents. Just as her fingertips grazed the edge of the files, a sudden loss of balance caused her to step back, inadvertently colliding with the rear wall. To her surprise, the subsequent step echoed a hollow sound akin to that of a hollowed floor tile. Taking notice of this peculiar resonance, she stooped down, tapping her hand against the tile surface."

"Intrigued by this discovery, Louise resolved to embark on a deeper investigation, employing her nails to trace the periphery of the tile. She discerned that the grout encasing the tile had detached from its neighboring counterparts. Seizing the opportunity, she triumphantly lifted the tile, unraveling my well-guarded secret. Sliding the tile aside, her gaze fell upon a timeworn stack of papers, firmly bound by a metallic attachment along one edge. It was not the chocolate cannoli stain adorning the front page that grabbed her attention; rather, it was the title inscribed as 'The Elvis Manual' that captivated Louise's imagination. She diligently perused its contents, repeatedly murmuring the words to herself."

"In her hands, she held the Elvis manual, which I considered to be my everything, my go-to guide from my future past. Exclaiming. What the hell is this EP? She couldn't resist her curiosity and began flipping through the pages. Her attention was immediately grabbed by the list of song release dates, accompanied by photos of Elvis Aaron Presley with each titled song. She continued flipping through and paused once more when she came across the movie titles, which were dated differently from mine. However, the movie star depicted in all the photos was still Elvis Presley, although he was not her husband. Little did she know it was the real Elvis Aaron Presley."

"By this point, Louise was thoroughly confused and couldn't even fathom the truth behind this secret book about her husband of 47 years. She flipped through more pages until she finally reached 'Elvis on the Ed Sullivan Show.' She flipped again and landed on the 'New Orleans Mardi Gras massacre' dated February 2, 1971. Moments of doubt filled her mind as she thought. Wait, that didn't happen. And indeed, it hadn't because that incident marked my first Superman rescue."

"Persisting, Louise continued to flip through pages that illustrated ever-occurring tragedies that never occurred. Her heart skipped a beat when she finally stopped at one that she distinctly remembered. It was the Space Shuttle Challenger disaster, when seven astronauts lost their lives, including a teacher. The date provided, January 28, 1986, was incorrect. She was certain that it happened much later in the year, and the death toll exceeded a thousand. It was at this moment that she realized my drug and alcohol addiction began around the same time."

"Still unaware of the magnitude of her discovery, Louise flipped through more pages and came across one dated the day after tomorrow, September 12, 2001. The headline from the New York Post read 'Act of War.' The article detailed the destruction of the World Trade Center and the loss of thousands of lives. Overwhelmed, Louise wondered, Oh, EP. What have you gotten yourself involved in? What is this about EP? This event is scheduled for tomorrow at 8:46 am. She couldn't take her eyes off the photo depicting the twin towers engulfed in smoke, realizing that the story she was reading hadn't even occurred yet."

"That night, Louise struggled to sleep as she went through the entire Elvis manual thoroughly. She couldn't help but wonder if her parents had been right in their initial concerns about her husband's mysterious background, suggesting that his lack of family might be for a reason. Louise even took the time to read John Cadman's birth certificate, which seemed to be legitimate. However, she couldn't help but question why a document from 1953 was on this modern paper. Could it be possible that her husband had assumed this identity? And why had he almost chosen the stage name of Elvis Aaron Presley? Suddenly, Louise remembered her husband had met Elvis in the Sun Records recording studio back in 1953, where they had met. He had deliberately attempted to meet him that day."

"With each piece of information, Louise pieced everything together. However, the idea of time travel hadn't even crossed her mind as there was no mention in the manual; Louise couldn't fathom the possibility of these events occurring. If only she had trusted what she was seeing, maybe she could have contacted the FBI herself and prevented the impending terror that was about to unfold."

"Following a restless night filled with tossing and turning, Louise finally made her way to the hospital and arrived at precisely 9:30 a.m. As she approached the nurse's desk to provide them with her husband's ID card, she immediately sensed that something was amiss. The desk appeared to be left unattended, and the abnormal behavior of the people around only heightened her suspicions. Peeking around the corner into the hospital ward, Louise noticed everyone had gathered, facing away from her, fixed on the television screen on the other side of the room."

"A man's voice emanated from the television, reporting on an incident that had just occurred in lower Manhattan. Although Louise couldn't see the screen from her current position, her curiosity led her to walk over and join the others in witnessing what captivated their attention. As she approached her husband's room, she glanced inside only to discover him lying on one side of the bed, overcome with uncontrollable tears."

"Upon gazing at the television screen that captured Elvis's attention, she took notice of the two World Trade Center towers engulfed in flames. Turning to the relevant page in the Elvis manual, she held up the photo in the realization that it depicted the future event currently unfolding before them. What followed would have a lasting impact on our lives. As I lay there, despondently fixated on the television, Louise approached me."

"Unbeknownst to me, she had been standing at the foot of my bed all along. Suddenly, a weighty object landed on my chest. Glancing down, I discovered it was the Elvis Manual containing the photo of the Twin Towers ablaze at that very moment. In the periphery, I could see Louise in tears, positioned at the foot of the bed. At long last, my secret was revealed. Without uttering a word, she climbed onto the bed, and we embraced each other while observing the unfolding events on the screen."

"At precisely 9:59 am, we bore witness to the collapse of the south tower, followed by the north tower at 10:28 am. Both were touched; Louise questioned what exactly was happening and how I was related to this unprecedented occurrence. In response, I could only ask where do I begin? I divulged every detail to Louise, just as I am doing now with you, and remarkably, she believed me. She acknowledged my past struggles with substance abuse were understandable, given the burden of possessing knowledge about the future."

"Louise had finally learned the truth about me, and our bond grew stronger. However, she expressed anger and disappointment, contending that I should have shared the truth from the very beginning. She believed that she would have believed me and provided help in my Superman rescues. She concurred with David Clements' statement that even more catastrophic consequences were possible, as exemplified by the Space Shuttle Challenger disaster."

"Several days later, I was released from the hospital, disregarding Louise's refusal to have me mentally evaluated. She understood the struggles I was facing, and despite my appearance of insanity, she firmly believed that no one else could have borne such a heavy burden any better. On the evening of my discharge, Louise and I sat by the fireplace. I held the Elvis manual, stained with chocolate cannoli, above the flames before letting go and watching it crumble into ashes. Louise demanded that I make a promise never again to attempt altering any more tragic events and never to stalk Elvis Aaron Presley any further. In her eyes, I had granted him a valuable extension on life, and she believed he deserved to be content."

Laughter erupted among the trio of men. "Louise is an extraordinary woman," Grandpa Elvis exclaimed. "I hope you and your family can meet her someday."

"Yes," added real Elvis, "I'd love to express my happiness and gratitude to her for ensuring my survival."

"Louise also understood that gaining any further knowledge about you, from that point onward, would serve no purpose. She knew that everything I had done since my return in 1953 was driven by comparison to you. I promised I would never seek you out again. And I kept that promise. However, today marks the exact day before I originally traveled back in time to 1953. Elvis, over the years, I have always intended to ease my guilt towards you. But the tragedy of your son's murder has changed everything."

"I have brought you up to speed on my actions, Elvis, and I hope you won't take this the wrong way. I came here today fearing your anger towards me for stealing your illustrious career. Yet you did even better than I expected. I assumed you must have endured what you did for a reason. The fame and wealth led you down a path of drug addiction, but that was your life during that era. Who knows? But the genuine surprise today is that you and Priscilla are still together. Despite the differences in your lives from the past, you found each other. Your daughter, Gladys, whom I once knew as Lisa Marie."

"Is that everything?" inquired the real Elvis, "because that lady you mentioned earlier gave me a peculiar glance the last time she visited. I believe it would be best for us to go outside and join the rest of the family."

"Ah, there's just one more thing," said Grandpa Elvis, "I wasn't planning on telling you, but I feel compelled to do so; well, this occurred long after your demise. Your daughter, Lisa Marie, married and divorced the singer Michael Jackson and married and divorced the actor Nicolas Cage."

"I don't understand," replied the real Elvis, "I can comprehend her marrying Michael Jackson since he was a talented singer, but Nicolas Cage? Man, I've never been impressed with his movies. But that's solely my opinion. I suppose he might still prove me wrong." The three men burst into laughter.

After spending several hours with the rest of the family, Grandpa Elvis and Elvis Aaron Presley moved to the rear of the property to have a private conversation. Grandpa Elvis intended to pose an important question to the real Elvis, but remained silent, lost in his thoughts. The real Elvis understood that his idol, Elvis, was contemplating something significant. His prolonged silence eventually provided the real Elvis with the answer he sought as he gazed upon his family in the distance, engaging in lively conversation and laughter.

"Elvis," uttered real Elvis, "I am exceedingly contented, man, despite the loss of my son, Jesse Garron. Just look around at my beautiful family. What could enhance my life when I already possess everything I could ever desire? Besides, I would have succumbed to a terrible drug addiction, gained excess weight, and perished in 1977. Why would I desire such a life when I possess this one?"

"Elvis, that is truly melodious to my ears because I deduced the same thing, but I needed to find out what your response would be."

The real Elvis stated, "My daughter would have been united in matrimony with Nicolas Cage." The men chuckled just as Priscilla, Emily, and Josh Cadman progressed towards them. "Well, Grandpa, it's 10:30," Josh uttered, "we had better leave since we need to find a motel."

"Hey, no," the real Elvis mentioned, "please stay here, we have plenty of room."

"Oh no," Grandpa Elvis replied, "thank you for the offer, but we must depart since I am returning home."

"No, Elvis," Priscilla asserted, "why stay at a motel when we possess the room?"

"Priscilla," Grandpa Elvis exclaimed, "if tomorrow weren't such a momentous occasion, I genuinely would have accepted your generous offer. Hey, you know what? Tomorrow is going to be my retirement celebration at Graceland, and all of you here are welcome to attend." Suddenly, jubilation ensued from the remaining family members who overheard the proposal and approached them, affirming that they would attend.

They all exited the front yard, and abruptly, the identical black van and SUV swiftly departed as they reached the end of the driveway. Grandpa Elvis and his grandson exchanged glances. "OK, everyone," Grandpa Elvis expressed, "see you all tomorrow at Graceland, approximately at 6 p.m." With a synchronized chorus of voices, they all exclaimed, "We shall be there!" Josh started the pink Cadillac, shifted gears, and departed amidst waving hands.

"Grandpa," Josh uttered, "can you believe that the two vehicles had just zoomed away the instant we ventured outside?"

"Josh, I am truly concerned, as I had already sent a message to your grandmother, only to discover that she was clueless about what I spoke of. Those individuals, whoever they were, must have remained present throughout the entire time there. Do you reckon you can drive us directly home to Graceland with no detours?"

"Undoubtedly, Grandpa, I can do that."

Entering a state of slumber for the rest of the journey homeward, Grandpa Elvis's snoring was a mere fraction of the racket that Josh had experienced while traveling to Little Rock. At precisely 1:34 am, they arrived at Graceland, where Louise, still awake, engrossed herself in some final preparations for the significant event. Upon hearing the opening of the front gates, she stepped outside onto the front porch to welcome them. The pink Cadillac paused at the entrance of the mansion's front breezeway.

Grandpa Elvis alighted from the Cadillac and strolled up to the front porch, embracing his wife. Louise yearned to know how the encounter unfolded with the genuine Elvis. With her grandson now possessing knowledge of his famous grandfather's truth, would he remain unaltered or undergo metamorphosis?

Chapter Twenty-One

A Foe From The Past

On the morning of November 20th, 2020, Josh Cadman awoke to the bustling sounds of caterers' trucks and marquee installers putting the final touches on the retirement party scheduled for later that evening. Realizing it was 9:23 a.m., he swiftly threw off the bedsheets, got dressed, and made his way downstairs to the kitchen, where his grandparents were enjoying breakfast.

"Good morning, Josh," greeted Louise, "take a seat and help yourself. We've got eggs, bacon, and some toasted bread."

"Josh, my boy, would you like to go on another drive today?" Grandpa Elvis inquired.

"But what about your party, Grandpa?"

"Oh, that's not until later. Besides, your father and grandma have already taken care of all the preparations. We are heading back to the place where it all began."

"And where might that be, Grandpa?"

"Brinkley, Arkansas; Josh."

"Brinkley? But Grandpa, you said you didn't want to interfere with your past actions."

"Correct, Josh. However, I want to observe young David Clements and myself from a distance as they step outside just before initiating the Elvisgate. We will approach them and advise my younger self to proceed, but before that, I will hand him some sheets of paper to add to the Elvis manual. These printouts contain information about the Fellino mafia. The FBI can handle them. By charging Martino and Gino Fellino with the murder of Sammy Navolla, they will be incarcerated. This plan should work, as it will prevent the Fellinos from obtaining the New York rail yard that Navolla owned. This property was the key to Fellino's future riches."

"All right, I'm leaving," Josh declared as he bid farewell to his Grandma Louise with a kiss, then went outside and started the car. "EP," Louise interjected, "you shouldn't underestimate the power of self-talk. Odd as it sounds, why don't you have young Josh give him the instructions while you wait outside? We ensure that even the tiniest alteration from the original reality doesn't put everything at risk."

"Louise, you're right," he replied. "Once my younger self departs, I will visit David and inform him that everything went smoothly. Once Peter steps through the Elvisgate, that's it—he'll be back in 1953 and on his way to secure the Elvis gig. After that, seeing David won't change a thing."

"EP, it's best for you to go outside. The car has been idling for quite some time now. And remember, if those black cars follow you, just come back home, and we'll have your backup plan ready." Grandpa Elvis embraced his wife tightly as if it might be their last encounter. Louise had experienced these emotions before without repercussions and suspected that her husband might be apprehensive about meeting his best friend. They shielded their eyes from the sunlight as they stepped out onto the front porch, waiting for the Cadillac to reverse. Reminiscing, Grandpa Elvis absorbed the same sunlight that had reflected off the Elvisgate 67 years ago.

At 10:07 a.m., they departed from Graceland for a drive to Brinkley. They headed towards the on-ramp of Highway 55, leading to St. Louie. Josh eagerly expected to see his younger grandfather, not because he needed proof of his story, but to witness him at the same age as himself. He wondered if such an encounter was even possible, considering that his grandfather would have already mentioned it yesterday. Grandpa Elvis was eager to reach Brinkley, but half an hour into the trip, he slipped into unconsciousness. His grandson glanced over to his right upon hearing his grandpa snore and chuckled, knowing that his grandfather couldn't stay awake.

Deep inside a slumber, Grandpa Elvis dreamed about a day when he was with his parents. It was Christmas Eve 2004, and they were all sitting on the floor in front of the fireplace. His parents played with him, his mother blowing bubbles and planting kisses on his belly while his father tickled him relentlessly, eliciting uncontrollable laughter. They were a small yet affectionate family, but tragedy had torn them apart because of an accident.

Upon waking up, Grandpa Elvis experienced a sudden realization of the immense changes that had occurred since his parents passed away. The guilt of not turning back the clock to 2006, just before their tragic car accident, plagued his mind. He couldn't help but imagine a life where he could have shared precious moments with his parents and Grandma Chris. Even if Grandma Chris had peacefully passed away, Peter's parents could have still savored a meaningful existence well into their retirement years and beyond.

The selfish act of stealing the real Elvis's career without considering the possibility of saving his parents weighed heavily on his conscience.

Nostalgia for Grandma Chris compelled him to assume the identity of Elvis, serving as a reminder of her. Bizarrely, he had planned to meet his encounter. These feelings towards his parents only intensified once he took on the Elvis gig, allowing him to reflect on his life's journey. Today offered a chance at redemption, as his ultimate motive for returning to Brinkley was to go back to 2006 as an 85-year-old.

He would still rely on his grandson's guidance to advise his younger self to travel back to 1953, seize the opportunity as Elvis, and confront the Fellino mafia. Today, he will sacrifice himself to save his parents from their fatal car accident by embarking on a one-way trip back to 2006. This plan only materialized this morning because of his belief that his close friend David Clements could input another date before the Elvisgate closed. He trusted that his younger self would still enjoy the same fulfilling life and that his loved ones would continue to be present in the future. Given his age and limited remaining years, this course of action seemed rational.

Louise sensed that something was amiss with her husband that morning when he hugged her tightly for an extended period. Unbeknownst to her, Grandpa Elvis had devised a plan, which he chose not to share to spare him the difficulty of bidding farewell to the rest of the family. The actual test would come later, at noon, when he would have to bid his grandson Josh goodbye.

Upon glimpsing the two same vehicles as the previous day through his rearview mirror, Josh swiftly picked up speed. "Josh, have you lost your mind?" exclaimed Grandpa Elvis. "Slow down before you lose control and crash. Let them overtake us, as we can't always outrun them."

The SUV zoomed past them, took the lead, and gradually decelerated while the van closed in behind, effectively trapping them between the two vehicles. They all gradually slowed down and eventually came to a stop on the side of the road. Four individuals, attired in black suits, emerged from the SUV and made their way towards the Cadillac.

"Josh, refrain from saying anything and let me handle all the talking," advised Grandpa Elvis.

"But Grandpa, they seem like FBI agents or something," said Josh hesitantly.

"Close, son. Private security officer, Kyle Tanner," stated the man in the black suit. "Sir, I kindly request that you follow me to the van behind you, as someone significant wishes to have a discussion."

"Get lost, secret service or whatever," Josh Cadman retorted. "You don't seem like one of the good guys."

"Sir, your grandson will be in danger," warned Kyle Tanner. "However, this depends solely on whether you comply with my instructions, and I assure you it's a promise." The three men aimed their handguns at Josh. "Hey, hey, hey, let's not do anything rash," intervened Grandpa Elvis. "I will come along and engage in the conversation, but allow my grandson to leave. You can even take his cell phone."

"No way I'm leaving you here," protested Josh.

"Let him go," pleaded Grandpa Elvis. "Listen, Kyle; he has something very important to attend to. Grandson, take these documents and convey to him what we discussed, all right? Kyle shook his head, smiled, and said, nice try, Mr. Presley. It's Peter Walker who is the reason you need to enter that van." Grandpa Elvis couldn't help but wonder how Kyle knew about Peter Walker, given that he had never mentioned his name.

"Please accompany me, sir," Kyle stated urgently. "Sir, time is of the essence, as we have gathered information regarding Peter Walker and David Clements." At that very moment, both grandfather and grandson comprehended they must have been surveilled at Elvis's residence.

"Agreed," Grandpa Elvis replied, "Kyle, you can at least release my grandson." Grandpa Elvis exchanged a secret signal with his grandson, instructing him to carry out the previously assigned task. "No, Mr. Presley," Kyle retorted solemnly, "We cannot permit that, and I am dead serious about terminating his life."

Withdrawing his firearm, Kyle pointed it directly at Josh Cadman's temple. Grandpa Elvis leaned down, opened his door, and slowly exited the vehicle, raising his hands in surrender. "No, Mr. Presley, that is unnecessary," Kyle interjected. Grandpa Elvis lowered his arms, moving behind the Cadillac and then proceeding towards the van. Kyle tapped on the door, which slid open to unveil the Texas Governor, Tino Fellino, accompanied by an elderly gentleman.

"Mr. Presley, I am..."

"I am well aware of who you are," Grandpa Elvis interrupted. "I never would have expected someone like you to stoop to such low levels."

"Mr. Presley, or perhaps I may call you Elvis," Governor Fellino began. However, Grandpa Elvis remained silent as his attention was fixated on the older man seated beside the governor. He had a sense of familiarity with the individual, yet struggled to recall where or how they had crossed paths.

"Elvis, you have certainly been keeping yourself occupied," Tino remarked. Despite hearing Tino's comment, Grandpa Elvis remained unresponsive, still attempting to recollect where he had encountered the other man.

"Elvis," Tino persisted.

"Or should I say, John Cadman, also known as Peter Walker," the elderly man added.

Finally, Grandpa Elvis recognized the voice, although he still couldn't recall the man's identity. This individual possessed knowledge of his two other aliases. He chuckled, removing an item from his pocket and displaying it to Grandpa Elvis. At that very moment, everything became clear. "Martino, Fellino." Grandpa Elvis uttered as he took the Apple watch from him and examined it.

"Yes, John, Peter, Elvis, or whoever you claim to be," Martino responded.

"So, you kept the watch, and it still functions. But how?" Grandpa Elvis questioned.

"John, let me explain," he said with a smile. "I kept that watch because back in 1953, I took it to a jeweler who was amazed by its advanced technology. He believed it must have come from another world, or maybe even the future. I didn't believe him then until I witnessed you transforming into Elvis Presley. That's when I knew you were from a different time."

"But Martino," Grandpa Elvis remarked, "you look so different. I mean, sure, you've aged, but you're not overweight like before. Are you still indulging in those cannoli like you used to?"

"No, Cadman. Type 2 diabetes put an end to that. Ah, those cannoli's from the old days," Martino reminisced.

"Yeah, you used to have two at a time, if I remember correctly. What happened to your uncle Gino?"

"He passed away in '92, and then I took over," Martino replied.

"So, you still have the watch, and it still works," Grandpa Elvis observed.

"Yes, only because I had a local Apple expert replace the battery just five years ago when they first came out. You already knew that, right? He informed me that the watch's serial number was registered to someone in Australia. Of course, this was registered to you, John, since you gave me the watch back in 1953."

"All right, Mr. Cannoli, the watch seems legit. But how would you know my past?" Grandpa Elvis questioned.

"John, that smart-ass comment you made about leaving the gun and taking the cannoli? That's a line from 'The Godfather' movie. And do you remember what you told my Uncle Gino? You said to let no one outside of the family know what you are thinking. Brilliant, John. But that wasn't your line; it was said in the same movie. Still, my Uncle Gino loved to claim that it was said in the same movie from his famous saying. I knew better, though."

"Perhaps I underestimated your intelligence, but how could you possibly know about my previous life?" Grandpa Elvis wondered.

"John, John, or should I say, Peter Walker, we overheard you telling the entire story to the real Elvis in his living room yesterday. Listening devices are in our possession. We heard everything you told the real Elvis and your grandson. We know your plans, but we have an even better plan."

"Let's be clear. What I told them yesterday was pure fiction, a mere figment of imagination," stated Grandpa Elvis.

"John," Martino inquired, "the 'Toy Story' themed watch, the iconic lines from 'The Godfather' movie, and the amusing story about overindulgence in cannoli's. Are these part of your fantasy? Not to forget the infamous Elvis manual, which supposedly guaranteed a winning outcome with 'Lucky Lucy.'"

"All right, you caught me, but 'Lucky Lucy' was a fluke," admitted Grandpa Elvis, "so what's next? Time is running out, as everyone here is aware of what is about to unfold."

"John, hand over the documents you were planning to give your younger self," requested Governor Tino Fellino. Unexpectedly, Kyle Tanner snatched the folded papers from Grandpa Elvis' top pocket.

"Thank you, Kyle," acknowledged Governor Fellino. "John, it seems you were prepared to alter the course of events."

"John, I'm disappointed," sighed Martino, shaking his head. "So, you intend to inform the police that I murdered Sammy Navolla, leading to the arrest of my younger self in 1953, and then..."

"What's the matter, Dad?" interrupted Governor Fellino.

"Tino, if I had been imprisoned for killing Sammy Navolla in '53, I would have been behind bars for at least 15 to 20 years. This would mean that you wouldn't have been born in March 1962..."

"Meaning, I wouldn't even exist, let alone be conceived," confessed Governor Fellino.

That's great, thought Grandpa Elvis to himself. Even after all these years, this former corpulent gangster can still do the math. Well, his uncle always claimed that he attended university.

"Brilliant plan, John," commended Governor Fellino. "Listen, that scenario won't happen because we have an even better alternative. We possess our message for your younger self, and here it is. John, we will strive for legitimacy, or at least a semblance of it. These papers contain a meticulously crafted plan to amass wealth in the future, starting from 1953. When we visit your younger self, we will present him with these papers instead of yours. They contain all sporting events and horse racing results for the next fifty years, beginning in 1953."

"Ha, this sounds like the 'Back to The Future' movie with the sporting almanac," Grandpa Elvis quipped, "Your wealth will flourish through wise investments. Your younger self will possess immense riches and credibility because of the acquisition of funds through games of chance."

"Now, John, you comprehend," Martino affirmed, "you must deliver these documents to your younger self, or else."

"John, it is presently 11:15 am," Governor Fellino informed. "If we are to arrive on time, we ought to depart." Recognizing his lack of options, Grandpa Elvis understood he had no choice but to comply, at least for now. He harbored a plan that he hoped would succeed, even if he were to impart the instructions from the mafia gang to his younger self. "Very well, let us proceed," Grandpa Elvis consented.

Kyle Tanner opened the entryway and extended his hand in help to Grandpa Elvis, who politely declined, not desiring any aid from this security employee affiliated with the mafia. Grandpa Elvis trod towards the Cadillac and settled into the front passenger seat while Kyle positioned himself in the rear, brandishing his firearm toward Josh Cadman.

"Grandpa, what happened, and why is this creep aiming his gun at me?"

"Josh, it is the Fellino mafia from the distant past. Let us depart, Grandson, for our timely arrival carries great significance." Josh drove away, trailed by both black vehicles. They were on their way to legitimize the mafia.

Chapter Twenty-Two

ELM STREET APARTMENT

In Brinkley, the pink Cadillac was only 5 minutes away from the Elm Street apartment. Grandpa Elvis, deep in his thought, remained silent as he contemplated the current situation. His original plan to sacrifice himself to save his parents had changed. Josh drove cautiously, mindful of avoiding any bumps on the road, as Kyle Tanner, armed with a gun, sat behind him. He was determined to prevent any accidental discharge of the weapon. As they turned onto the main street of Brinkley township, Grandpa Elvis would have normally been excited, but the menacing, gun-pointing individual had dampened his spirits.

On their left, they passed by the Palmerston Hotel, but both grandfather and grandson averted their gazes, uninterested in reminiscing at that moment. They were in a predicament and remained silent, conveying their thoughts to each other without uttering a word. Though Josh was eager to act, his grandfather gestured for him to wait, signaling that he had a plan.

The Cadillac gradually slowed down and came to a halt 200 yards before reaching the corner of Elm Street, followed closely by two black vehicles. The three men disembarked from the car, with Kyle trailing behind to open the van's door. Governor Tino Fellino handed Kyle a set of papers, instructing him to deliver them to a young Peter Walker, along with directions to pass them on to Gino and Martino Fellino upon their arrival in 1953. "That wasn't part of the original plan!" Grandpa Elvis protested.

"Well, it is now!" Governor Fellino demanded. "Kyle will follow your younger self as insurance to make sure young Peter Walker sticks to the plan."

"But the slightest change could alter the future." Grandpa Elvis stated.

Kyle and the Fellinos smiled, embraced, and shook hands. He then closed the van door and activated his vest camera, allowing the Governor to observe and listen to everything without arousing suspicion from any curious neighbors. The driver gave Kyle a thumbs-up to show that the video and sound were functioning properly. Moving towards both grandfather and grandson, Kyle gestured for them to proceed onto Elm Street. Fortunately, the day was peaceful, and no one paid them any attention. However, the Governor was not inclined to take any risks.

Upon arriving at Elm Street, Grandpa Elvis noticed that something was amiss. He questioned whether his memory had become dulled after 67 years. Josh eagerly expected to see the other pink Cadillac, but when the three men peered around the corner, it was nowhere to be found.

Grandpa Elvis asked his grandson if they were in the right location, and Josh assured him they were. Kyle wondered if they were being deceived and deliberately delayed, hindering their progress with the

Fellino plan. He, along with Elvis and his grandson, felt uncertain as they inspected the street signs. Governor Fellino, through Kyle's earpiece, inquired about the issue, and Kyle relayed that something seemed different from Grandpa Elvis's original reality.

Grandpa Elvis examined the door of the basement unit and then glanced at the large green electrical transformer box behind it, which held the power cable. Reality struck when he looked at his watch—it was 11:43 a.m. The cable should have been visible, but it was nowhere to be seen. The pink Cadillac should have been parked right in front of them.

"Well, it is now 11:51 a.m.," Grandpa Elvis remarked. "We should have encountered David and me by now because, in less than 9 minutes, the Elvisgate will open the wormhole in the atmosphere. Or will it?"

"It seems like there is no activity at all, Grandpa, as it is now 11:55 a.m." Grandpa Elvis had a thought and suggested, "Perhaps I didn't purchase this car because it wasn't available for sale. Yes, it makes sense now. The original car was sold by the original Elvis estate long before I bought it from a collector. Therefore, it's logical that the car is not in sight."

"But, Grandpa, even if your theory is correct, where's the power cable? Look at that electrical transformer; it has been untouched for years. I must admit, Grandpa, I feel uneasy now." Josh anxiously observed his right hand, checking if he was fading. "Please, Josh, avoid looking at your hand," Grandpa Elvis chuckled. "See? Your hands are still solid. It's now 12:01 p.m., and there wasn't an electrical explosion like 67 years ago. Where is that delivery guy who gave us the legal envelope?"

"You're right, Grandpa, the one who provided you with that envelope. Hey, Grandpa, whatever happened to that envelope?"

"I suppose it got destroyed when I threw the Elvis manual into the fire." Kyle was engaged in a conversation with the governor. "All right, enough of this nonsense," Kyle stated. "My microphone is going off because the governor is becoming impatient. I feel the same way, Mr. Presley. My boss wants us to investigate by knocking on the door."

Grandpa Elvis gazed down Maple Road and saw the pink Cadillac with the two black vehicles stationed behind, then returned his attention to his grandson, who was still present, alive, and well. He wondered what could have altered from the past and why things were different this time.

"Let us investigate," Kyle instructed. "It is now 12:08 pm, and no signs of any activity are emanating from that apartment." He gestured for them to cross the road. "I have a hypothesis," Grandpa Elvis stated, "but it requires verification. Initially, I had no intention of encountering my younger self in the presence of David Clements today, as I solely desired to speak with David alone after my younger self departed. However, I will never find out the accuracy of my theory until we knock on that door."

Kyle grew impatient and aimed his weapon at Josh's head. "Lower that firearm, Tanner," Grandpa Elvis admonished, "let us proceed with the investigation. Josh, please remain silent and allow me to handle all communication. Oh dear, I now comprehend what might have transpired. Why, oh why, did I not perceive it earlier?" Grandpa Elvis delicately guided Kyle's hand, which held the gun away from his grandson's head.

They crossed Elm Street and approached the green electrical transformer to confirm the absence of any activity. They approached the apartment door. "Very well, I shall knock," Grandpa Elvis declared, "and then we shall discover what precisely is transpiring." He knocked on the door, and after a few moments, it swung open, revealing an elderly lady instead of Peter Walker or David Clements.

"Greetings, hello, oh my," the lady exclaimed, "do I recognize you? Ah, you must be him, am I correct?"

"Yes, ma'am, I am Elvis Presley, and this is my grandson Josh Cadman, and beside him is Kyle Tanner, my security guard."

"Oh, my goodness, I cannot believe it, and yes, I perceive the resemblance," the elderly lady remarked.

"Thank you kindly, ma'am, and what is your name?" Grandpa inquired.

"Blanche Masters."

"Very well, Blanche," Grandpa Elvis replied. "We apologize for troubling you, but could you inform us of the whereabouts of Peter Walker and David Clements?"

"Well, I'm sorry, Elvis," Blanche responded, "but you must have the wrong address. I have lived here for almost a year, and I have encountered no one by the names of Johnny Walker or David Clementine."

"Ah, ha, ha, it's Peter Walker and David Clements," stated Grandpa Elvis with a chuckle.

"Grandpa, shall we go?"

Kyle Tanner stepped back, using his microphone to communicate with the governor, requesting a background check on Blanche Masters. "Why don't you all join me for a beverage? Blanche kindly proposed.

"No need; we must return," replied Josh.

"Blanche, if you don't mind, we will accept your offer," Kyle said.

"This way, gentlemen," Blanche gestured toward the entrance.

"Grandpa, we must return to Graceland before Grandma contacts us. When will the security team decide for us? Josh inquired.

"Leave Grandma to me, Grandson. You're right about our security measures. However, Tanner wishes to witness everything for himself. Besides, I want to show you this place since my last visit was 67 years ago," explained Grandpa.

"Please have a seat on the sofa, gentlemen. I will bring us some refreshments," Blanche offered.

"Thank you, Blanche," expressed Grandpa. "Josh, look over there, where the wall is. That's where Elvisgate was built. Do you see how high the ceiling is here? It just fitted in perfectly. And right here, where we are seated, is where the ramp entered the gate. Oh, and do you notice those two bedrooms over there? The one on the left used to be mine." Grandpa Elvis shared nostalgic memories while his grandson observed with interest. Meanwhile, Kyle discreetly relayed information to the governor through his microphone.

"Here we go," Blanche announced, presenting a tray with drinks. "Enjoy some homemade lemonade."

The three men expressed their gratitude, saying, "Thank you, Blanche." Suddenly, the doorbell rang, prompting Blanche to approach with a smile. However, Kyle interrupted his conversation on his microphone and cautiously reached into his jacket to retrieve his gun, just in case. There was a mischievous look on Blanche's face as she opened the door, revealing two elderly ladies outside. The moment they noticed the iconic rock legend, they exchanged high fives, with Blanche joining in. Despite their age, they acted like teenagers. Josh realized Blanche must have secretly communicated with them when she went to fetch their lemonades.

"These are my best friends, Betty Allan and Carol Granger, Elvis," Blanche introduced them with a smile. "They play gin rummy with me. That's why they are here."

"That's perfectly fine, Blanche," replied Grandpa Elvis. "You don't need an excuse to introduce me to these delightful ladies." The three ladies blushed with excitement. "Elvis," Blanche interjected, "would it be all right if we took a picture or a selfie? Our families won't believe us otherwise."

"Absolutely," Grandpa Elvis agreed. "And you know what? Don't worry about a selfie because my grandson Josh can take the photos for you. Or better yet, have Josh join in the picture while Kyle handles the photography." The three ladies happily embraced the opportunity for a personal photoshoot with Elvis Presley. Josh forced a smile into the photos, feeling the urgency to escape from the clutches of the mafia gangsters and return to Graceland for the party.

After a satisfying 20-minute conversation, photo session, and autograph signing, it was time for the three men to leave. Blanche and her friends expressed their gratitude for the visit and photos, waving goodbye as the men crossed the road. The two black vehicles were parked nearby on Elm Street. The van's door slid open, and calmly, Governor Tino Fellino addressed Grandpa Elvis, saying, "I suppose neither of us can change the past. So, for now, goodbye."

"Hey, cannoli man," laughed Grandpa Elvis, "I know you broke your hand on that brick wall back in '53." The van door closed, and the two government vehicles sped off discreetly, avoiding any unwanted attention.

Chapter Twenty-Three

A FAMILY REUNION

Inside the Cadillac parked on Maple Road, both men sat in silence. Grandpa Elvis experienced a mix of sadness and relief. His original plan was to depart from this reality and journey to the year 2006. In his mind, altering the course of his parents' tragic car accident would have rectified things. However, his plan had dissipated, for there was no trace of David Clements, Peter Walker, or even the Elvisgate. Something had gone awry in the initial reality, causing Grandpa Elvis to retrace his thoughts.

"Josh," he voiced, "this all aligns because, like Peter Walker, I was born in 2001. Through time travel, I lived an additional 67 years, arriving at the same juncture in time."

"Yes, but why were there two Apple watches, yet only one of you and the pink Cadillac?" Grandpa Elvis pondered the same question until, suddenly, he realized. He explained, "Josh, you see, the Apple watch present in this reality was brought by me from my previous one. Although I introduced an object into this reality, the company still produced the same watch with the same product number, as no alterations were made. Regarding the car, it was constructed anew in this reality, as I purchased it brand new in 1953, while the one from my previous reality remained behind. Thus, only one currently exists here."

"That sounds logical, Grandpa."

"Josh, I finally get it!" he continued. "The reason my younger self and David Clements weren't at the Elm Street apartment is that, in this reality, I had replaced the original Elvis Presley. So, my grandmother had never met Elvis back in '62. Maybe there's another Peter Walker out there, only 19 years old. Considering our identical appearances when I started my Elvis career, he should have revealed himself by now. I suppose he must have checked my younger profile on the internet."

"Grandpa, it also appears that David Clements may never have encountered your younger self during his school years. Perhaps David was not even aware of the rare occurrence that takes place every 150 years."

"Maybe. Let's proceed, as I would like to show you Grandma Christine Smart's house before we head back to Graceland. It's not far, just past Elm Street, the fourth street on the right called Heysen Street. Number 48 is where I used to live with her until that fateful day in 2014." Josh skillfully maneuvered the car away from the curb and proceeded past Elm Street. They reached Heysen Street and made a right turn. "Number 48 should be on your left," Grandpa Elvis directed, pointing ahead. However, he suddenly froze upon catching sight of his Grandma Chris's house. The Grandson quickly parked the Cadillac on the other side of the road. His grandfather was in a state of shock, and it wasn't solely because of the sight of the house. His grandson was unsure of how to proceed since he did not understand the situation unfolding before him.

"Grandpa, what's wrong? What's happening? Please, talk to me," Josh implored. He deliberated whether he should shake his grandfather out of his daze or embrace him. Ultimately, he chose the latter because his grandfather was 85 years old.

"Grandpa," he implored once more, "what's the matter? I've never seen you like this. Well, maybe yesterday when you brought up the Space Shuttle disaster." Finally, Grandpa snapped out of his trance-like state and responded, "Grandson, this is reminiscent of my Space Shuttle disaster."

"Space Shuttle disaster? Grandpa, what do you mean by comparing this to your Space Shuttle disaster?" Grandpa Elvis pointed towards the house. "Observe the car parked in the driveway," he stated. Josh leaned forward to gain a clearer view. "Yes, the black Chevrolet from the 1990s."

"That's the same car in which my parents perished in 2006," Grandpa Elvis revealed. "Look at those license plates, 'BFY-947.'"

"Oh, do you think they are here, Grandpa?"

"After the accident, the car was destroyed. However, to my surprise, it is here before us now, leaving me unsure of what to make of it."

"Should we venture inside and uncover the truth, Grandpa?" Without hesitation, he replied, "Indeed, I believe it would be wise for us to explore further." With memories of crossing Elm Street together not too long ago still fresh in their minds, the two men cautiously crossed the road in search of answers.

Upon reaching the car, Grandpa Elvis paused and reached out his left hand to touch it, gently sliding it along the roof. He found it difficult to fathom that this was the same car; its appearance hinted at its antiquity, with some surface rust near the front window and significant damage to the bonnet, likely incurred over countless miles of travel. Grandpa Elvis knew it to be his father's car. It sat parked at Grandma Chris' house, awakening nostalgic emotions within him. However, the mystery of its presence lingered. Resolutely, they proceeded towards the front door. Josh, without hesitation, pressed the doorbell, and he could hear movement within.

Suddenly, a figure materialized behind the frosted glass panel. As the door swung open, Grandpa Elvis locked eyes with his father, whom he hadn't seen since his childhood. Overwhelmed, he nearly stumbled backward, clutching onto his grandson for support. The passage of time was unimaginable; here stood his father, the man he lost at the tender age of five almost eighty years ago.

"Good day, gentlemen," the man greeted. "Wait a moment, aren't you that famous singer? Yes, you are Elvis Presley. Maxine, Maxine, come here! You won't believe who is at our door." Grandpa Elvis felt a surge of excitement upon hearing his father utter his mother's name. "Brian Walker?" he exclaimed.

"That's me," Brian replied. "But how would you know my name?"

"Let them in, Brian, my lord," Maxine Walker exclaimed. "It's unthinkable not to fully open the door for the king of rock and roll." Grandpa Elvis was initially bewildered upon seeing his mother. She appeared different, not as he had remembered her. The fragrance of her perfume triggered memories of his youth. Maxine pushed the screen door open and stepped outside before embracing her son, whom she did not know of. They were his parents. It was beyond his imagination that they would be alive and living in this very house.

"We are avid fans of your work, Elvis," Maxine stated.

"Elvis, how are you acquainted with my name?" Brian inquired.

"Brian, don't be absurd," Maxine exclaimed. "We have never crossed paths with the king of rock and roll before. Oh, if only my mother were still alive because..."

"Christine Smart?" Grandpa Elvis interjected.

"Oh, that's correct, but how?" Maxine questioned.

"You're Brian Walker, aged 52, and you are Maxine Walker, aged 51," Grandpa Elvis declared.

"Well, that's nearly eerie because Brian's age is accurate, but mine is not. I'm only 49. However, you are Elvis Presley, the rock star, aren't you?" Maxine asked.

"Yes, Mum, I mean Maxine," Grandpa Elvis responded.

"Mum?" Maxine inquired. "Well, why don't you come inside? I would like you to meet our son, Peter." Grandpa Elvis couldn't believe what he had just heard from his mother. His mind was in a haze, having just met his supposedly deceased parents. Now, his heart raced as he learned about their son, Peter. He had contemplated meeting his younger self, and his theory was soon disproved. "Pardon me, Maxine," Grandpa Elvis asked. "Did you mention that your son's name is Peter?"

Maxine responded, "Indeed, it is Peter. He's a massive fan and only 19 years old."

Grandpa Elvis inquired, "Was he born on September 27th, 2001?"

"Certainly, Elvis, he was. But how did you know that?" Brian asked, "Elvis, you seem to possess much knowledge about us."

Their son approached the door; he interrupted, "What's happening here, Mom, Dad? Hold on, isn't he the Elvis guy?"

"Yes, it is Peter," Brian confirmed. "Elvis was about to explain something to me."

Both Grandpa Elvis and Josh had assumed that they were about to meet a younger version of Peter Walker, who had traveled back in time 67 years. However, Peter Walker looked entirely different. "Well, both of you, please come inside," Maxine offered. "Perhaps, Elvis, you can share your story with us. But who is this handsome young man?"

"This is Josh Cadman, my grandson."

"Please, have a seat," Maxine invited. "Oh, and don't worry about the condition of the house. This is my son's residence, and he lives here alone. Originally, this house belonged to my mother, who passed away. Peter inherited it, and we are here today to visit and help clean it up."

"Grandma Christine Smart," Grandpa Elvis stated, "and she passed away six years ago, right here in this house?"

"Well, yes. But what is your connection? Brian asked curiously.

"And do you still live at 19 Berry Hill Drive, Berry Hill, Nashville?" Grandpa Elvis inquired.

"Dad, this guy is giving me the creeps," Peter commented.

"You're right, Peter. It seems like he has been studying us or something," Brian remarked.

"More like reverse stalking, Dad," Peter added.

"Now, now, you two," Maxine interjected. "Enough of that. Elvis promised to explain himself. So, gentlemen, please have a seat and clarify how you come to possess so much knowledge about us."

Both men settled at the kitchen table while Brian, Maxine, and Peter sat across from them. Grandpa Elvis began revealing the truth, realizing that they must be part of his life, even though he was much older than his parents and even his brother Peter. He needed them because he had had a non-immediate family since his Grandma Chris passed away. Despite his advanced age, he desired their presence, as he longed for the same sense of family.

The story began the same as the previous day, with a focus on Elvis Aaron Presley. As Grandpa Elvis narrated his life story and the reasons behind his decision to travel back in time, the audience experienced a rollercoaster of emotions, from tears of joy. Their hearts sank as he revealed the tragic death of his parents in a car accident in 2006, followed by the passing of Grandma Christine Smart in 2014, leaving him all alone. But on November 20th, 2020, everything changed when he journeyed back to 1953 and assumed the identities of John Cadman and, eventually, Elvis Presley. He then recounted his encounter with Gino Fellino and his notorious gangster nephew.

The listeners hung on to every word that Grandpa Elvis uttered, identifying with him deeply because of his extraordinary journey across time. They delved into the highs and lows of his life, marked by his heroic efforts to prevent major disasters like Superman, thanks to his knowledge of the future. Initially skeptical, they gradually grasped the full magnitude of his revelations as he continued his tale. He clarified he had specifically visited today to visit the house where he once lived with Grandma Christine Smart.

In hindsight, they pondered how things might have unfolded differently if their son, Peter Walker, had not fallen ill on that fateful day in 2006. Perhaps they would never have made the trip back to Brinkley to collect him from Grandma Chris's house, to avoid the fatal car crash. Grandpa Elvis finally deciphered the truth: his original birth had been replaced by another son, as his sole existence had already been transported back to 1953. The alteration forever changed the course of events, resulting in a different fate for his parents.

Grandpa Elvis arrived at this theory upon noticing the missing pink Cadillac he had given David Clements before his time travel. This Cadillac, which his grandson owned, had already been acquired by him in 1953, unlike the previous reality. If he could successfully bring David's Cadillac through the Elvisgate, two of the vehicles would be present, akin to the double Apple watches.

Today, the truth could have been concealed by him from his parents and brother, but he felt obligated to disclose it. The family he had built with Louise could now find closure, knowing that their husband, father, and grandfather did indeed have a family. Louise had made several unsuccessful attempts to unearth her husband's familial roots over the years.

At last, Grandpa Elvis experienced a genuine connection with his past life. He comprehended the mechanics of existence, having been born once and subsequently aged into an alternate reality. Although he and his brother Peter shared DNA from their parents, they manifested themselves as distinct beings. This makes each of us unique in the world.

As the day grew late, he and his grandson disregarded phone calls from the rest of the family. By now, Louise would probably be furious because time was running out, and the guest of honor would be absent from his party. "Apologies for the interruption," Josh interjected, "Grandpa, I just spoke with Grandma, and she is, I believe she said, livid." Grandpa Elvis chuckled, having witnessed her explosive moods throughout the years.

"Grandpa, it's already 4 pm, and we should head out as your guests will arrive at 6 pm. I'll start the car. It was lovely to meet you all, ah, Great Grandad Brian and Great... you know what, maybe I'll call you uncle and auntie for now because..." Young Josh felt puzzled after meeting his grandfather's relatives and pondered as he made his way outdoors what their future relationship would be like.

Grandpa Elvis didn't want to bid farewell so soon, so he devised a plan to expose his secret to the rest of the family. He invited them to his retirement party, explaining that they had not been together since he was merely five years old. He had waited over 80 years to express his love for them. Brian argued it was too soon as they had only just met, but Grandpa Elvis couldn't postpone it any longer and instructed them to pack an overnight bag. He offered to chauffeur them in the pink Cadillac. He wanted them to spend the night at Graceland, as he had over fifty bedrooms, and in the morning, he would arrange for them to be taken home via limousine.

The Walkers felt apprehensive about how Elvis's family would react once they found out about their existence. They believed that Elvis's family might view them as opportunistic individuals pretending to be his parents. It seemed highly improbable that these individuals, who were much younger than Elvis, could be his parents and brother. Despite this, Peter expressed a strong desire to see where Elvis Presley lived, and the prospect of good food also enticed him.

Grandpa Elvis was pleased, but he understood that introducing these people to his family would be a challenging task. He would need to convince his family collectively, which would prove one of the most difficult things he had ever done. Considering his children's distinct personalities, they would surely have many questions. Perhaps the timing was not ideal, as they were all gathered to celebrate his retirement rather than to hear and comprehend an unbelievable story.

Even Louise was oblivious to what was about to unfold, but Elvis didn't mind because, ultimately, it had turned out to be the best thing that could have happened. His original intention had been to leave his family behind if the Elvisgate had occurred at the Elm Street apartment.

CHAPTER TWENTY-FOUR

A LONG-LOST FRIEND

With the skills of a professional driver, Josh maneuvered the Cadillac with speed and precision. Breaking the speed limit as they made their way to Memphis, they aimed to reach Graceland before the guests. Throughout the journey, they engaged in discussions about the former life of Grandpa Elvis, delving into intriguing details about Grandma Chris that set her apart. In the original timeline, Christine Smart encountered Elvis Aaron Presley backstage after a concert in 1962. It was possible that Christine still had a deep affection for this man, even years after his passing.

However, in the altered reality, Christine Smart had never met this Elvis Presley behind the scenes following one of his performances. The cities he had toured, and the timeline of events differed from the original reality. If Grandma Chris had indeed made her way backstage, he would have recognized her as his very own grandmother. She never appeared. Frankly, it was for the best, considering that Elvis would be her grandson in the future.

Amidst laughter, Josh comprehended the fact that his grandfather's brother, Peter, was now his great-uncle, even though they were the same age. They collectively agreed not to share this information with everyone at the party, except for Louise. They revealed that Brian, who is the nephew of Grandpa Elvis, is the son of Martin Walker, Grandpa Elvis's long-lost brother. Given that Martin was the name of Brian's father, it was a simple detail to remember. Although this arrangement seemed misleading, explaining the truth to many individuals at the party proved to be an impossible feat. Hence, Grandpa Elvis's role was to introduce nephew Brian, niece Maxine, and great-nephew Peter to the rest of the family.

At precisely 5:35 p.m., they approached their destination just in time, which was fortunate because Louise's incessant messaging was driving her husband crazy. As they reached the boulevard, a long line of cars extended far from Graceland. Realizing that some cars in the queue were familiar, Josh halted the Cadillac. Grandpa Elvis lowered his window to engage in conversation, as the person inside was none other than Elvis Aaron Presley.

"Hello," greeted Grandpa Elvis, "why are you in this line, Elvis?"

"Elvis, we arrived early," responded the real Elvis, "but it seems they won't allow entry without a proper invitation."

"Of course," acknowledged Grandpa Elvis, "that makes sense since you don't have one, given that I only invited you yesterday. All right then, everyone, follow us in. Oh, and Elvis, I would like you to meet my parents, Brian and Maxine Walker, and my brother, Peter Walker."

"Hey, aren't they?" The real Elvis remarked. "Didn't you mention that____?" Grandpa Elvis's plan to remain silent until after the party crumbled as he unintentionally confused the real Elvis and his family.

"Yes, Elvis," clarified Grandpa Elvis, "they are alive and well, and this is Peter Walker, their son, and my brother. Ha, ha, I'll explain everything inside. Please follow us in." The pink Cadillac took the lead, heading towards the main gates. As the security guard spotted their arrival, he promptly opened the renowned gates of Graceland.

"Mr. Presley?"

"Joseph," addressed Grandpa Elvis, "keep the gates open and guide all these cars to the backfield for parking." Joseph swiftly obeyed, and all the guests found themselves within the gates in no time. Josh drove directly to the front breezeway of Graceland. Louise had no patience for excuses. She was furious that her husband had gone to Brinkley against her wishes and was now late. She was ready to voice her discontent because he had ignored her many calls and messages. "Hey Grandpa, Grandma looks pissed."

As the doors opened, Louise braced herself to face her husband and grandson. However, when the back doors opened and three individuals stepped out, she remained silent as her husband approached her to explain. "EP, you have quite the audacity," she proclaimed.

"Louise, I apologize, but I would like you to meet some people. Allow me to introduce Brian, Maxine, and Peter Walker. Louise, please meet your father, mother, and brother-in-law."

"What? How can this be, EP?" she exclaimed. "Didn't they perish in a car..."

"Honey, in this reality, they didn't experience that fatal car crash in 2006. Instead, they had a son who was born on the same day as me, named Peter. Although they are my parents, he looks slightly different, don't you think?" Louise was shocked, even though she had many things to say before their arrival. However, she could never have imagined this situation and felt that it would be impolite to express it. "Oh, my apologies, Mum, Dad, and brother-in-law," she said. "Oh my, this is quite overwhelming."

"What's overwhelming, Mum?" Lisa Marie inquired as she and her four siblings approached the front porch. They had heard their mother refer to these strangers as mum, dad, and brother-in-law. They were now interested in the situation unfolding, and it was too late to conceal the truth any longer. "Mum, you must explain," Lisa Marie demanded. "You just called these people Mum, Dad, and brother-in-law."

The plan that Grandpa Elvis had concocted on the journey to Graceland had just been killed off, as the secret was now revealed. What could he do? He did not have three hours to recount his story once again. His party had already begun, but he had to clarify himself. "Lisa Marie," he stated, "please meet my parents, your grandparents, Brian and Maxine Walker, and your uncle, Peter Walker, my brother."

"Well done, Dad," John Cadman commended. "Please enlighten us on what is happening."

"Dad, it's true," Josh confirmed. "They are your grandparents, and this gentleman is your uncle, your father's brother."

"Josh Cadman," Christine interjected, "What have you been drinking? It must have been quite something."

"Oh, no, Auntie Christine," Josh replied. "I..."

"No way, son," John Cadman asserted confidently. "They don't even share the same last name as us, do they?"

"Well, Dad." Josh replied confidently, "Grandpa was originally born as Peter Walker in the original reality in the year 2001."

David Cadman addressed young Josh, expressing his belief that intervention was necessary because of Brian and Maxine Walker as their grandparents and Peter Walker's supposed role as their uncle. Grandpa Elvis halted the conversation, urging everyone to gather inside for an explanation. He had already disclosed the truth about his authentic life and identity to Elvis Aaron Presley, his grandson Josh, and the Walkers. Bewildered, John Cadman inquired about the identity of

Elvis Aaron Presley by asking, "Who in the hell is Elvis Aaron Presley?"

Grandpa Elvis invited John to the jungle room for a detailed account of his secret life. Recognizing the urgency, Louise raised concerns about the guests and band members as the marquee was filled with eager fans. However, their children were anxious, having been convinced by Louise and Josh that these people were their family. He realized he could no longer postpone revealing the truth to his children and came up with a solution. Gathering everyone's partners, he arranged a family meeting in the jungle room while allowing the Walkers to accompany him to the marquee. He had to inform the marquee attendees that an important family gathering was taking place and encouraged them to begin the celebration without delay.

"What about the band, and who will be the one singing?" Louise inquired, addressing her husband. It finally dawned on him that one of the most crucial elements of his retirement celebration was the last performance of him and his band. "Louise, I have an idea," he proclaimed confidently. Leading his parents and brother towards the rear of the house, there was an eruption of cheers from the gathered guests as they approached the marquee. Expressing his gratitude with a smile, he instructed the Walkers to enter and find a table where they could help themselves with food and drinks.

Moving towards the front of the marquee, Grandpa Elvis conversed with his bandmates, informing them to begin their performance without him. Once again, a wave of cheers surged from the crowd, prompting him to express his gratitude and briefly explain the family gathering while encouraging everyone to make the most of the festivities.

Elvis Aaron Presley, who was seated in a corner with his family, captured Grandpa Elvis's attention. Guiding the real Elvis aside, he made a personal request. Initially, the real Elvis hesitated, but after further persuasion, he ultimately agreed, sealing the deal with a handshake. Then, Grandpa Elvis crossed paths with a passing waiter, and a glimmer of recognition flashed through his mind. Although he couldn't quite recall where he was from, he speculated the waiter might be one of his grandson's friends because of their similar age. Stepping out of the marquee, his astonishment grew when he read a sign affixed to one of the catering trucks parked behind the house. The sign read Clements Catering. He couldn't believe his eyes, for that was the name of Steven and Natalie Clements' catering business.

Could it be? Grandpa Elvis pondered to himself, as it matched the name of their enterprise. Suddenly, memories flooded his mind from when he and David toiled away on weekends during their high school years. They had worked on many events together, but this one was especially significant. Before he could even consider the possibility of encountering his long-lost friend. A voice called out from behind.

"Mr. Presley, Mr. Presley." It had been over 67 years since Grandpa Elvis had heard that voice, yet he knew exactly who it belonged to. Slowly, he turned around, and there stood his long-lost friend, David Clements. "Ah, Mr. Presley," David nervously stammered, "my name is...."

"David Clements," Grandpa Elvis interjected. David was both surprised and honored that the most famous man uttered his name. "Ah, yes, sir," David responded. "Hey, how do you know my name? Oh, my parents must have mentioned me to you."

"Parents?" Grandpa Elvis exclaimed with excitement, "Steven and Natalie, are they here?"

"Well, Mr. Presley," David confirmed, "they are currently in the kitchen at the rear of the marquee, preparing the food. That's why I came to find you; I wanted to inquire about the timing for serving the main course. One of our staff members informed us that there has been a delay."

"Apologies for the delay," Grandpa Elvis admitted. "Please take me to your parents; I'd love to see them."

"Well, yes," David responded. "However, the events manager explicitly instructed us not to interact with the guests and not to bother you."

"Meeting me wouldn't exactly be considered mingling," Grandpa Elvis argued. "Besides, I'm the owner of this place, and the events manager works for me." David chuckled. "You make a good point, sir. My mother has been eagerly expecting this event, and she's been talking all week about how she'd love to get an autograph or a selfie with you."

"Ah, a selfie," Grandpa Elvis remarked. "Of course, your mum is welcome to take a selfie with me." They strolled alongside the marquee, and David forged ahead, lifting a flap on the canvas cover. This startled his parents, who were diligently preparing food on plates. Steven and Natalie were even more startled when they realized that the king of rock and roll was standing right behind their son.

"Oh, oh, oh," Natalie struggled to find words.

"Natalie, please don't worry," Grandpa Elvis reassured. "I'm delighted to see all three of you here."

"Mr. Presley," Steven interjected, "we were just finishing up the appetizers to be served."

"No, Steven," Grandpa Elvis clarified. "That's not why I'm here, but it's great to see you again." Grandpa Elvis unintentionally revealed too much, as the Clements did not know what he was referring to. He had never initially planned to seek out his former teenage friend from a different life because of their significant age difference. Explaining the story to a teenager would be difficult, and coming from an elderly rock icon, it would seem nonsensical. However, David and his parents were here by chance, and he couldn't resist.

"Mr. Presley," Steven said with curiosity, "you mentioned seeing us again. I'm pretty sure that if any of us had met you before, we would have remembered."

Grandpa Elvis expressed his confusion and suggested that David should be present at a family meeting inside the mansion. He believed David should share the connection they had years ago. Steven and Natalie exchanged puzzled looks, as they were unaware of any connection between Elvis and their family. Because of the significant age difference between David and the rock icon, they found it unlikely. Natalie agreed to the proposal, but only if David wanted to go inside. David, unsure of the reason behind Elvis's request, wanted to join the family gathering and explore the famous mansion.

He asked his parents if they would manage without him, to which Steven replied that David's involvement was minimal because of his preoccupation with astrological research. David jokingly questioned if he contributed at all, and Natalie assured him that Damien, Jack, and Lance were assisting them. Upon hearing these names, Grandpa recognized the young waiter and realized that Damien Frost was the same individual he encountered in the marquee. "You mean Damien Frost, Jack Gallon, and Lance Denney?"

Something seemed off to Steven, Natalie, and David when they heard Elvis correctly identify their three employees by name. How could this iconic rock star possess such intimate knowledge about them? It was a perplexing situation they couldn't wrap their heads around. "Now, Mr. Presley," David ventured, "this is getting weird. You just mentioned the names of my high school friends, who also are our employees, with perfect accuracy. How is this possible? David contemplated whether he should retreat inside, as this stranger seemed to possess an uncanny depth of knowledge about him and his family."

"Well, David," Grandpa Elvis paused thoughtfully, "I know that the four of you attended the same high school. I know Damien was the leader of a bullying trio, which included Jack and Lance."

"Mr. Presley," David retorted, "how could you possibly be privy to all of this? It occurred a long time ago, sir. I had to seek counseling because of the relentless bullying. However, as we grew older, they backed off, and we developed a friendship."

"Yes, Elvis," Natalie interjected. "How is it you possess such detailed knowledge about David's and his friends' experiences?" Grandpa Elvis realized it was probably best for the three of them to join the meeting inside. However, he couldn't entrust the catering duties to those bumbling fools that he vividly remembered. Even though he needed to explain himself, his guests had to be fed and fed properly.

"David, please come inside," he said. "Once I have explained my true-life story to you and my family, you will comprehend. Then you can inform your parents. I'm certain you will be here tomorrow to pack up because of my past occupation. But never mind." Grandpa Elvis almost mentioned that he used to work alongside them as a family member, but there was no use in wasting any more time until he shared his story with David and his family. Revealing now would only further confuse them.

By now, David was even more captivated by the tale this iconic rock star had to tell. "Well, Mr. Presley," he said, "I suppose I have nothing to lose and everything to gain in terms of knowledge about you, sir."

"Perfect, David," Grandpa Elvis responded. "We should go inside now before my children look for me." He shook hands with Steven, but when he faced Natalie, he embraced her. Natalie was a mother to him, and Steven was a father. He deeply missed them and felt that he should have said farewell to them in his original reality. They left the area where the Clements were preparing the food and strolled toward the entrance of the marquee. Grandpa Elvis glanced at the crowd and pointed out Damien, Jack, and Lance to David. He wanted to see them because he hadn't seen them since he left high school all those years ago.

Together, they entered the house through the kitchen and proceeded down a hallway. Out of the corner of his eye, Grandpa Elvis caught sight of Emily, the lovely granddaughter of Elvis Aaron Presley, standing at the foot of the staircase. Suddenly, a man's arm reached out towards her, and she took hold of it, ascending the stairs with him. The identity of the mysterious man was concealed by a wall where he was standing. Grandpa Elvis grew concerned that Emily Presley might be up to no good with this man. He was about to investigate when Sarah, his 18-year-old granddaughter, called out, "Grandpa?"

"Oh, Sarah," he said, "I was just contemplating something, and I need to go upstairs to retrieve my glasses from my room. Oh, and Sarah, this is David Clements, the caterer's son, and he needs to be present for the family meeting." If David had any secret feelings for Tracey Mathews from the original reality, then it was unfortunate because, in this reality, nothing could prevent him from admiring Sarah. He was drawn in by her beauty, charm, and remarkable smile. "Oh, hello, David," Sarah greeted.

David had also caught her attention, and Grandpa Elvis noticed the connection between them. He seized the opportunity to investigate Emily's actions, but before he could go upstairs, his daughter Lisa Marie appeared in the hallway. She called him, "Dad, what are you all doing here in the corridor? We have been waiting for you."

"Auntie Lisa Marie," Sarah interjected, "Grandpa was going to his bedroom to fetch his reading glasses."

"Yes, Sarah," Lisa Marie replied sarcastically, "I can see you didn't bring him to the jungle room as you said you would, since you're all here. Oh, and who is this young man?"

"Lisa Marie," Grandpa Elvis points out, "this is David Clements, the caterer's son. He will join us for the meeting."

"Hello David, nice to meet you," Lisa Marie greeted. "Hey, Dad, didn't you say this meeting was meant for family members? No offense, David." Grandpa Elvis knew he had to address the situation with Emily later to prevent his grandson from becoming infatuated with her. "Lisa Marie," Grandpa Elvis explained, "once I have shared my life story, you will understand why David needed to be present."

"OK," Lisa Marie conceded. "Let's go inside now, as they are considering taking control of your affairs, Dad."

"Affairs?" Grandpa Elvis inquired.

"Power of attorney because of your eccentric behavior, Dad," Lisa Marie clarified. Grasping the need to set things straight with his family, Grandpa Elvis realized their concerns were justified. His actions since returning home had given the impression that he had lost his sanity. "All right then," he conceded, "since everyone is already in the jungle room, let's proceed."

"Dad, I didn't mean to imply that you were losing your mind, but these people are our age, your children. They can't possibly be your parents!" Lisa Marie exclaimed.

"Let's go in," Grandpa Elvis said. "I need to share my life story, and then you will understand."

"But Grandpa," Sarah realized, "what about your reading glasses? I can go upstairs and get them for you."

"I don't require them for my narrative, Sarah," he remarked, wanting to prevent Sarah from discovering Emily and the mysterious man in a compromising situation. They all proceeded to the jungle room, where his children, partners, and Louise had a heated argument. Their attention was diverted upon sighting Grandpa Elvis.

Instead of joining the commotion, Grandpa Elvis surveyed the room and realized that his grandson, Josh, was absent. It brought a smile to his face as he deduced that the man who offered his hand to Emily and led her upstairs must have been his beloved grandson. While he knew this Emily girl was involved in something unsavory, he felt at ease knowing it was with his kin. That they harbored genuine emotions for each other and wished to explore them privately upstairs put him at ease. He also expressed gratitude towards his daughter, Lisa Marie, for preventing him from stumbling upon the two lovebirds in that situation; it would have been rather awkward. "All right, everyone," he announced, "where should I begin?"

"Dad, who is this gentleman?" inquired John Cadman.

"John, this is David Clements, the caterer's son," Grandpa Elvis responded. Louise exchanged a glance with her husband, having now discovered that he had found his long-lost friend, whom she was only vaguely aware of. Everyone greeted David, and just as his children were about to pose further questions, Grandpa Elvis's band began playing one of his songs, accompanied by a singer performing 'Burning Love.' It bore a striking resemblance to Elvis, albeit with a slight difference.

"Dad, who is singing your song with your band?" Christine asked.

"Well, Christine, I had not intended to divulge this individual's identity just yet since I had not started my story. However, the marvelous singer whom you can all hear is none other than the authentic Elvis, Elvis Aaron Presley."

"Dad, he's not bad. Judging by his vocals, he's rather impressive. But who on earth is Elvis Aaron Presley?" Peter Cadman exclaimed.

"Let me start over, Peter," his father expressed as he gestured towards the man singing outside. Grandpa Elvis then fetched a chair from the side wall of the jungle room and sat in front of the family, who were seated on the lounges. Standing behind her husband, Louise placed her arm on his shoulder, which he clung to with his right hand. He engaged in conversation with his children and their partners, starting with the beginning of his tale. Initially, he received the same reaction from his grandson as he did the day before. However, as he continued recounting his real-life story from 67 years ago, a silence fell upon them all. It was then that David comprehended how this exceptional performer possessed such intimate knowledge about him and his family.

Over the next two hours, the only audible sounds were those of Grandpa Elvis narrating his story, accompanied by the resounding voice of the real Elvis in the background. The crowd erupted in applause and cheered for the stand-in Elvis. They were unaware that the man before them was the authentic entertainer rather than the impostor Elvis they were familiar with. Inside the jungle room, tears mixed with felicity, stemming not from the customary movie screening but from the account their father had just shared. Finally, they grasped the burdens their father had endured, which extended beyond the usual afflictions of fame and fortune suffered by rock and roll stars.

For most individuals, living with the guilt of such misdeeds would have proved impossible. However, fortune smiled upon their father, allowing him to emerge triumphant. They felt a profound sense of gratitude that he had acted as he did, since it led them all to the sanguine existence they presently enjoyed as a close-knit family. Grandpa Elvis, who had experienced the loss of his parents at a tender age, now found that everything he had forfeited was unexpectedly restored. He had at long last unburdened himself with the secret from his past, experiencing a weight lifted off his shoulders.

Having missed the initial portion of the retirement celebration, Grandpa Elvis and his family proceeded towards the marquee. Resolute in his decision, Grandpa Elvis abstained from singing that night, feeling indebted to Elvis Aaron Presley, the undisputed king of rock and roll. The genuine Elvis enjoyed the festivities, visibly immersed in his element. The Elvis impersonations from years past had equipped him with the tools of the trade, and the original band felt at ease in his presence.

In a corner of the marquee, Josh Cadman and Emily Presley found solace in each other's presence, much to the astonishment of his family. However, this revelation did not come as a surprise to his grandpa, who had received confirmation that his grandson was the one who accompanied young Emily upstairs. Oblivious to the onlookers, their love consumed them as their gaze remained fixated solely on one another.

Grandpa Elvis's children approached the Walkers and embraced their newfound relatives, showering them with affection and kisses. Adjusting to the age difference would require some time, yet they were delighted to extend their warm welcome to these new family members.

Chapter Twenty-Five

ONE LAST PERFORMANCE

Elvis Aaron Presley and Grandpa Elvis have engaged in daily conversations for the past three years. Having nothing left to prove, Grandpa Elvis officially retired on the day of his party. With his remaining time, he planned to prioritize his immediate family, which he had been without since the age of five.

On Saturday, August 19th, 2023, Grandpa Elvis and Elvis Aaron Presley prepared in the backstage dressing room of the Nashville Convention Center. This area served as a waiting space for singers before their performances in the grand conference room. Seated in front of their respective mirrors, both men anxiously awaited their call to the stage for their first and only duet performance. The real Elvis felt nervous, as he had never sung alongside his idol, Elvis Presley.

As they gazed at each other, both men pondered how the audience would react to their joint performance. They were about to sing to a crowd who were familiar with them individually, yet they were breaking new ground with their duet. Grandpa Elvis laid two glasses on the nearby bench and carefully poured Kentucky Bourbon into them. "You know, Elvis," the real Elvis spoke up, "after I pass away, the only thing I will miss is this authentic Kentucky Bourbon. The charcoal essence and smoothness linger in your throat."

Grandpa Elvis chuckled. "Indeed, Elvis. That is why it's beneficial to loosen your vocal cords before a performance." Suddenly, there was a knock on the door. Louise and Priscilla Presley entered the dressing room. "Is the Kentucky Bourbon necessary?" inquired Louise of her husband.

"Hello, Louise," replied the real Elvis. "Elvis mentioned it is crucial for our vocal cords."

Priscilla chuckled. "Nice try, Elvis, but you still drink it at home, right?"

"Then, EP," Louise proposed, "why don't you pour two more glasses for Priscilla and me? I have never felt so nervous before."

"Me too, Louise," added Priscilla, "because this is Elvis's first genuine performance, apart from the retirement party in 2020 and his previous impersonations of your husband." Grandpa Elvis reached for a drawer by his side, extracted two more glasses, placed them on the makeup counter, twisted the bottle open, poured some bourbon into the glasses, and presented one to each of the ladies.

"EP," spoke Louise, "our reason for being here is to inform you that they are ready for both of you to come out. The master of ceremonies will introduce you, and then you will make history by performing together."

Ten minutes later, the two men entered the stage, hidden by a lowered curtain. The members of the Elvis Presley band were in their positions and nodded affirmatively to signal their readiness. Louise and Priscilla bid their husbands good luck with a kiss before returning to their tables with their children. They patiently awaited the announcement. Grandpa Elvis had lived in two distinct realities, and now he was on the cusp of going out to perform with his idol. The moment arrived as the master of ceremonies prepared to introduce them to the audience.

"Ladies and gentlemen," he proclaimed, "we have a remarkable surprise in store, as one of these men is the king of rock and roll, Elvis Presley, but we also have another Elvis. I am proud to announce the first-ever performance of Elvis Presley and Elvis Aaron Presley." As the curtain lifted, the band began playing 'Love Me Tender.' Grandpa Elvis sang to the delight of everyone in attendance while the two men observed that the newlywed couple, Josh and Emily, were married earlier that day. Both grandfathers stood on the stage, singing at their wedding reception.

In the spotlight, Grandpa Elvis took charge, and once they each sang their part, distinguishing between them became impossible. Descending the stairs from opposing sides of the stage, the two gentlemen approached the sweetheart's table with caution. Emily and Josh headed towards their grandfathers while the crowd, rising to their feet, erupted in song. Such was the power of the men's performance, a truly magical spectacle.

The families were now united through the bond of marriage. Another surprise twist emerged as David Clements and Sarah Cadman took the stage to announce their engagement, planning to tie the knot the following year. Thus, Peter Walker would soon gain David Clements as his grandson by marriage.

The following morning, in the wake of the celebrations, they all remained at Graceland, Grandpa Elvis and Elvis Aaron Presley sat basking in the sunshine alongside their wives, awaiting the emergence of their children and grandchildren for a post-wedding luncheon. As for Josh and Emily Cadman, they luxuriated in an exclusive Nashville hotel and planned to embark on a romantic European honeymoon once lunch had concluded.

Gradually, the other family members emerged to join them, Grandpa Elvis read aloud an intriguing news story from the morning papers. It detailed the unfolding political events of Governor Tino Fellino's arrest, carried out by the FBI. The governor faced charges linking him to the murder of Governor Jesse Garron Presley. The United States Attorney General, Anthony Fraser, presented compelling evidence to the Supreme Court. This evidence suggested that Fellino had directly orchestrated the murders of political figures and mafia associates.

Adding to the saga's complexity, yet another twist emerged: Attorney General Anthony Fraser is the grandson of the legendary mafia boss Sammy Navolla. In 1953, Sammy Navolla was killed by Martino Fellino, the 91-year-old father of Governor Tino Fellino, who is currently serving a life sentence. Evidence against Martino had only surfaced with an enigmatic tip from a concerned citizen.

Louise asked, "Who alerted the police?" Grandpa Elvis lowered his newspaper and glanced at the real Elvis, who was pleased with the news. Both men chuckled. "So, Elvis," the real Elvis remarked, "you told me you won two Academy Awards, but I have been to your house many times, and I didn't see them on display anywhere."

"I won those awards," Grandpa Elvis confirmed, "but I suppose I never felt the need to showcase them like some trophy. Despite being a fifty-room mansion called Graceland, it's simply home to me and my family. I suppose I have many cherished trophies and collections of gold records. I must have struggled to find a suitable place to exhibit them because they are kept securely in my walk-in safe in the bedroom."

"I would love to see them someday. It has always fascinated me how winners lift them and comment on their weight."

"Well, why don't I retrieve them?" Grandpa Elvis suggested. "We still have some time before the children arrive."

"No, stay put, EP," Louise interrupted. "I will fetch them for you."

"I will come with you, Grandma," Sarah Cadman offered. "You can hold on to your glass of champagne, and I'll help with carrying them."

"All right let's retrieve the Oscars," Louise agreed. Sarah wanted a private conversation. "Here you go, Grandma," she said, offering her hand. "Pass me your drink. I want you to be careful and hold on to the handrail. Grandma, I wanted to ask if Grandpa has ever experienced, you know, that feeling?"

"If he felt unsettled because you would marry his childhood friend."

"Yes, Grandma, David, and I are content, and we know that in Grandpa's original reality, he had a hidden affection for that girl."

"Tracey Mathews."

"Yes, Grandma, the one he left behind for you."

"Grandpa omitted that part of his story when he shared it with me. Listen, Sar Bear, that was at another time, and your David has never encountered Tracey Mathews. Tell me, Sar Bear, does David have any concerns regarding this matter?"

"Well, no, Grandma, it's just my insecurity because he had a secret crush on a woman he has never met."

"In that case, there's your answer. In this reality, you, Sar Bear, are David's not-so-secret crush, and now that he has put a ring on your finger, which should be sufficient for you not to harbor any mixed feelings about some girl who doesn't even exist in his life."

"I appreciate it, Grandma."

They entered the bedroom and proceeded towards the safe. As the light illuminated the room, the two Oscars could be seen on the back shelf, concealed behind a stack of CDs. Louise carefully positioned her champagne glass next to the CDs, intending to tilt both Oscars, causing no objects to fall. However, she inadvertently bumped into the CD piles, causing her glass to plummet to the floor, shattering upon impact. Both crouched down to assess the extent of the damage, discovering that the champagne had seeped into the floor tile that had previously concealed the Elvis manual.

Sarah began collecting fragments of broken glass and noticed that one piece had slid underneath the bottom shelf. She leaned down to reach it, and while retrieving the glass fragment, she stumbled upon an envelope. She picked it up and showed it to her grandmother. Louise held it in her hands, tilting it to examine the worn-out appearance under the light, noting that it was addressed to Peter Walker.

"Can you believe it?" Louise exclaimed. "This is the envelope your grandfather received at the Elvisgate before he traveled back in time. It must have slipped out of the Elvis manual and gone unnoticed, eventually settled underneath the bottom shelf. Look at the name and address."

"Wow, Grandma, this is insane! I remember the story of how you discovered the Elvis manual. And to think that this envelope, which is over seventy years old, was lost and now found!"

"Lay that broken glass on the shelf for now, Sarah, and I'll take care of it later. Can you grab the Oscars? I'll hand this envelope to Grandpa so he can finally open it. He had many opportunities throughout the years, but never did. It's finally time," Louise instructed. Sarah picked up the Oscars, and together, they walked outside. When they approached Grandpa Elvis, Louise handed him the envelope. He was speechless. The Oscars were placed on the table, but everyone's attention was solely focused on what he held in his hand.

"Louise, where did you find this?" he asked. "I was convinced that it got burned when I threw the Elvis manual into the fire after I was discharged from the hospital following the 9/11 attacks."

"It must have slipped out and ended up underneath the bottom shelf in the safe, EP," Louise replied. "It remained there until I accidentally dropped my champagne glass, and a piece of glass landed next to it."

"Could you please show me, Dad?" John Cadman asked, lifting it to the sunlight and discovering that the envelope contained something inside. Lisa Marie walked beside her brother to get a closer look. "Hey, sis," John remarked, "there is another envelope inside with the address, but I can't decipher it____."

"Let me have a look at that, John," Lisa Marie requested, snatching it and examining the front of the envelope. She held it up to the light, pressing it to see the writing on the inner envelope. "Peter Walker, 48 Heysen Street, Brinkley, Arkansas_____."

"Wait there," Maxine Walker remarked. "This is my mother, Christine Smart's handwriting." Grandpa Elvis recognized it was indeed Grandma Chris's handwriting when he realized the answer was written on the front of the inner envelope itself. 48 Heysen Street was her home address.

"That's where I currently live," Peter Walker stated. Peter received the envelope, turned it over, and noticed a connection with the inside envelope. "Look here," he exclaimed, "this envelope was sent out and then returned to the sender."

"Could it be Abercrombie and Associates, Lawyers?" Grandpa Elvis inquired.

"Yes, Elvis, they most likely sent this initially on September 28th, 2019."

"That was one day after my 18th birthday," Grandpa Elvis stated. "This could have been part of an automatic mail-out, possibly activated the day after I turned 18. Since my last known address was Grandma Chris's house, it was delivered there first. It was then sent back to these lawyers, and a year later, just before I entered the Elvisgate, they probably discovered my current address, and it finally ended up in my hands coincidentally."

"Well, Dad!" John stated with enthusiasm. "We might as well open it to solve this mystery." His father nodded, and John ripped the ends of the first and the second envelopes, carefully pulling out two folded pieces of paper and handing one to his father. Maxine requested John to hand her the one in his hand, as it was a handwritten letter from Christine Smart, her mother. Tears streamed down her face when John handed the letter to his grandmother. She read, "Dear Peter. If you are currently reading this, it means that I didn't make your 18th birthday. Happy Birthday, Peter. I love you wholeheartedly. The reason I waited until you reached this age was because I wanted you to be mature enough and able to comprehend why I___."

Overwhelmed with emotions, Maxine stopped reading, knowing that her mother's letter confirmed another existence with her son in a distinct reality. Lisa Marie kindly offered, "Let me read the rest so that you can listen instead of reading." Maxine handed her the letter, and she continued reading, "To understand why I kept the truth hidden from you, because of the trauma of losing your loving parents at such a young age. Peter, having you with me reminded me of someone who touched my heart many years ago. Despite the void in my heart that existed for a long time, having you gave me a reason to keep going."

Grandpa Elvis shook his head as Louise embraced him from behind, offering comfort. Lisa Marie proceeded with the reading, "Peter, I hope when you discover what I left for you, you will comprehend why my heart was always dedicated to this man. I fell in love with the wrong man. I was young and naïve. Peter, when my precious daughter Maxine died, I was prepared to depart this world, for I should have gone before her. However, having you by my side kept me going every day."

Lisa Marie paused, taking a deep breath. "Sis, let me have a turn," John Cadman suggested. "Peter, when you became part of my life, it was because I was your only living relative. We never discussed our family lineage, and in hindsight, I should have informed you earlier. But you had me, and I had you." Louise leaned over to kiss her husband on the cheek, feeling a pang of guilt as her parents had often inquired about her husband's family, unaware of the truth.

John continued, "Every day, Peter, you resembled your grandfather more and more, and it brought me great joy. I hoped that by the time you discovered the truth, I would be around to witness your reaction. Peter, you have an extended family, but I urge you not to seek them out because the past should always remain in the past. I will always love you, and hopefully, one day, after a long and fulfilling life of your own, your parents, grandfather, and I will reunite in heaven. Forever yours, Grandma Chris...xxx."

After finishing the mysterious letter, John and the rest of the group fell silent, lost in their thoughts. While Christine Smart's letter brought comfort to her grandson, Peter. They also realized that it failed to mention his grandfather by name, leaving them with lingering questions. Grandpa Elvis directed his attention to the other folded piece of paper in his possession. This note immediately captured everyone's attention. Slowly, he unfolded it, and only he and

Louise could decipher its contents. At that moment, Louise was left speechless, her hand covering her mouth.

"Mum, Dad, what's going on?" Lisa Marie asked curiously. "Tell us what it says." Her father handed her the note. "Hey, it's a birth certificate," she exclaimed. "It belongs to Maxine Smart, born on May 13th, 1964. According to this, her parents are Christine Smart and… wait, what?"

"Give that to me, Lisa Marie," John demanded, snatching the birth certificate from her and reading what his sister couldn't. "Father___, I can't believe it. It says that the father is Elvis Aaron Presley." Shock and astonishment couldn't describe the emotions filling the area. They had just witnessed the most incredible twist in Peter Walker's family history.

"John, are you sure?" Peter Walker questioned. "My mother was born much later than that, and besides, my grandfather wasn't Elvis Aaron Presley."

Suddenly, Grandpa Elvis realized why this Maxine Walker looked slightly different from the person he remembered. He realized Maxine, his mother, had a different father than this Maxine and that father was none other than Elvis Aaron Presley.

"It comes to my attention," he expressed, "that my mother, Maxine, and you, Maxine, are distinct individuals since my Grandma Chris indisputably had more than a causal relationship with Elvis Aaron Presley in my existence. She likely conceived a child with him, a fact she probably kept hidden. This explains why she mentioned an extended family in her letter, which has now been identified as the Presleys from my original reality. This was the driving force behind my Grandma Chris's infatuation with the man present here, whom I now believe to be my biological grandfather."

At last, comprehension dawned upon everyone as members of both families exchanged glances. They listened attentively as Grandpa Elvis disclosed, they were all connected through blood, igniting a new chapter of entertainment and excitement.

Chapter Twenty-Six

KISSING COUSINS

To the astonishment of everyone, Grandpa Elvis and Elvis Aaron Presley rose and embraced each other. They accepted the truth that had been unveiled and now recognize their kinship through the uncanny likeness of their appearances and the harmonious blend of their voices when they sing together. Grandma Chris had always longed to confide in her grandson, but she believed he was still too young to grasp the intricate complexity of being the grandson of the legendary rock star Elvis Aron Presley.

At 18, she disclosed this secret to her daughter Maxine, deeming that the right time had arrived for her to comprehend the intricacies of such a connection with a man who departed in the year 1977. Grandma Chris sought no material gain from Elvis Aaron Presley, and revealing the truth years later would have impeded them from leading a normal life, overwhelmed by the clamor of the media and scrutiny that would have ensued. Eventually, she wished for her grandson to grasp the reality of the romance she encountered during her youthful years.

She discerned the essence of Elvis Aaron Presley within her grandson. As he entered adolescence, she became apprehensive that others would perceive the resemblance and eventually unravel the family ties. Those acquainted with Christine Smart were aware of her infatuation with the renowned rock star and had heard whispers about their clandestine affair.

The families stood in silence, gazing at each other, still trying to comprehend the revelation that had been disclosed. Concerned, the two older men who remained standing feared that the other family members from both sides were strategizing their response. And, as always, if someone from the Cadman family had something to say, it would be Lisa Marie who would break the ice.

"All right, all right," Lisa Marie chimed in, instantly capturing everyone's attention. "So, that means that, oh well, we are cousins."

"Hold on," Vernon Presley interjected. "If my father is your father's grandfather, then that would make us great nephews and nieces, perhaps?" Laughter erupted. "No, no," John Cadman confidently corrected. "That would label us as great cousins."

"But what about us?" Peter Walker pondered. "If my brother is your father's grandson, then my family, the Walkers, are, um, um... Oh boy, this whole situation is so perplexing."

"Now, listen up," Gladys interjected. "My father, Elvis Aaron Presley, is the grandfather of Elvis Presley or Peter Walker from the original reality. Christine Smart conceived a daughter with my father. Oh boy, this is all so strange. However, Maxine Walker, you are not related to this Elvis-slash-Peter Walker because you had a different father. But your husband is still his father, and your mother, Christine Smart, was genetically his grandmother. Does that make sense?"

She indeed had a valid point, but confused everyone even further. "Hold up," Christine Cadman intervened. "If my father is the grandson of your father, then we would be great nephews and nieces, I believe."

"Yes," Lisa Mathews agreed. "That's correct, Christine. We are your great-aunties and uncles, and we have already established that fact. But isn't it mind-boggling to consider that if this letter had not been discovered today, none of us would have had any clue about our shared ancestry, would we?"

Frantically gesturing, Sarah Cadman pointed at David Clements and herself and questioned, "Are we related?" Laughter erupted when they all realized that Sarah had nothing to worry about, as the Clements were not related. Elvis Aaron Presley and Grandpa Elvis settled back into their chairs. "Hey, Grandad," Grandpa Elvis exclaimed, "that's weird." Laughter erupted once again.

"Not any stranger than calling you Grandson," the real Elvis responded. "It seems like a mess you've created by going back in time because I would have still been your grandfather."

"You couldn't even write something like this," Grandpa Elvis remarked, "and yet, here we are, witnessing it unfold."

The famous gates of Graceland suddenly opened, reminding everyone of the purpose of their presence, as they spotted the pink Cadillac waiting beyond the gates. Everyone rose swiftly, pondering how to break the news to the newlyweds about their connection. "Oh no," John Cadman exclaimed, "what do we tell the kids? We haven't even discussed their relation to each other."

"John," Lisa Marie interjected, "we must inform them now that they are cousins or distant cousins."

"No, hang on," Lisa Mathews suggested. "Why spoil this beautiful moment right before they leave for their honeymoon?"

"No," Lisa Marie insisted, "they deserve to know the truth; otherwise, they might never forgive us."

"Listen," Christine Cadman calmly proposed, "let's wait and observe. Either way, whether they know or remain clueless, the outcome might be the same."

"What do you mean, Christine?" Lisa Marie inquired.

"Well," Christine explained, "let's see how they feel about each other after their wedding night, and maybe they will reveal the answer to us." Both Grandpa Elvis and Elvis Aaron Presley exchanged glances and nodded in agreement. The Cadillac had just pulled up near the front porch, and normally, they would have all rushed up to greet the newlyweds with excitement. However, this time, they remained in their seats. Lisa Marie was the only one who objected to the plan. "No, Dad," she insisted, "how can you withhold the truth for the next two months?"

With a joyful chuckle, Lisa Marie's father exclaimed, "Oh, Lisa Marie, I possess the ability to maintain a secret for much longer than that!" Laughter filled the air as everyone rose from their seats and made their way towards the newly married couple. Exiting the car, an act of excitement was put on display by all, although the young couple sensed that something was amiss.

"My dear Josh and Emily, my two favorite people," Grandpa Elvis affectionately greeted them. Embraces and kisses were exchanged not only by him but also by the others present. Lisa Marie did her utmost to continue the charade. She offered her congratulations, but Josh and Emily couldn't help but notice the subtle signs that all was not as it seemed, particularly with Lisa Marie. "Very well," Josh interjected, "let us bring our bags inside, freshen up, and reemerge approximately ten minutes from now."

The newlyweds stepped foot into the elegant mansion. "Hey, Emily," Josh whispered, "did you observe anything weird about everyone? They all wore weird expressions as if something had just occurred."

"Well, maybe," Emily reasoned, "let's remember that some may be tired or nursing a hangover, or maybe both."

"Yeah, you may be right." Ascending the stairs, they reached their bedroom and gently placed their bags on the bed, when suddenly the sound of arguments could be heard drifting through the open window. "Listen," Lisa Marie said, "how can we conceal this significant news from them? If it were me, I would prefer to know immediately." The newlyweds quietly listened to the conversation revolving around them yet remained oblivious to its content.

"Lisa Marie," Lisa Mathews interjected, "under normal circumstances, your suggestion would be appropriate. However, today is the day following their wedding. We ought to provide them with some time alone, free from confusion." Emily and Josh exchanged glances, perplexed by the unfolding events. "Emily," Josh whispered, "this is disconcerting. They possess knowledge about us."

"Shush," Emily cautioned, "the argument is still happening, and we must remain quiet." Alas, it was too late, as Christine Cadman overheard their whispers from upstairs. "Hey, everyone, keep the noise down," she admonished. "I believe I just heard whispering and noticed a movement of a curtain from an upstairs window."

"That is my son's room," John Cadman added.

Emily and Josh locked their eyes, realizing they had been caught eavesdropping. Hastily, they sprinted downstairs, ventured outside, and joined the rest of the family. "Here come the love birds!" Lisa Mathews exclaimed. Suddenly, a burst of excitement filled the air as everyone rose to their feet, applauding and whistling. It was as if they should have greeted the newlyweds in such a manner from the start.

However, this sudden display of enthusiasm now only seemed more suspicious.

"Oh, I thought you guys were fed up with us already," remarked Josh Cadman.

"Not at all!" Grandpa Elvis rebutted, beckoning them to take a seat. "Come and join us; lunch is about to be served." The love birds obliged, sitting close together and intertwining their fingers, which delighted the onlookers who were eagerly searching for any signs of trouble. Most of them had agreed to disclose the revelation after the couple's two-month honeymoon, but Lisa Marie had other plans. Tension filled the air, and the lovebirds could sense it. Then Lisa Marie broke the uneasy silence with a question directed at her father, "Hey, Dad, how do I go about watching one of your movies in the jungle room?"

"Well, Lisa Marie," Grandpa Elvis huffed, "why would you want to do that now when we're all gathered here, about to enjoy our lunch?"

"I simply wanted to watch one of your films, Dad," she replied cunningly, a sly grin appearing on her face. "I believe it's titled 'Kissing Cousins'." It took a moment for everyone to grasp the full meaning behind Lisa Marie's words. Some roared with laughter, while others were horrified by her explicit reference to the newlyweds. Even Josh and Emily were bewildered by her comment, causing the rest of the crowd to erupt into laughter. Frustrated, Josh slammed his fist on the table and demanded, "What is happening? You must reveal what on earth is going on, as you are not the same people we once knew."

In an instant, silence fell upon the crowd as everyone struggled to convey the news of their shared bloodline. "Dad," Lisa Marie implored, "May I disclose the truth? They have sensed something amiss, and if we delay any further, their enjoyment of the honeymoon will be compromised. They might even reconsider going once they find out what we all know."

"Excuse me," interjected Josh Cadman, "are you suggesting that we might reject the idea of going on our honeymoon?" Grandpa Elvis scrutinized the real Elvis, his newfound grandfather, recognizing that it was indeed time to disclose the truth. With her father's blessing, Lisa Marie turned to Josh and Emily, presenting them with Grandma Chris's letter. "What's this all about?" Inquired Josh.

"Josh, it's a mislaid letter that Grandpa received right before he entered the Elvisgate, embarking on his journey back in time," Lisa Marie explained.

"But Auntie Lisa Marie," he responded, "wasn't it inside the Elvis manual when Grandpa disposed of it in the fire after his release from the hospital?"

"No, Josh," she clarified, "it must have slipped out of the Elvis manual and settled beneath Grandpa's safe's lower shelf when Grandma Louise initially discovered the manual. We only stumbled upon it this morning and, upon opening it, uncovered something that affects all of us here."

"What did you discover?" Inquired Emily.

"Emily," Lisa Marie began, "please read it and then observe the other letter I have here in my hand." Josh and Emily exchanged perplexed glances, wondering about the significance of the letter. Josh read aloud, and as the minutes ticked by, they were overcome with emotion because of Grandma Chris's profound love for Grandpa Elvis. Lisa Marie handed the other document to the lovebirds, and Josh and Emily concentrated their attention on the birth certificate. "All right," he announced, "this is the birth certificate of Maxine Smart, born on May 13, 1964. The listed parents are Christine Smart, check, and the father is..."

"Grandad," Emily inquired, "are you his grandfather?" The newly married couple exchanged bewildered and speechless glances, attempting to comprehend and manage emotions that would normally repel them. However, Josh had something to express, "Grandpa, this man whose career you took by going back in time was always your grandfather?"

Emily finally comprehended Auntie Lisa Marie's allusion to the film 'Kissing Cousins.' She and her husband exchanged incredulous looks, realizing the long-kept secret that they were blood relatives. "Ha, ha, so, we're cousins?" Josh Cadman chuckled to his wife.

At that very moment, everyone feared the newlywed couple, who had only been married for one day. Yet, just as they believed their union would face trouble, Emily gripped her husband's collar with both hands and planted a passionate, unexpected kiss on the lips. He reciprocated with equal enthusiasm, and the entire crowd erupted in cheers, realizing that their relationship was not an issue.

Josh Cadman grew excited and exclaimed, "Emily, if my Grandpa Elvis is your second cousin, what does that make us?"

"Wow, wow, and wow," Emily exclaimed. "So, that means if your father is my father's great-nephew, what are we?"

Lisa Marie pleaded with Emily, "Emily, let it go. At worst, you two are distant relatives. As long as you two maintain the flame of love, none of that stuff matters."

The two aging men who bore the name Elvis shook hands, their faces beaming with delight upon realizing their familial connection. The revelation of their shared bloodline would likely have remained hidden had it not been for the fortuitous incident involving Louise's clumsy handling of her champagne glass. Subsequently, a dispute arose as they engaged in a discussion regarding the intricacies of their kinship. The elderly Elvis duo maintained a stoic silence, oblivious to the surrounding bickering. They gracefully rose from their seats and strolled towards the mansion, engrossed in conversation. The argument escalated when Lisa Marie, contrary to her previous agreement, ventured out alone.

Unexpectedly, both older men leisurely hastened to the pink Cadillac, smoothly entering the vehicle with Grandpa Elvis confidently assuming the driver's position. It went unnoticed by the others that they were absent until the engine of the pink Cadillac emitted a thunderous roar. In one swift motion, they departed from Graceland as the renowned gates swung open.

Josh dashed towards the closing gates, closely followed by the rest of the crowd. Pausing momentarily, he turned towards them and expressed his gratitude, uttering the famous words, "Thank you very much, ladies and gentlemen. Elvis has left the building."

The End......